# The Life They Deserve

Linda Van Meter

D1373870

Copyright © 2019 by Linda D. Van Meter
All rights reserved.

Cover design by Linda D. Van Meter

No part of this book may be reproduced in any form or by any electronic or mechanical means including information storage and retrieval systems, without permission in writing from the author. The only exception is by a reviewer, who may quote short excerpts in a review.

This book is a work of fiction. Names, characters, places, and incidents either are products of the author's imagination or are used fictitiously. Any resemblance to actual persons, living or dead, events, or locales is entirely coincidental.

Linda D. Van Meter

Printed in the United States of America

First Printing: November 2019

**ISBN:** 9781697701586

*This book is dedicated to the women who share in the accomplishment. Michele and Michelle; your willingness to encourage me, read my sporadic pages and talk through ideas made all the difference. A special note of appreciation for my biggest fan; Jerry. My dream to do this happened because you've always believed in me.*

*Thank you to my readers. Your enthusiasm for my stories fills my heart!*

Books by Linda Van Meter

*Worth Losing*

*Whispered Regrets*

*After The Show*

# *Prologue*

*The mother lion carefully grasped the leg of the wildebeest in her mouth, trying to drag the heavy limb across the plain. She was taking it back to her den, a slightly enclosed space in a cragged rock formation. Here, her two cubs were waiting for a meal.*

*She stepped over a fallen tree and the hoof caught on a root. The lioness tugged, but the bloodied limb stayed lodged. She let go of it and climbed onto the tree to pull it from a different angle.*

*That's when it happened. The whoosh of the bullet followed the crack of its release from the gun. The next sound was a gurgle from the lion's throat. The bullet had pierced her jugular; she fell. Her own blood mixed with that of the wildebeest.*

*Celeste hit replay on her phone three more times, until her eyelids stung, and her heart ached. Finally, she closed her eyes and took a deep breath. It always worked. Now she could make those calls. It was her life's purpose to save the cats.*

# Chapter 1

Annabeth Muldoon lay in the awkward vertical position particular to a dentist's chair. She clasped her hands on her stomach, pleased to note it was now nearly flat. Giving up fast food and bourbon shots, compounded with several days at the gym each week, trimmed off some serious pounds.

The dentist's drill buzzed in her mouth. She tried to look beyond his masked face, just inches from hers. At one point she closed her eyes, but immediately, the assistant asked if she was okay. Now, she focused on the tiled ceiling and replayed the conversation with Rikki.

Her agent called while she headed to her root canal. Carrots weren't always healthy; one caused her to crack a molar. Rikki was pushing her to choose her next book subject. There were some interesting possibilities. As the dental assistant used a tiny vacuum to clean tooth debris from her mouth, Annabeth considered.

Rikki's favorite was the young politician shaking up

Washington with her strong, controversial proposals based on statistically sound reason. She was changing laws and her future looked fairly presidential. Rikki was right in thinking this book would be a big success both financially and to continue to grow her name as a top biographer in the country. However, Annabeth wasn't into politics. The job required quite a lot of homework. Did she want to spend the next six months in DC?

Her second option was a six-time gold medal Olympic skier who overcame multiple bone fractures in a jet ski accident. He was back on the slopes now, training for the next winter Olympics. This would force her to be where there was a lot of snow. New York City winters were bad enough, she wasn't a fan of icy mountains.

The final option was a former film star. She made many successful movies; mostly romcoms and a few dramas. In fact, she'd won an Oscar when she portrayed a serial killer's daughter. A few years ago, she'd sold her LA mansion and invested all her money in a big cat sanctuary in North Carolina.

She now lived there with her husband, a veterinarian, and spent her days caring for lions. How did one give up the celebrity lifestyle for that? Annabeth got to live in that world on her last assignment. She had fond memories of a Malibu beach house she shared with a few rock stars.

Her ruminations worked, the dentist announced, "All done."

****

"I didn't plan on this," Annabeth couldn't believe she was attempting to justify her next assignment.

Chase scowled at her, then took a swallow of his beer, "What do you mean you didn't plan on this? You chose the assignment."

Now it was her turn to look irritated. "I meant this," she moved her hand between them indicating their relationship.

They'd met two months ago both leaving the gym at the same time. They happened to be headed two blocks north to the same bar to meet different people. He held open the door and Annabeth nodded a thank you. They turned left on the sidewalk. She knew he was behind her and after half a block it made her feel slightly uncomfortable. Stopping on the pretense of tying her shoe, she squatted down.

He wasn't fooled. He stopped too and spoke, "I'm not trailing you; I'm meeting some friends at the Westend which is this direction."

Annabeth stood and grinned, "Me too."

He tossed out the names of his friends, she shook her head, "Not them."

When he smiled, she noticed he had a small dimple on his left cheek. "What are the chances? I'm Chase."

"Annabeth."

"Shall we walk together?" They headed down the street. The conversation flowed easily. Annabeth learned that Chase was an IT Engineer for New York Health and he had lived in this area for three years.

When he realized that she was the author of rock star Jack Corey's biography he practically jumped in the air. Apparently, Chase was a big fan. In fact, he'd read the entire book in one weekend. He filled the rest of their walk with endless questions about the band and her experience. Their arrival to the bar came too quickly. Chase looked disappointed as they picked out their separate tables. He took a deep breath, "I'd love to talk more."

Annabeth was incredibly flattered and wanted to see him again, "When will you be at the gym?"

"On Thursday, would you like to grab a drink afterwards?"

"Sure, you can follow me after your workout." They both laughed. Annabeth liked his smile and noticed it aimed in her direction across the room, several times throughout the evening.

They continued the routine for three more gym visits, then decided it was time for a real date. Two and a half months later Annabeth had strong feelings for Chase. The call from her agent, telling her that the flight was scheduled for next week to her new assignment just came today.

Annabeth invited Chase to dinner. They'd eaten curry and drank IPA's overlooking the Chelsea skyline. She told him that her research and time with the subject of her newest biography would take at least a month. Chase was not taking the news well.

Annabeth took a slow drink of her own pale ale. "This is the process. I must immerse myself in their world. It's how I write."

Chase walked to the steel railing and was quiet a moment, then he turned. His eyes were apologetic, "And that's why your books are so great."

"Books?" she raised an eyebrow.

"I finished the twin one and I'm on your second one." His interest in her work pleased her.

She moved closer and put her hands on his chest, "I hate

leaving now too. This is a surprise; a good one."

He pulled her close for a kiss. "A month is too long. Can you come back on weekends? Can I visit?"

She felt lightheaded; this smart, handsome man didn't want to go a month without seeing her. "I'd like that." They kissed longer. Annabeth blew out the pillar candles in the lanterns and led him into her bedroom.

# Chapter 2

If Annabeth hadn't flown out of JFK this morning, and it was just early afternoon, she'd swear she'd landed in an African savannah. She was steering her rented SUV on roads surrounded by dry, dusty expanses of land. The wind was blowing the dirt and grass so strongly that twice she'd turned on the wipers to clear the debris that blocked her view. The directions took her off the highway twenty minutes ago and onto a sparsely covered stone lane. This would be a nightmare in a heavy rain. The many ruts that her vehicle bounced through would be deep and treacherous puddles.

The road took a sharp turn to the left and after a long curve, ascended a hill. Behind her, the sun moved past a small cloud and its glow spread out across the vista in front of her. She arrived at the *Peaceful Pride* sanctuary. "Oh!" she said aloud. A large house was nearest her. Across the path a body of water sat, somewhere between a pond and a lake. The water was a blue akin to that of a coastal gulf shore. Beyond it, she spotted several rooftops that perhaps housed the animals. Strategically placed tall grasses hid the area. Yes, that must be the animal pens.

Curious if she could hear them, Annabeth turned off the radio and powered down her window. She heard the leaves blowing on the many trees that lined the road. There were clear calls of a variety of birds but no roars or growls.

The car traveled another quarter of a mile when she came to a twenty-foot fence and an equally tall gate. She hadn't noticed it at the top of the hill. Of course, there would have to be a fence. Her car came to a stop. A security camera was visible at the top. Next to her was an intercom with a call button. A voice responded immediately after she pressed it. "Yes?"

"Hi. I'm Annabeth Muldoon."

It was a woman's voice, "Yes. Bring your car to the front doors. We can get you unpacked, then Abe will put your vehicle in the garage." As the mystery woman gave instructions, the gates rolled open.

The house was not at all what Annabeth expected. She imagined that a celebrity turned big cat owner would have built a home resembling something from an African plain. This place looked more like a southern plantation; white, stately with large columns adorning a long front porch.

A woman, who looked to be in her early sixties, came out of the grand double doors as Annabeth shut off her engine. Her skin had the deep creases of someone who'd spent most of her life in the sun. Her hair was thick, mostly gray, pulled back in a low ponytail. She wore jeans and a sleeveless t-shirt adorned with birds. On her feet were Birkenstocks. Annabeth thought this woman looked like her kind of person.

Behind her came a young man perhaps in his late teens. His skin was the color of coffee. He was tall and slim, dressed more like she expected in khaki cargo shorts, work boots and a t-shirt with the sanctuary logo on it.

Annabeth stepped out of the vehicle and stretched. The hour and a half drive from the airport made her stiff. She realized as the two people approached that both towered over her 5-foot 3-inch frame.

"Hi Annabeth, I'm Shannon." The young man stepped beside her, "This is Abe. We'll get your things and then he can move your car."

"Thank you," Annabeth clicked her key fob, and the two began pulling her luggage from the back. By the time she'd gathered her phone and purse from the front, they were next to her with her suitcases. She reached for the large bag that Shannon had over her shoulder, "I can get that."

Using her head to point, Shannon responded, "If you can get the suitcase, we'll send Abe to the garage." Annabeth nodded, took the handle of the wheeled bag from Abe and followed Shannon up the porch steps.

The foyer was grand; marble floors lead to a large open staircase. On the left appeared to be a sitting room, on the right a dining room. Both were filled with elegant, antique furniture, the kind that looked rarely used. To the left of the steps, was an open hallway leading to the back of the house. Annabeth suspected that the real living areas were back there.

Shannon moved up the steps. She trailed her, once again bumping her unwieldy suitcase, glad that she'd built up her biceps at the gym. The second floor appeared to be divided into two wings. Against the wall in the middle was a wooden bench, resembling a church pew, next to an old-fashioned washstand. Behind both a large framed mirror hung on the wall. Shannon turned left down the hall, there were four closed doors. At the last one on the left, she opened it and entered.

It was a large bedroom with a four-poster bed on one side near the windows. Across the room sat a love seat and an overstuffed chair. Shannon showed her the attached full bath and walk-in closet. The interior design amazed Annabeth. She'd expected a new and contemporary structure. "Is this the house that Miss Barlow's grandparents lived in?" She knew that the sanctuary was built on land that Celeste inherited when her grandmother passed away.

Shannon looked at her, thinking a moment. "Let's have a talk. I'll try to give you some pointers." She motioned to the chair and sat on the loveseat.

Surprised, but obedient, Annabeth settled into the chair.

"First, Celeste goes by Unina here at the sanctuary. It's Zulu for mother." Annabeth's fingers itched to write this strange information down. "This house was built just three years ago. Unina wanted it to match her grandmother's furnishings."

Annabeth nodded, "It looks very authentic."

Shannon took a deep breath, considering her next words

carefully, "I know that you're here to write a book about Unina. MJ brought you here hoping this book will make money. She knows that the sanctuary is struggling financially. Unina thinks the purpose of the biography is to raise awareness of the plight of the cats." She paused. "You're being placed between them. It could be tricky. Unina isn't the person you're used to seeing on the movie screen or television."

What did she mean? Did Celeste or Unina think she was writing a different book than they hired her to write? Annabeth looked at Shannon. "So, this will be a challenge?"

Shannon nodded, "I just wanted to be honest with you. I hope this works out. Come to me with any questions. And please keep this conversation between us." She stood with an uncomfortable expression on her face, as if she'd said too much.

Annabeth stood also, "Thank you for the name explanation and the heads up. I don't want to offend her when we meet."

Shannon left the room, closing the door behind her. *Well, this will prove interesting*. Annabeth changed into jeans and a short-sleeved navy top. She put on her white Converse tennis shoes, uncertain what terrain she'd be walking on.

Seeing no sign of Shannon, she headed out the front door. The wind picked up for a moment bringing to her nose the distinct scent of animals. This made her turn toward the tall grass and the buildings it surrounded. She hadn't gone too far when she heard footsteps behind her.

It was Abe. He did a slight jog to catch her. "Where are you headed?" His voice was strong and deep, revealing that he must be in his twenties not late teens as she'd suspected earlier.

"Well, I figured the cats must be this way as well as Unina." The name still felt strange on her tongue.

Abe stopped, angling his body in front of her. "They are, but you can't go out there."

"Why?"

"She must invite you."

"I have been invited, that's why I'm here."

He ran his hand over his eyes, "You've been invited here," he indicated the property with his other hand. "But you can't go to the sanctuary without her permission."

Annabeth tried to tamp down her impatience, "Does she know I'm here?"

"Probably."

"Please tell her I'd like to see her and the lions."

His expression was dubious, "I'll go. Promise me you will head to the house."

It was in Annabeth's nature to argue, but this was the beginning. She would have to develop respect and camaraderie with the staff to write a good book. "Okay." With that she turned and headed from the direction she came.

# Chapter 3

Twenty-four hours later, Annabeth's patience wore dangerously thin. She was still not permitted to see the lions or talk with "Unina."

Abe sat with her at the "watering hole" their name for the luscious blue body of water. Shannon served them iced coffees and still warm, pillowy soft biscuits. Abe wolfed them down, two bites at a time. "Unina doesn't eat processed food or white flour. Enjoy these while you can."

Annabeth decided one with butter and honey was allowable if the rest of her meals would be strictly meat and vegetables. She turned her phone to record, but also opened her laptop "Usually I use a pen and paper for interviews, but there are some things I've researched that I want to ask you about."

Abe, she discovered, was a graduate student in veterinary medicine at the University of North Carolina and this position was his graduate program. He'd been here for six months.

"I'd visited before. Though Unina refuses to open the sanctuary to the public, she welcomes the zoology and veterinary professors and students here."

"Are you the only vet at the sanctuary?"

Abe swallowed another half biscuit before answering. "No, Udok is a veterinarian who specializes in exotic animals."

"Udok?" Annabeth clicked a tab on her screen, "I heard that she married Dr. Christian Mendoza."

An unreadable expression passed across his face. "Udok is short for doctor in Zulu, her name for him." Annabeth attempted to hide the raise of her eyebrows with a swallow of coffee. "Ben McKinley works here full time. He was hired to maintain the property, but the cats know him enough that he also cares for the pens."

"Let's talk about the lions," Annabeth's hands were poised above the keyboard ready to take notes.

"We currently have seven. It's a large number. Three females and two male adults. We also have two female cubs, well they're barely still cubs."

Annabeth consulted another screen, "The information I saw said only four." Abe frowned. "Is there a legal limit?"

"No. It's just a great deal of lions for a small group to care for."

Not looking up, Annabeth nodded, her fingers flying. "I would imagine that's a lot of mouths to feed."

"It certainly is."

"What do you feed a lion?" Though this would not be a book about lions, she wanted to know how the place functioned, how Celeste Barlow became an animal guru.

"The main source is a commercial product that is made with the proper nutrients needed by a lion. Captive animals lose out on certain vitamins and minerals. It's important to find the right product. This is a frozen meat mixture which looks kind of like sausage. We also give them fresh chunks of meat; beef, chicken, rabbit or lamb."

"So, they don't hunt for anything?"

"No, but we try to give them carcasses of animals regularly. The activity of shredding the bones and meat is healthy and a source of activity."

Annabeth wondered where one found animal carcasses, slaughterhouses? She decided that she didn't want to include any information that could stir up animal activists, unless she uncovered information that showed Celeste was mistreating animals. Her goal was to show a positive light on the sanctuary. She leaned back in her chair away from her computer. This caused Abe to relax too. He took a drink of coffee.

"So, Unina has learned how to care for the animals from her husband?"

"No, when he came here, she already had two cats; Nova and Luna. Udok was a professor at UNC. Nova was injured and there were no local vets qualified to treat her. Unina found Udok."

"A movie star who owned her own lions, what veterinarian could resist?" Annabeth hadn't meant to muse aloud, but Abe laughed. "I've been here for a day and not seen a peep of her. Does she spend all of her time down there?" She pointed toward the mystery buildings.

"Yes."

"Doing what?"

Abe looked uncomfortable, "She just likes to watch them."

"Can she pet them?"

"They do recognize her as their caretaker. Cats of all sizes are social animals."

Annabeth returned to her notes, "Does she get in their enclosures?"

Abe's face said yes, with an expression of disapproval, but his loyalty forced him to say, "Sometimes it's necessary."

****

It was just after six in the evening, Annabeth had had enough. She was not going to be held captive there and not get any work done. Abe gave her the name of the nearest restaurant. Now she was bouncing down the lane toward the highway.

North Carolina was hot, but Annabeth wasn't accustomed to being seen in public in shorts. Last summer, on the rock tour, she remembered her friend Paige looked good in white jeans. The new, thinner Annabeth was wearing a pair. She added a black gauzy top.

On the drive in she called Chase. "Hey," he sounded distracted.

"Can you talk?"

"Yep, just getting dressed for the gym."

"Wish I was going."

"Me too," he sounded pouty, then tried, "How's lion girl?"

"I wish I knew."

"What does that mean?"

Annabeth explained the absence of Unina.

"She goes by a South African name? Wackadoo."

"Maybe," the GPS app on her phone cut in to tell her to turn.

"So, you're wasting your time there?" his voice was unhappy again.

"No, I've interviewed staff members, done research. Now, I'm headed to town for dinner." They talked a while more then said their goodbyes. She wasn't sure Chase would be waiting for her when she returned to New York. He was not supportive of any of this.

Twenty minutes later, she pulled into the parking lot of the Carolina Cantina. Annabeth took a seat at the bar. On the right side of her was an empty stool, on the left, a group of four men were finishing up their dinner; laughing and talking. She ordered a Corona with a lime. The bartender asked her if she would like a menu and she took one. As she was looking over it, most of the men got up to leave. They were issuing farewells and slaps on the back to the remaining gentleman.

The bartender asked him if he wanted another whiskey. With an affirmative nod, he glanced at Annabeth perusing the menu. "Having trouble deciding what to eat?"

She nodded her head, "Yes, I haven't been here before, any recommendations?"

The man smiled, "Absolutely, go for the seafood enchilada."

Annabeth liked the sound of it. "Thank you."

The man was handsome, of obvious Hispanic descent; dark eyes, dark hair, dark skin. He reached out and shook her hand, his was a strong rough hand of someone who worked for a living. He was dressed in dark jeans and a blue button shirt. "Welcome to the Carolina Cantina."

He hadn't offered his name, so she didn't either. "Thank you."

Together they snacked on the chips and salsa placed on the bar. When the bartender stopped at their spot again, the man asked for the spicier salsa, "It's amazing," he confided.

She waved the dish away, "No thanks, I can't do super spicy."

His eyes got big, and he laughed, "Uh oh."

Her own widened, "Are the enchiladas going to be spicy?"

He chuckled. Annabeth noted he was incredibly handsome when he did that. His dark eyes sparkled, "Well, *I* don't think so."

She was about to protest when a steaming plate of food was placed before her. The dish looked delicious with shrimp visible at the ends of the rolled tortilla, covered in a cream sauce. Annabeth picked up her fork and hesitantly lifted a tiny bite of the enchilada. Putting it in her mouth, she carefully touched it with her tongue. "It doesn't seem hot to me," she said and swallowed. Suddenly, she covered her mouth. "Oh, the heat follows." After another small bite, Annabeth put her fork back down on the table.

The man lightly laid his hand on her arm, "This is my fault. Let me order you something else."

"No, seriously. I'm fine."

"I insist," he then turned to the bartender and spoke in Spanish. "This will be much better."

She eyed him, "Should I trust you?"

He laughed again. With his hand on his heart, he spoke, "I promise. Now let me get you another beer to wash away the heat."

# Chapter 4

Annabeth was up early the next morning and considered going for a run but was still unfamiliar with the area. Wouldn't it be nice to take a walk past the lion compound? She finished her shower, dried her hair and was dressing when her cell phone buzzed. It was Abe; they exchanged numbers before she left for dinner last night in case she got lost. His message was quick, *Unina is at breakfast. Get down here.*

Annabeth was glad she'd already gotten ready, slipping into flip-flops, she headed down the steps. Voices could be heard toward the back of the house. They were in the informal eating area near the kitchen. Annabeth stood at the entrance of the room and glanced at the large table. There sat, in her mind, Celeste Barlow. Across from her was a dark-haired man, presumably her husband, and Abe was next to him. Shannon carried in a pitcher of juice and said good morning to Annabeth. She then gestured to the woman she placed the pitcher in front of, "I'd like you to meet Unina."

Unina looked up at her and gave a brief smile. "Hello," she said in her deep, quiet voice, then took a bite of melon.

Annabeth admitted being a tad starstruck. This was the woman she'd seen in many movies, the woman who'd won an Oscar. She was tiny, delicate like a bird. Her skin, though pale in all her movies, now had the glow of someone who was in the sun frequently. Her luscious, long brown hair was braided, and the braid sat just over her left shoulder. "Nice to meet you," Annabeth suddenly felt shy.

Unina pointed her hand toward the man across the table, "And this is Udok." The dark-haired man turned around and made eye contact with Annabeth, a sheepish expression on his face. It was the man from the night before.

Udok? Why hadn't she recognized him? In truth, there were few photos of him with his wife. They never talked about the sanctuary or her purpose for being in North Carolina or what he did. This was Celeste's husband, the zoology professor and veterinarian. She hoped her face hadn't colored when she looked at him.

Udok spoke innocently, "Very nice to meet you." Okay, so they'd never exchanged names. How could he have known who she was?

Shannon saved the day by returning to the dining room with a pot of coffee, "Can I get you a drink?"

Abe pointed to the seat next to him and she sat down. He was scooping food onto his plate from the platters of eggs and fresh fruit as he asked her if she found the restaurant, she was looking for last night.

Unina silently finished her juice and looked about to rise from the table. Annabeth couldn't let her leave without a word. She looked at the other woman and forced eye contact, "Can we get together this morning and have a conversation? There are so many things we need to talk about for the book."

Unina looked up, and Annabeth saw her expression was one of rejection for a moment, then she relinquished. "That would be fine. Why don't you come up to my room in thirty minutes?" With that, she stepped away from the table, acknowledging none of the others, and moved out of the room.

****

Annabeth was now back in her room preparing to see Unina. She had pointedly not spoken to Udok, waiting to see if he would give her some explanation of why he hadn't said who he was or that he hadn't realized who she was. Either way, it was very uncomfortable. Nothing untoward happened last night, but there was some flirtation.

She gathered up her laptop, checked her phone, got her notebook, pen and left the room. In the hallway, she passed the bench and the washstand and turned to the other wing. Shannon said which was Unina's room, so Annabeth knocked on the first door of the right wing.

Unina responded with a quiet, "Come in." Annabeth attempted to hide her shock at the furnishings of the room. This was double the size of the one she was staying in and everything in it was white, silver and contemporarily furnished.

On the wall were four massive glass doors, two of them currently opened to a grand terrace. Unina was sitting on a long wicker couch, gazing out at the vista before her.

Annabeth walked in and closed the door behind her, still amazed that besides the giant bed that sat in what looked to be a large white box, there was also white furniture and silver end tables. Everything in the room was contemporary. The walls were adorned with canvas prints of lions. There were pictures of groups and individuals. These must be the cats living just outside the house. As she thought that, she heard a sound that must certainly be a lion's roar. It was crystal clear, directly out on the terrace.

Once through the door, she could see the lion sanctuary. Enclosed in a fence was a large grassy area; with trees, and rock cliffs and water, it looked like a real African plain. In it, lions were moving about; one laying in the grass, two others were walking around. She couldn't at this point see all of them, but she saw the recognizable swish of a lion's tail swatting at a fly in the tall grass. Annabeth stood mesmerized, this was the sanctuary, and this is what Unina could do; sit and watch her lions.

It took only moment of standing there, taking in the splendor of the scene, for her to feel is if she was in fact part of it. The sun on this beautiful June morning felt warm. "It's marvelous isn't it?" Unina spoke from the couch.

Annabeth mentally shook herself, her smile unstoppable, "They're beautiful. It looks as if they're in complete freedom."

It was the wrong thing to say. She saw a pained look on Unina's face before she responded, "If only they could be." The mother of lions, adorned in a white caftan, her bare feet tucked under her, motioned to the chair at the right of her couch, "Have a seat."

"Thank you," Annabeth said. "I'm so glad to finally talk to you."

Unina didn't make apologies nor give explanations, she simply said, "The time isn't always right, but I know how important it is that we get this message out."

Annabeth paused; *get this message out?* There it was again. The book was a biography on how movie star, Celeste Barlow, became lion sanctuary owner, Unina. Was that considered a message? Shannon indicated that Unina's manager, MJ, had different motives. Annabeth felt the need to tread carefully. She didn't want the opportunity to at long last sit and talk with the woman to end too hastily. She pointed at her phone, "Is it okay if I record on this? It helps me because sometimes I get caught up in the conversation and my notes aren't thorough."

Unina seemed to consider this and nodded. Annabeth clicked it on, setting it on the glass table between them. "Thank you." She opened her notebook, clicked her pen, then looked over the questions she prepared. "Unina, would you tell me in your own words, why you left your California celebrity life to come here?"

There was silence as Unina closed her eyes for a moment, then looked out and silently watched the cats. Her eyes followed a female who moved toward the middle to squat down and drink out of the watering hole. "Yes, seven years ago I went on a safari in Africa with some friends. They said it would be a great adventure: seeing elephants, giraffes and lions. It was beautiful. We stayed in condos right out in the middle of the plain. Our tour buses were safari vehicles. It wasn't at all what I was expecting. I remember an adorable baby giraffe following behind his mother. I recall being fearful when the big elephants stormed past us with strength so powerful that it shook the wheels of our vehicle. But I also remember the lions.

"Our guide explained to us that over the last twenty years, the population of lions has halved. They fascinated me, they were so beautiful and regal. Watching them was all I wanted to do. I didn't want us to continue. That night I was able to convince our guide to make calls until he found someone to take me back and spend time with the lions. I made a sizable donation to a research team from here in the states and spent a day with them. While we were there, I watched a mother lion shot down by a poacher, taking a meal to her cubs."

Annabeth could see the tears on Unina's cheeks. "The research team was committed to keeping everything in its natural habitat, therefore they would not feed those cubs. Instead they would let them die." Unina reached for her glass of water on the table, took a slow drink, wiped her eyes and then took a deep breath to compose herself.

"When I returned home from the trip, I wanted to see more lions. I looked up where big cats were kept here in our country. Some zoos have reasonable enclosures for lions, others don't. There are private animal farms where lions are kept in the equivalent of big dog cages; horrible conditions. I wanted to do something about it; to have a place where lions, who were living in homes that they shouldn't have been or lions who were neglected, could live like they were meant to live. I wanted to do something in Africa too, but there was so little to do other than send money."

Annabeth was scribbling fast, wishing she'd opened her laptop. This was exactly what she wanted to hear. "In less than a year, I found two lions who needed removed from an animal farm in the Midwest. The authorities shut it down for neglect. This is the land my grandmother left me in her will. North Carolina doesn't have laws against owning lions, and this was my chance. If I couldn't save those cats in Africa, I could save the lions here. It wasn't easy. I was fortunate to discover the zoology department at the University of North Carolina."

"And," Annabeth said the name that was strange on her tongue, "Udok?"

"Yes, he was very helpful and now  the interns are vital too."

# Chapter 5

From her bedroom window a few days later, Annabeth could see the rain pouring down. It formed large puddles and ruts on the gravel drive up to the gate. This was a good day to stay right here and get some writing done.

Breakfast was just she, Shannon and Abe. The three relaxed; none of Unina's moods which could run from morose to irritation at any given moment. Annabeth didn't wish to see Unina's husband, either. As this thought crossed her mind, he stuck his head in her door, "Good morning."

"Hello, Udok."

He gave her a grin, showing lots of white teeth and sparkling eyes. "Please, call me Christian." She nodded, preferring that name. "What are you up to?"

"I've got some pages to write."

He frowned, "Are you sure? Unina will be in the pens all day; she worries about them in the rain. I was going to head into Raleigh, and I thought you might want to come with me."

Annabeth knew she shouldn't, she was feeling mildly uncomfortable about their time at the restaurant. He hadn't mentioned it to anyone, nor had she.

To compensate for her guilt, she tried to engage in a flirting text conversation with Chase last night. It wasn't very successful. She needed to take a weekend soon and go home to New York, but it was tough. Right now, Unina had been more open to talking, and MJ would be here this weekend. Annabeth wasn't going to miss the opportunity to talk to her also.

Today, it would be nice to go into the city. She would love to do a little shopping for herself. Annabeth's prediction of deep puddles was accurate. He drove slowly in his Range Rover, heading out of the bumpy lane across the small highway until they got to the main interstate.

Conversation was light. They talked easily to one another. As they laughed over something, he flashed his smile at her, Annabeth felt warm inside. She mustn't take it the wrong way; it was better to treat this like work time. Reaching in her bag, she pulled out a small steno pad and a pen. "Can I ask you some questions while we're on the road?"

Christian frowned, but he relinquished, "Go ahead."

"Tell me how you met Celeste Barlow."

He considered it a moment. "I remember well. I knew she was in town building her sanctuary and had been at the university. It's all anyone in the department talked about. The first cat was injured, and Celeste came into the zoology building frantic. One of our students tried to talk to her, but she was inconsolable; insisted she needed to speak to an expert."

"And that was you, Dr. Mendoza."

He nodded in agreement. "Yes, she was crying. Nova was limping, she explained. Her tears weren't because the cat was in danger, but because she was in pain." From her side of the truck, Annabeth saw his mouth crinkle into a smile. She knew this was a fond memory and probably the point when he fell for his wife.

"I relinquished and raced to the sanctuary with her." He laughed lightly, "It was nothing more than the old tale of the thorn in the lion's paw, and I was the mouse that removed it."

Annabeth was delighted at his analogy and laughed, "So you're saying *that's all she wrote.*"

The humor left his face. She watched him closely. "Something like that. Though for her it may have been more of a convenience; a guarantee that I would always be there for the lions. I'll admit it I was starstruck by the movie star, also thrilled at the opportunity to live in my own home with lions to care for. I did exactly what she wished. And then she began to change."

Christian stopped for a moment, stared out at the road hard and then glanced at Annabeth. She could see that he was struggling with the decision to tell her how he truly felt about the way Unina was. He swallowed and continued on, "I don't know what I think about you putting these things in the book. I'm not sure what to do."

Annabeth was accustomed to this concern. "It's my goal in writing this book, to attract readers with a fascinating person that they feel already familiar with. I have no desire to write a

Hollywood tell-all book."

This satisfied Christian, and he began to talk. "MJ was still coming here frequently. I think she was sincerely convinced she could get Celeste," he said the word carefully as if it had been a long time since he'd used that name, "to still do movies. She even tried to get her to be the face on some animal products." Annabeth recalled her being the face of a pet food. "Celeste felt she was done with all of that. Her focus was the lions and she wanted to rescue every one that she heard of. We had to force our hands; me and the interns. Getting more cats was defeating the purpose that she wanted, and the state of North Carolina may not have laws, but there are limits."

Annabeth wrote down information then looked at him, "So have you invested your money in this property too?"

Christian shrugged, "Well, I'm obligated to pay for our home. When I resigned from the University, my income ended."

They arrived in Raleigh He looked at the time on the dash, "How about some lunch first?"

They headed into a cafe. "This rain gives us a good excuse to get away. How about we split a bottle of Rosé."

Against her better judgment, Annabeth agreed. Interview time was over, and they sat together as a man and a woman who enjoyed each other's company; talking about their childhoods, their travels, and avoiding the sanctuary all together. Soon the meals were eaten, and the wine bottle sat empty in the bucket of melting ice.

Christian looked at his watch and said, "Well, shall we get

shopping?" As they walked out, he kept his hand at the small of her back. She was ashamed how much she enjoyed the warmth of it on her. It was such a proprietary action that she wished she hadn't allowed him to do.

In the parking lot, he opened the door of the truck and she held on to him as she stepped up. As Annabeth turned to close the door, he was still there. Christian reached up and with his left hand pulled her face to him. He gave her a quick kiss. Annabeth looked at him, "I think we better avoid wine at lunch from now on."

Christian tilted his head back and laughed, "You're such a breath of fresh air." His comment reminded her of exactly who they were and where they were.

She tilted her body away from him. "Christian, you can't do that again." He looked down, nodded his head and then lightly shut the door.

Annabeth sat back facing the windshield, wondering what was wrong with her. She was no longer a lonely, desperate woman who would randomly make out with someone else's husband. She surreptitiously glanced over at Christian. It didn't matter how attractive and charming he was. She almost chuckled aloud imagining that someone this handsome would be interested in her. It was a case of location over attraction. She was, after all, the only woman within his same age range, besides his possibly crazy wife, for miles.

Too bad, kissing or anything else would not occur after two-and-a-half glasses of wine at lunch. The alcohol wasn't giving her the proper mood or emotion or objectivity to even consider her own relationship. She would deal with that later, for now she pulled out her pen again and made a list of things she wanted to pick up at the store. When they parked somewhere, she'd tell him she would go her way and he could go his. This was not and would not be a day date.

Christian parked at Target. Annabeth jumped out of the vehicle before he could arrive at her side of it. He seemed unaffected from the kiss or her rejection. They walked into the store, side by side. He pulled out a big red cart, "Okay, where do we begin?"

She couldn't find the fortitude to tell him to leave her alone. Instead, Annabeth pointed towards the beauty section. "I need some things over here." He stayed by her side. It was absurd how they moved row to row, each putting things in the cart. Their conversation was light and meaningless.

In the outdoor living section, they bought three swimming rafts; a wine bottle shape for her, a slice of pizza for him and a donut-shaped raft for Abe. No mention was made of what Unina would want.

Christian bought himself a set of stars and stripes swim trunks and a tank shirt with a popsicle on it. Annabeth chose a lemon covered tank top. She stepped into the dressing room and tried on several bathing suits, refusing his offer to judge which looked best. In fact, she chose the most modest; a one-piece blue.

When he got distracted in the electronics department; looking at outdoor speakers, Annabeth wandered over to the book section. Perhaps she'd pick up a novel. She needed to keep herself occupied in the evening; time spent with him was too fun. As was her habit, she couldn't help but peek at her own books. *After The Show, The story of Jack Corey*, was still sitting on the shelf with *New York Times* bestsellers.

"Wow, I forget, you're a star in your own right," Christian's voice just over her shoulder, was sincere.

She flushed with the compliment, but brushed it off, "No, I write about stars."

He touched her arm. "Seriously, you are. I saw you on television with him," he motioned toward Jack Corey's name. "You're just so authentic that I forget you're kind of a big deal."

The word "authentic" stung. She thought Chase would disagree with that statement if he could see her now. Grabbing the week's number one novel, a thriller, from the shelf above, Annabeth turned away. "Are you all done?"

Christian sensed the mood change. "Yep, have you got everything you need?"

They paid for their purchases and loaded them into the back of the Rover. Annabeth intended to return to the interview on the trip home. The waning effects of the wine and her confused emotions left her drained. Christian turned country music on the radio. She leaned her head against the seat, and simply listened to the music, telling herself to ignore the handsome man just inches from her.

# Chapter 6

MJ's appearance at the compound caused quite a stir. Unina had been downstairs earlier, grilling Shannon on what food was being cooked. She'd scolded Ben for not keeping up on the yard. Annabeth sat at the table with a cup of coffee, surprised at this change in her book's subject. Ben apologized, and she was tempted to remind Unina that she forced him to spend the entire last two days cleaning the pond in the lions' enclosure, there'd been no time for landscaping.

Abe came in to inform her he fed the cats, then sat down with Annabeth for some breakfast. "Where is Udok?" Unina asked him.

"He drove to the university."

"Fine," she said as she left the room and headed up the stairs.

Shannon brought Abe some muffins that had not previously been out for breakfast; contraband carbs. He grabbed one up. Between bites he rolled his eyes at Shannon, "So the wicked witch is flying in?"

Though her lips twitched, she admonished him, "Abe stop

that. Annabeth will work with her today. Don't give her a bad impression of the woman."

****

Melissa Jo DeSantis, known as MJ in this house, was Celeste Barlow's agent. She'd represented Celeste for twenty-two years. It was MJ who contacted Annabeth's agent about the possibility of a biography. Ever persistent, she'd asked for Annabeth's personal number trying to convince her to take the project.

The agent drove onto the compound in a rented Mercedes, dust flying as she raced down the lane. Annabeth was sitting at the patio table near the pond, facing her laptop. The day was breezy; an unusually comfortable day for North Carolina in June. MJ left the car running, obviously expecting some sort of valet to take care of her. Adjusting her black and white ankle length pants, then shaking out her black hair that sat at her shoulders, she looked over at Annabeth. She was as rail thin as Celeste. Her outfit was a sleeveless turtleneck with the stylish pants, and tall black sandals, closed at the toe. On her face were large sunglasses.

Shannon stepped out of the foyer; a false smile on her face. MJ spoke briefly to her and walked towards Annabeth. From her vantage point, Annabeth could see that MJ didn't even bother to collect her purse. Instead, the older woman was removing an overnight bag from the trunk of the car and MJ's purse from the front seat.

Annabeth didn't have much interest in those who were impressed with themselves. She took charge, pushing back her chair, and standing, "You must be MJ."

"Annabeth, nice to meet you." She sat opposite of her, "How's it going?"

"Good. I've gotten some strong interviews. Spent a lot of time with my research. It's shaping up."

"Has Unina talked to you?"

"Yes, just a couple of times. We sat on her terrace."

MJ looked concerned, "Only twice? Did she say much?"

Not wanting to share her information before it was written, Annabeth said, "Yes. We talked about how she ended up here, the safari and the creation of the sanctuary."

"Well, that's very good. I'm going to be here for three days. We can do a lot of talking."

"That would be helpful. Everyone here is nice about answering questions, but I'd like to talk to someone who can give me honest answers."

MJ raised an eyebrow, "Honest answers?"

"Was she always an animal activist?" Annabeth returned to her laptop.

The woman scoffed at the notion as she placed a frosty glass of unsweetened tea on the table. Shannon brought drinks after serving as valet. "Celeste barely took responsibility for her Persian cat. She hired a pet nanny to feed her and clean her litter."

"Then what changed?"

"The safari was something her friends took her on to get over her divorce from Tate O'Rourke."

Annabeth recalled the marriage. The two darlings of the silver screen began dating while filming a romantic comedy that took place in Barcelona. The press had a field day with their budding off screen romance. The relationship seemed manufactured. It was something actors sometimes did to promote their upcoming film. Many would take it nearly to the altar and split. It surprised Annabeth when Celeste and Tate married after the release of the film. "Did she take their divorce hard?"

"No." MJ held back for only a moment, "It was the three miscarriages in their two-year marriage that tore her apart." This was news. "The third one required surgery that resulted in her inability to ever get pregnant again."

Using the pretense of typing to let in all sink in, Annabeth was drawing conclusions quickly about Celeste becoming Unina. "Did it work?"

"That's when she saw the lioness get shot."

"And her cubs left to starve." Annabeth nodded remembering the details.

MJ sighed, raising her sunglasses off eyes that had been surgically altered to remove all the lines that a woman in her fifties would have. She leaned back in the chair, allowing, only for a moment, the sun to heat her face. "I was in talks with a big studio where she was up for a role in a three-picture deal. It would have been gold."

For who? Annabeth wondered. MJ sat up and placed her large glasses over her eyes. "That was the beginning of the end for the film star, Celeste Barlow. She came home and spent every moment worrying about the lion. Crying over the ones lost. Her therapist said it was a viable outlet for her to seek to find healing over her inability to be a mother."

"She could've adopted," Annabeth mused, taking a gulp of her own tea. She watched two dragonflies flit over the water.

"I suggested that. I think she misunderstood because that's when her idea for this place became her life's purpose. I'll admit the first two lions were adorable. She purchased a motorhome to live here, insisting that the animal shelter be complete before construction on her home."

"She's invested a lot of money," Annabeth said this with her eyes on the screen. Most people didn't want to discuss finances.

"You mean *all* of her money. I've tried to convince her she needs to do another picture to keep the place afloat, but she refuses."

"She was the face of *Healthy Beast Multivitamins* a few years ago."

"That was a nightmare. She insisted on having research done to make sure the company did zero animal testing. I told her the project was to help her sanctuary. At length, Celeste agreed. She did it with the understanding that her mission for lions would be on each package. It cost her almost half the projected earnings."

"Most places like this allow paid admission to help cover expenses."

"I know," MJ's response was accompanied with a heavy sigh. "She refuses."

Annabeth glanced over her notes, "Are the interns paid?"

"Thank God, no. That's how these graduate programs work."

"And Christian provides medical care."

MJ, who was looking down at her large white watch, spinning it around her boney wrist, stopped what she was doing and looked at Annabeth. "Christian?" Her tone made the name sound illicit.

Annabeth felt as if she'd revealed her personal friendship with him. "Do you call him Udok?"

"Everyone here calls him Udok. I've only ever heard him called Christian by her, before she became Unina."

Annabeth attempted a casual shrug, "I guess no one has corrected me."

MJ was sizing her up, her eyes, mostly hidden by sunglasses, took in Annabeth's unruly honey colored hair; pulled up in a messy bun in the heat. The Annabeth who toured with the rock band had been thirty-five pounds heavier. Her petite figure was toned by her hours in the gym. She was wearing light blue gym shorts with white trim. Her top was a thin-strapped tank of royal blue. There was the beginning of a tan on her bare arms and legs, a glow begun with the North Carolinian sun.

She would never be the breathtaking beauty of Celeste Barlow, nor would she be the well-coiffed attractive woman of MJ. Annabeth, however, learned to appreciate herself. Too many years of not being respected by men, both professionally and personally, made her tough. She was a brilliant writer who gained success in recent years. Her confidence was suddenly strong. Though she carried some guilt over her time around Christian, she would not give anything away.

MJ said conspiratorially, "I guess you're aware that their

relationship is unusual."

"Was it always?"

The other woman shrugged, "Honestly, Celeste was drawn to him because of the cats. She was more enamored by his vet skills than anything. He, of course, saw her as a movie star."

Annabeth pretended to look at her files, "But they got married."

"Believe me, I well remember the wedding of Unina and Udok." The names sat on her tongue like a bitter taste.

"I'll be honest," Annabeth looked at MJ, "When I did my research, I imagined I would meet a married couple who worked as a team. She seems to be down at the compound or on the terrace in her room, alone, most of the time."

MJ stood and stretched, as if the topic bored her, "She needs him for the cats and he's clueless of what she needs." She emphasized the word *he*, indicating that she knew better. "I'll go see her. Annabeth, this book must sell. The sanctuary and Celeste's survival depend on it."

# Chapter 7

Christian knew he was trying his best to win the affections of Annabeth when he brought her out to the watering hole, the next evening. He'd put a couple of beers and a bag of tortilla chips in a bag along with fresh guacamole that he'd convinced Shannon to make. Ben hooked up the outdoor speakers, and he played some soft music from his phone.

Annabeth bought into his offer to talk more about the sanctuary, but one look at the blanket in the grass with the late-night picnic and she was unhappy. "This is supposed to be a time for me to gather information on the book, it looks like a seduction."

He smiled, but she didn't respond in kind.

"I'm getting tired of repeating myself. You're a married man. I'm here to write about your wife's life. This is all wrong."

No one needed to tell him how messed up his life was. He wasn't certain how much he was willing to share with Annabeth today. They'd all agreed on discretion.

Celeste Barlow was so animated and passionate when he'd met

her. As intoxicating as this vibrant woman, who he'd watched countless times on screen and admired in photos, appeared, he was also enthralled with the compound.

No expense was spared on building the place. She ordered the best enclosures money could buy from a specialty company. This included all the gating and chutes required to make feeding and moving safe. There were four separate small enclosures for new lions to get adjusted or any other issues when lions needed separated.

Christian had been to Africa and Australia. He'd witnessed animals in the wild. Celeste worked with the best designers, contractors and landscapers to create the habitat. She had rock cliffs constructed that looked authentic. Her landscapers planted just the right vegetation so that some would give the lions visual privacy and others comfortable footing. There were trees large enough to offer shade and be able to withstand a lion scratching on the trunk. The watering hole was a massive thing, designed to look natural but using the best technology to have a filtering system for hygiene.

As a veterinarian, he knew the thoughts and feelings of animals were important. What were the lions' responses to this place that instinctually must have felt it was how they should always have lived? She created a world for her lions that was a utopia.

After the "critical" paw treatment to Nova, Christian began to visit the compound weekly. Celeste regularly text him with questions. Two of her cousins from North Carolina were living with her. She was providing room and board, along with a salary for helping care for the animals.

By this time a male, named Maximillian, arrived from a small circus. Despite neglect, he was a healthy five-year-old. She was in talks with an exotic farm in Ohio to rescue the next two cats. Christian became a fixture at the house as well as the sanctuary. Their dinner conversations and eventually pillow talk focused on the cats.

The Ohio lions arrived in a cattle truck. The owner also sent an older female. She was weak and very ill from the 10-hour trip. Her name was Mable, and her condition was so severe that she allowed Christian and Celeste in her pen right from the start. Celeste spent virtually every hour with the lion's head in her lap. She scooped water in her hand and gently ladled it into Mable's mouth.

Christian put in back-breaking hours caring for the other five cats. It was obvious an extension of the enclosure was needed. He rehired the contractors for the new structure. On top of this, he was driving the near hour-long trip to the university to teach his graduate classes and take care of administrative duties as chair of the Zoology Department.

Eight days after they'd carried Mable off the cattle truck, she took her last breath. Celeste was inconsolable. Her crying rants blamed the laws that allowed unfit proprietors to own animals, the poachers in Africa who killed the lions, making them such a desired possession in the states, even some at Christian for not being able to do anything. Most often, she was angry at herself. If only she'd gotten her sooner. If only she'd got more water and food into her. If only.

Her complete collapse frightened Christian. She seemed so fragile. He was taken by her ability to love. One night he found Celeste, in the rain, sitting on the fresh mound of dirt, where they'd buried Mable, her tears mixing with the gathering puddles. He asked her to marry him. She needed a strong person to take care of her.

Two weeks later, they had their wedding on the front lawn of the house. MJ stood up with Celeste. Christian's brother, Carlos, from San Antonio, stood with him. As the Justice of Peace from the courthouse faced them, Celeste spoke solemnly, "From this day on we are a family to our cats. Their ancestors originated in South Africa; therefore, we will take names of the native Zulu tongue. I am Unina, the mother of our sanctuary. You are Udokotela, doctor of our family."

Behind him, Carlos choked on a laugh. "I will not be called Udokotela." Her face was crestfallen. He couldn't make his bride cry at their wedding. "How about Udok for short?" Her brilliant smile was catching. Though those in attendance raised their eyebrows, Christian was now deemed Udok.

True to her word, from that day on she never spoke his real name. The entire staff and any who entered must address them by their Zulu names. She took her role of mother seriously.

There was no honeymoon, they could not entrust the cats to anyone. Her next demand was that he leave his job at the University. Shortly after, two new cats were scheduled to arrive from an independent circus in Miami. Unina spent hours on her computer or the phone working out the details. Her business lawyer was at her side constantly. Fortunately, that deal fell through, but she had not yet decided to quit rescuing lions.

His hesitancy to leave his job brought scorn from her. Her constant emotional manipulation won. He resigned his position and spent his days at the sanctuary. Unina changed too. After the death of Mable, her concern for the animals was almost manic. If one seemed ill or in a bad temper, she'd spend the entire day at the enclosures. Even before the death of Mable, there were nights when he would go out and find her asleep on the concrete pad near the pens.

While she prepared the wedding, he planned a surprise. Christian had a camp room constructed in the storage building. A bed, bathroom and mini kitchen was installed. Unina wept with joy proclaiming this the best wedding gift she could have ever received. What kind of wedding gift allowed a bride to sleep away from her husband?

****

For two days after their lunch trip, Annabeth focused on her research. Unina allowed her to spend another hour on the terrace with her. She expressed her desire to meet the lions.

Unina began discussing them; their names, their histories. It seemed when the hour was over that she would in fact invite Annabeth down to the compound. That morning, she ended the conversation insisting that she must go down, Annabeth thanked her for her time, stood and said, "Perhaps tomorrow?"

Unina responded, "Perhaps." Her smile indicating that it was a strong possibility and Annabeth was relieved. This was going to happen.

Soon after, she was in her room typing notes with the door open and she heard footsteps on the stairs. Unina must have been headed out to the compound. Annabeth continued writing.

Several hours later, it was nearly dusk, and the North Carolina sun was beating down. Outside the temperature read in the mid-90s. Christian had sent a message up with Shannon for her to come out to the watering hole for a swim. He promised they would talk about the book.

Her initial reaction was to refuse. She didn't to spend an evening swimming with "Udok". The heat of the night, however, changed her mind. Annabeth dug her bathing suit out of the bag, put it on, and grabbed her short summer robe, wrapping it around her.

Out at the watering hole, she was pleased to see all the swim floats were blown up. This was where she found Christian. The music, food and drink looked suspiciously like a seduction. "Don't even think about it!" Annabeth pointed at the man who was attempting to give her a Corona.

He held his one hand up, feigning innocence. Ignoring the beer, she scooped up the inflatable wine bottle and popped in the water. It was wonderful, she immediately felt relaxed and refreshed. Annabeth stretched out on her back. Her eyes were closed, her body was wet and cool. There was a slight breeze, and the heat felt good. The music was soft.

The sound of movement in the water made her raise her head slightly. Christian grabbed his pizza slice raft and paddled out to join her. “A swim before we eat?”

“I’m not hungry,” she refused to look at him.

“The water feels great, swimming first.” He allowed them to float in silence only a moment before he tried to engage her in conversation. “What have you been doing today?”

“I met with your wife.” Annabeth said the word *wife* strongly. “And then I got some writing done. You?”

Christian floated up alongside of her. He lay on his stomach, his hands leaning on his crossed arms. “Oh, I had to check in on Beau and make sure his ear was fine. He was scratching it yesterday.”

For several minutes they both floated in silence. She realized the time for interview questions was never going to happen. Annabeth could almost feel herself starting to drift off to sleep, when suddenly a warm hand touched her cool arm. She jumped somewhat out of her reverie and in the process practically upset her balance on the raft. Christian grabbed her arm to steady her. The ensuing maneuver dumped them both into the water. As she emerged, her hair now soaked, Annabeth looked at him.

“What?”

She gave him an accusing smile, “Did you dunk me on purpose?”

He chuckled, “Absolutely not.”

Grabbing her raft with one arm, Annabeth spoke, “Well, it feels wonderful.”

Christian unabashedly eyed her in the water. Annabeth turned her back on him for a moment. Hanging both of her arms over the raft, she peered back at him, "Christian, stop it. I think this is a game for you. There's a woman here, who's not your wife and you're enjoying the flirtation. But it's not okay with me."

His smile disappeared instantly. His eyes were dark and serious, "Annabeth, you're wrong. I truly enjoy being around you."

"At the home of your wife."

"It's my home," now it was his turn to look away. "I don't have to tell you this isn't a normal situation."

Annabeth interrupted, "It's not my concern. I'm also involved with someone. I won't come here and be that person."

Christian sighed, he reached over and gently stroked her shoulder, "I know you're not. I know you're too good for that. I'm sorry." He looked in her eyes, "I'm truly sorry." Slowly climbing back up on his raft, he closed his eyes.

Annabeth followed suit. So funny that he'd say she was too good for that, she'd never been too good for that. She'd been the other woman before and she'd always justified it, but this wasn't okay. Besides what about Chase? She had her doubts about him. The relationship probably wouldn't survive; she was ruining it right now. How could she stay with him, if she so easily responded to the very next man who looked her way?

They both floated on their backs in silence, as the warm air dried their suits. She thought perhaps Christian was asleep. Annabeth tipped her raft slightly to the side and rolled gently into the water. When she did this, Christian woke up. He turned and looked at her, his expression was one of sadness. Annabeth hated how it affected her.

He was watching her and read her thoughts. Slowly dropping into the water, in the small space between their rafts, he wrapped his warm arms against her bare midriff. She allowed his lips to meet hers. The kiss was slow. Annabeth didn't even recognize her own hands that were stroking his back, his shoulders and even his chest. He was doing the same to her. Suddenly there was absolutely no chill to the water, it became a boiling pit of desire. Their kissing increased.

Annabeth thought, *we're going to do this, we're going to take off our suits and do this right here in the water, right here in the front yard of the compound.* She shook her head, and it seemed to return them both to awareness. Christian pulled away and turned his back, gaining his composure. She also turned, grabbed her raft with both arms and began to paddle to the edge of the pool.

Annabeth stepped out, laid her raft against the patio table and scooped up a towel. She had just wrapped it around her body, when Christian also stepped out. Reaching for his towel, he looked at her, his eyes very serious, "I'm sorry, but I'm not. I don't know what to say other than I don't want to stop this. I want this to go further." With that he walked away from her and headed into the house. Annabeth dropped into the chair.

# Chapter 8

That night when she text Chase, she was pleased that he asked if they could FaceTime. This was just what she needed; to see the man she cared about. When their screens both revealed them, she saw he was in his apartment on his couch; most likely watching television. Still in his work polo shirt with the *New York Health* logo in the right corner, Chase looked familiar, adorable, and someone she could appreciate.

He smiled widely at her. She wore a tank top, her damp hair tied back in a band. Fortunately, she'd applied mascara and eyeliner before she sat down to work and received his suggestion. "You look tan," he said.

"Yep, it's pretty hot here in the African savannah." Annabeth winked, "But they have a pond right out front."

"How are the lions?" she frowned at his question and he looked perplexed, "You still haven't seen the lions?"

"Nope. Hopefully tomorrow is my big day."

Now Chase almost looked angry, "I don't understand why you

had to be there all this time, when you haven't even seen the actual animals that the book is about!"

Annabeth rushed in to correct him, "No, my book is about Celeste Barlow, who I have been meeting with. I've also met with her husband, her agent, her intern; who works with the animals, and her housekeeper. Sometimes those are where the actual information for the book comes from. I have met with her a few times. She has to decide that I have earned my right to see the animals."

Chase rolled his eyes, "Yeah, she definitely sounds like she's a little off her rocker." He reached down and grabbed a bottle of beer off the coffee table and took a slow swig. "It doesn't sound like the Celeste Barlow I've seen in the movies."

She gave him a smile and whispered conspiratorially, "Trust me, she's not."

He nodded, "Well, I guess that's what makes a good book."

"Exactly, tell me what you've been up to."

"Not much, new project at work. It's going well. Looks like I might have to head to Boston next week for a couple of days. I've been kind of bad about not going to the gym." Now he gave her a longing smile, "It's just not as fun."

Annabelle felt her heart pound a little faster. Her tone was sincere, "Thank you. I miss you too."

"When can I see you?" his eyes were serious.

Annabeth was quiet a moment, thinking maybe a weekend away would be smart. Unless Celeste decided it was time for her to see the lions, she should leave the compound and distance herself from Christian. She looked at the screen, "How about this weekend? What have you got going on?"

Chase grinned, "Nothing, are you coming back here?"

She nodded, "Absolutely, I think that's a good idea. It'd be good to check on the apartment."

"Oh, I see, it has nothing to do with me." He offered her a flirty grin.

She didn't tease him back, in fact her expression was very serious, "Yes Chase, I really want to see you."

****

The next morning, as Annabeth was taking her coffee cup into the kitchen and having a conversation with Shannon, Unina appeared. She was in khaki cargo pants, rope flip flops and a *Peaceful Pride* T-shirt with the sleeves rolled up over her shoulders. She glanced at Annabeth's outfit, jeans and a *Rolling Stones* T-shirt. Unina gave a half nod as if the outfit met her approval. She looked at Annabeth, her expression serious, "Would you like to come down with me to see the lions?"

Annabeth's heart was pounding out of her chest with excitement, but she maintained a calm voice, "That would be wonderful. May I bring my camera?"

Unina shook her head, "No, not this time. Let's let them meet you first, before you take pictures that might make them uncomfortable."

"Just let me grab my sunglasses."

"No, I don't want you to wear sunglasses. I want them to see your eyes. You must gain their trust," once again Unina shook her head.

Behind her, Annabeth could see Shannon do a slight eye roll and then turn her focus toward the kitchen sink. It didn't matter whether it was ridiculous, Annabeth agreed. This was a big moment.

The two women headed out the door which lead to the garage below. Unina pushed a button that opened the furthest door, there sat two utility vehicles; one was a four-seater, and the other had a long flat bed. These were the compound vehicles. She led Annabeth to the four-seater, climbing behind the wheel.

As the women rolled slowly down the trail, Unina talked about the lions. "I'm glad you're coming this morning. They'll be hungry, then after their morning meal they're ready for attention. Amra and Kyra are especially playful."

Annabeth was already jotting things downs, "They're your young cubs?"

"Yes, just ten months old, they've been with me for three."

"Where did you get lions so young?"

"The farm that we first received Nova and Luna from, foolishly got two more." Unina smacked the steering wheel in frustration. "They seemed so grateful when we took the girls. They were malnourished. I could see their ribs." She paused a moment. Annabeth could see with a sideways glance that she was trying to compose herself. "They had infections in their eyes. Those people promised they'd never get exotic animals again. I foolishly paid the price they were asking to save those lions."

"Normally, does a sanctuary pay for the animals they rescue?"

"Absolutely not, and that was the last time I did it. It's a poor idea because monsters like them immediately get new animals and attempt to sell them."

"Did you have to pay for Amra and Kyra too?"

They were getting closer to the buildings; Annabeth could hear the sounds of animals; an occasional roar and grumble. She felt her pulse increase in excitement.

"No, this time I brought the local animal protection with me, this was Abe's suggestion. It worked perfectly. They handed them over to avoid being fined. Later they signed legal documents stating that they could no longer have animals on their property. Fortunately, the cubs hadn't been there long. They were still healthy."

She parked the vehicle near the first building. Turning to Annabeth, she spoke firmly, "Just do as I say. Don't attempt to touch any or approach them."

Shaking her head, Annabeth spoke, "My purpose here is to watch you interact with the cats."

This pleased Unina, "Good. If you just stay back and let me take care of my pride, it will be fine."

They walked around the corner of the building. The enclosure was impressive. The fencing stood fifteen-feet-high and took up an acre of space. Annabeth had seen from the terrace that there were several trees in the enclosure, some small slopes and rocks stacked like cliffs. The watering hole was large enough for three to four lions to get in at once. The landscape varied from tall grasses to bare spots and short grass.

As Unina approached the gate, an incredibly large male leaped off a large boulder and bolted toward the gate. The females stirred from where they were scattered but did not yet move to the fence. Out from the tall grass strode the other enormous male. The half-grown cubs appeared from near the watering hole.

The first male to arrive at the fence was making a noise that sounded like a huffing noise. The change in Unina was shocking. She began to coo as her face broke into the gorgeous smile that Annabeth had seen grace many magazine covers. "Oh Maximillian, you gorgeous man, are you hungry?"

The 450-pound beast began rubbing his giant lips and equally massive teeth along the fence. Unina moved close and ran her hand against his fur. Annabeth nearly gasp when he pushed his mouth close to her fingers, then laughed aloud as his huge pink tongue licked the other woman's fingers.

Maximillian noticed her for the first time, froze and stared at her. Unina whispered to him, "It's okay Max. She's our friend." By now Beau moved near the fence too and was rubbing his head along the chain links, hoping for a touch. She moved to him and scratched his long brown mane that was poking through the steel wire. Without looking, she said quietly, "Annabeth, they both want attention. Why don't you give Max a scratch?"

Annabeth couldn't believe this was happening. She was being asked to approach the king of the jungle and pet his head.

Her heart pounded and her hand trembled as she edged closer. His big nose pressed against the fence as he sniffed her. Unina moved near, the massive male lion heads were next to one another.

"That's it, check her out."

To her complete delight, Max must have found her acceptable, because in the next moment, he tilted the side of his head against the fence, attempting to make contact with her hand. Annabeth, tentatively, let her fingers touch the coarse fur.

Unina's voice was quiet, calming. "Just use the palm of your hand to rub his head. Don't stick your fingers in the cage."

She didn't need to be told that, but as her palm connected with Max, Annabeth melted. She felt just a pinprick of the thrill that must have made Celeste Barlow fall in love with these big cats. She watched the two males almost touching head to head. "Do they ever fight?"

Unina moved away, heading into the building. "Oh, they did at first. It was quite terrifying." She paused; Annabeth could hear her opening doors. The lions apparently knew she was preparing their food, they both stood side by side, eyes to the door. They were making low rumbling noises, almost like a deep hum.

"Step way back," Unina ordered. She emerged from the building pulling a wagon full of meat. Beau and Max now separated and stood at different gates. Unina pulled out a monstrous chunk of ground meat and opened a sliding panel. "These are their food chutes. They have their own and know to stand at it."

Annabeth began to record on her phone in her pocket. She was too intrigued by all of it to be taking notes. Max was eating noisily, Unina now slid the same portion into Beau's chute. She then moved to the other side of the enclosure where three more chutes were placed. The females were all soon eating.

When the wagon was empty, Unina rolled it to the building. "So, they fought at the beginning?" Annabeth retrieved her notebook from the vehicle.

"Yes, it was incredibly stressful to go through the process of introduction. In the wild, it would be near impossible to have two unrelated males live in the same pride. It helps that we sterilize them."

"Are all of your cats sterilized?"

"They are," Unina used a hose to spray off the wagon. She then got down a tray and was putting what looked to be vitamin supplements into chunks of meat. She attached the pieces to long wooden skewers, seven of them. "I am not equipped to deal with breeding. Plus, this is not the environment to bring in new cubs. It would be marvelous if new cubs could be introduced to their motherland. Unfortunately, even in South Africa there are too many difficulties to guarantee their survival. The cubs have already been sterilized."

"Does this also help with the males getting along?"

"Absolutely. They need not claim the females as their own. But when they first met, we kept them in separate enclosures."

"How did you know that it was safe to put them out together?"

Unina was setting the skewers in a large bucket, almost like a meat bouquet. This she placed on the wagon and began to roll it out. "They were in neighboring pens. When they would lay side by side, with only a fence between them, we knew they were accepting of one another." While she spoke, Annabeth followed her to the fence.

The lions knew exactly what she was doing. Max approached, apparently the first alpha and greedily gobbled the chunk of meat off the stick. She then moved to Beau, who did the same thing. Mealtime was over. Max returned to his rock cliff and despite his large size leaped up onto it with seamless effort. Beau ambled out to the water and squatted down for a drink.

The women moved to the side where the females were, each of the three adults approached for their meat vitamin. Unina continued her story, "It was distressing when we released them. Udok had a tranquilizer gun ready, just in case. They didn't need it. Both were born and raised in civilization. After a few wary sniffs they moved their separate ways. Beau was eager to check out his new world."

The older females moved away and the young ones; Amra and Kyra, were standing on hind legs, eager for the treat. Unina sat on the ground and patted next to her for Annabeth to join her.

She laughed out loud and her voice was that of a loving parent, "Come here, girls. Our friend, Annabeth, will help me with your vitamins." She handed a stick to her.

The two young lions tried to stick their noses through the fence. "Step back so you can get these, sillies," Unina reached in and pushed the chest of one. Both cats moved back and gobbled the meat. Annabeth loved the feel of the large mouth pulling against the skewer. When it was plucked off, she pulled the stick back and sat it on the ground with the others.

They eagerly swallowed the treat down and then approached the fence. “These two act like overgrown puppies. It’s okay to reach in and scratch them.” Amra and Kyra seemed to know what she said. They both collapsed against the fence.

Annabeth used her fingernails along the spine of one of the young lions. “Who’s this?”

“That’s Kyra.” Unina had her face against the fence, kissing the forehead of Amra.

“Hello, Kyra. Aren’t you a good girl?” The lion was sliding her body against the ground, so that Annabeth could scratch her entire spine.

It wasn’t long before the entire pride became sleepy. Everywhere she looked, Annabeth saw napping lions. Unina glanced at her, “You look very hot. It takes a while to get used to this weather. Why don’t I drive you to the house?”

Annabeth thought she was being politely dismissed. That was fine, she would not disagree. Things went so well. In fact, she was eager to go back and write about the experience. “No thanks, I’ll walk. I could use the exercise. I feel as if I’ve been inactive for days.” Both women stood, “Thank you so much for bringing me here. This has been one of the best moments ever.”

Unina seemed very pleased. “Next time, I think it would be fine if you brought your camera.”

# Chapter 9

Annabeth entered through the front door. She'd stood out on the porch for a moment swatting off dust that was clinging to her jeans. Her t-shirt felt sweaty and her eyes took a moment to adjust to the inside light after the brightness of the sun without UV protection.

Shannon walked into the foyer, “You look beat.”

“I am, it was hot.”

“Why don't you splash some water on your face, put on something cooler and I'll get you some lunch and a nice cold drink.”

Annabeth smiled gratefully at the other woman and jogged up the steps. She looked at her laptop. It would be wise to sit down and begin writing, but she was warm and hungry. When she tossed on shorts and a t-shirt, she also grabbed her notebook and pen. If Shannon would sit with her while she had lunch, this might give them a chance to talk too.

Soon she was back down in the kitchen where Shannon had a

plate prepared with fresh melon, strawberries and chicken salad. Next to it was a frosty glass of iced tea. Annabeth sat on a bar stool at the open counter. Shannon was putting the supplies away from the quick lunch she'd made. After Annabeth took a long swallow of the tea, she spoke, "So Shannon, how did you end up working here at *Peaceful Pride*?"

The other woman took a rag and was wiping the counter slowly. "Unina's grandparents were friends of my parents. My mother and her grandmother both grew up around here."

"I bet everyone here was pretty impressed with the celebrity that Celeste became?"

Shannon nodded her head, remembering life before she was dealing with Unina. "Oh yes, it was amazing. I can recall when she had her first TV appearance and then her first movie. In fact, her grandparents had an Oscar party when she won the Academy Award. They invited me to it right on this land."

"Did you know Celeste before the compound?"

"No, but I'm over twenty years older than Unina. They never invited me to meet her on the rare occasions that she was here; and they were rare. She was here for her grandfather's funeral and for her grandmother's. I attended the funeral with my mother."

Annabeth swallowed a bite of her sandwich, "Is your mother still alive?"

"Yes, she is. She lives in an assisted living home in Chapel Hill."

"So, when Unina was looking for people to help here, she found you?"

Shannon shrugged her shoulders, "I lost my husband six years ago to lung cancer." Annabeth murmured her sorry. Shannon nodded accepting it, "And my grown son lives in Texas. So, I was bored, alone. I took care of my dying husband for eighteen months. I agreed to come in, do a little cleaning. It was supposed to be for five hours a day, not a problem."

Annabeth was certain that now Shannon lived here. There was never a time day or night when she hadn't seen her here. In fact, she was certain that Shannon's room was just across the hall from hers. "Don't you live here full-time?" she asked.

"Yes, I have for the last two-and-a-half years."

"So how did that come about?"

"Well," Shannon poured herself a glass of iced tea and sat on the stool opposite of Annabeth's, "as the lion numbers increased, it was obvious that Celeste needed more help. Her only focus was the cats." Annabeth felt that there was more she could say but didn't. "And then Udok came and things were even busier. In fact, the doctor invited me to live here."

"Do you have your own home?"

Shannon shook her head, "No, I sold it. There was no need to keep it. It didn't hold happy memories for me anyway, it was where my husband passed away. If this job ends someday, then I'll move on when my mother passes. There's probably the biggest chance I'll go to where my son is."

"When did," Annabeth considered her words carefully searching for the right ones, "Unina begin to..." she couldn't find the words.

Shannon understood the question and said, "The death of the

older lion made her feel inadequate."

Annabeth glanced back through her notebook, "You're referring to Mabel."

"Yes, she told you about her?" Shannon looked surprised.

Annabeth almost said no, Christian told her, but remembered MJ's response and instead said, "The doctor told me."

"With the first two lions, her intent was to devote as much time as she could on the care of the cats. When the next three arrived and the elderly lioness was so very ill, I didn't see Unina for days. I had Ben take food down three times a day. He insisted she was hardly eating, but I just kept trying. And when Mabel died, well it was as much a place of mourning as when I lost my husband."

****

Annabeth hated calling Chase two days later to tell him that Unina was allowing her daily visits to the lions, and that changed everything. Her only words that offered him any hope was that the increased time with Celeste was giving her more information and could mean the sooner she could return to New York to write the book in its entirety.

It was true, she'd been able to be with the cats three more times. Annabeth loved every minute. The biggest thrill was yesterday. The young ones were due for shots. Both Unina and Udok were there. She felt that at the compound she must force herself to think of him as Udok. Christian was the man that she fought hard to keep out of her daydreams.

She watched the process of getting a lion into the shift pen from the enclosure. Kyra was first, she was friendly enough so they could easily get her into the small space. Unina then climbed in with her and placed a large collar and leash around her neck. The lion was thrilled to have her "mom" so close and rubbed all over her, even standing and placing her front paws on Unina's shoulders.

Udok was not amused. "She will scratch you up or break a bone, Unina."

She didn't even look at him, her smile and laughing voice directed at the playful cat, "I'm fine."

"Maybe if you ate something once in a while, you'd be strong enough to handle this."

Now Unina frowned at him, "Don't ruin my fun." Udok gave up and opened the cage door. The cat bounded out, and he had to take the leash from his wife.

Annabeth watched from a distance, discreetly taking photographs. She forced herself to look at them as a married couple who devoted their lives to this sanctuary. Though they didn't act like a pair of lovers, they operated well as a team in the handling of Kyra. Soon they got her into the building. She readily jumped up on the examining table, her attention now on the leash. Her large paws batted at it as if it was a ball of yarn.

Unina waved Annabeth to her. They stood on each side of the lion. Annabeth loved being able to scratch the cat behind the ears. Kyra rubbed her cheek against Annabeth's hand. Udok vaccinated the cat, while she was focused on the women surrounding her. The curls on Annabeth's head caught her attention, and she reached out a paw to swipe at one.

Udok's hand shot out and grabbed at the claws, "Kyra, no." His voice was harsher than necessary.

"She's just a baby, she wouldn't hurt her," Unina protested.

"Those claws could have done serious damage to Annabeth's face," his voice was sharp.

Annabeth looked down, embarrassed when she saw Unina look from her husband to Annabeth. "We wouldn't want that."

# Chapter 10

On Saturday morning, she felt confident enough in her acceptance at *Peaceful Pride* that when she woke up and saw a nice breeze was blowing, decided to take a walk near the compound. Annabeth pulled on shorts and a shirt and added her tennis shoes. She grabbed her phone and earbuds. A long walk would do her muscles some good.

Just to be careful, she moved quietly as she left the house. She wasn't certain if Abe spent the night, but she didn't want him stopping her from walking along the trail. She respected Unina's rules and would not go down to the cats. However, there were some nice trails around the yard and near the trees. Annabeth found her favorite station, classic rock, and put it on shuffle.

Moving at a steady pace, she felt the stretching pull of muscles. She hadn't been exercising enough. It felt good. Though it was already warm, it wasn't humid. She walked at a quick pace, marching to the beat of *Baba O'Riley* by the Who, when a sudden movement caught her peripheral vision. She froze, instinct telling her not to move. Could it be some sort of wild animal? It wouldn't be one of the cats, right? Something moved, and it was good-sized. Annabeth stood silent for a moment, waiting to see it move again. Nothing.

Her imagination made her crazy. Was it just a rabbit or a bird perching on a large branch? Suddenly, she felt something move up behind her and grab at her waist. It wasn't a creature; it was the hands of a man and he turned her around. Christian gave her the grin she found irresistible.

She smacked his chest lightly; the sound coming out of her mouth a mixture between a scold and a laugh. He scared the hell out of her. With no remorse, he chuckled, "I'm so sorry."

Annabeth stepped away from, "I seriously doubt it."

He pulled her to him, his lips inches from hers. Her hands were at his chest, she was close. She wanted badly for their lips to meet, but she laid her hand lightly on his cheek. "No, none of that."

Annabeth stepped back. This time something else caught her eye. She looked to the left of them and in the distance, she could see Luna and Nova. Both cats were pressing against the fence toward the shelter. This was what they did when a human was near; and they wished to be scratched. Was Unina standing there? Had she seen them?

****

It was a rainy day, the kind of rain that would last for hours. MJ was back. She apparently went out to the compound in her car, because a drenched Unina climbed out of the passenger's side and headed straight up to her room.

When she came back down, she was wearing loose white linen pants and a flowing top to match. Her hair looked as if she dried it with a towel and brushed it out. She looked like the starlet; Celeste Barlow.

Annabeth was with Abe and MJ, sitting at the table, in the late afternoon, drinking coffee. Abe was eating cookies off a china plate. At the appearance of Unina, Shannon swiftly took the plate back into the kitchen and brought out of a bowl of fresh fruit.

Unina looked at all their mugs and shook her head. "Shannon bring me a bottle of vodka."

MJ clapped her hands together and laughed, "A much better choice for a dreary afternoon. Shannon, do you have some tonic and lime out there too?"

They left the table and settled themselves on the sofas that surrounded an immense coffee table which looked to be a slice of a giant tree.

It shocked Annabeth to see that Unina was quite a drinker. The woman sucked down her beverage as if it was a glass of ice water. She wished she had her notebook. Her instincts told her this would be a time to glean some good information. Instead, she surreptitiously set up her phone to record and had it ready. Christian wasn't at the compound today which wasn't unusual. The four women and young Abe relaxed on their own.

Because of her tiny diet, the vodka seemed to affect Unina quickly. She didn't wait for the tonic and lime and swallowed down her first glass. She was pouring her second while the others turned theirs into cocktails.

MJ began sharing some Hollywood gossip with the group. Abe launched into a tale he'd heard about a rap star making an upcoming spy thriller. Unina jumped in when she heard the name, apparently drink number two loosened her tongue. "Oh, he could definitely be a successful actor. He's been faking his way through marriages for years." She poured her third glass.

Abe laughed at this and asked her if she knew him. To Annabeth's delight, the woman became sharp-tongued Celeste Barlow. Annabeth discreetly hit her phone to record. The subject of her book shared stories of Hollywood as smoothly as she downed the vodka.

It wasn't long before MJ rose and retrieved a fresh bottle from the liquor cabinet. She joined Unina in spinning tales of the days gone by. Even Annabeth's own days at *Rolling Stones Magazine* allowed her to take part in the conversation.

MJ mentioned a man who'd splashed the covers of most magazines with his success in movies and his lack of success with women. She stretched her legs out on the couch, so that her toe nudged Celeste. "I always hoped that you two would do a picture together. It most certainly would have been a success. I could actually have seen you two as a couple, as well."

The other woman clanged her empty glass on the table, "Oh stop it, MJ, you're boring me with all of this talk."

Her manager was undaunted by the reprimand, "Well it shouldn't bore you. A movie with him would bring a fortune to keep this place afloat."

Unina turned and looked at her manager, "Shut the hell up!"

Annabeth exchanged surprised looks with Shannon. MJ, however, remained unaffected by the comment. "I'm not kidding. You're a great actress and you've let these years go by. Now the motion picture industry could use the mature Celeste Barlow. You could be making pictures, you're at a great age to do so."

"I'm not going back to that world, my world is here," Unina looked almost pouty.

"What I'm telling you is that you can make a few million on one picture. And you have people around here who could take care of the cats while you go on location for a few months. Think about the money you could bring in for the sanctuary."

Annabeth silently applauded MJ for making a strong point. If the situation was that they were desperately trying to afford to keep the sanctuary healthy, a movie deal would be an enormous one.

Unina looked at her empty tumbler on the coffee table, after a moment's hesitation, she grabbed the bottle of vodka, pouring the remaining liquid in her glass. "MJ, you know how I feel about this. I cannot leave my family for a couple of months."

Annabeth felt as if she was watching a sparring match and her eyes went right to MJ waiting for her next statement. MJ didn't argue, apparently her many years being the management of Celeste Barlow taught her a more successful way of dealing with the actress. Instead, she took a sip of her own drink and put on a sweet smile. In a soft voice she said, "Unina darling, I'm sorry. I didn't mean to upset you. You know my concern is for the well-being of your sanctuary. There are things you'd like to do to make their lives better. You need lots of money in case of an emergency. It's just the best and quickest way to get that money."

Unina's eyes clouded over for a moment as she considered, then she drank the rest of her vodka and her angry mood returned, "It's not happening. I'm not leaving. This is where I belong!" She looked around the room at the others, her eyes settling on Annabeth. "What do you think Annabeth Muldoon? Is that why you're actually here, to convince me to go back on the screen?"

Across the room, Annabeth shook her head. "Absolutely not. I'm here to write about you; your life from the beginning of Celeste Barlow to you as Unina, the mother of the lions." She patted herself on the back for saying that with a straight face. "And the point of this book is to make money to help you finance the sanctuary."

She thought she was saying the right thing, but apparently, she hadn't, because once again Unina slammed down her empty tumbler and the vodka bottle with nothing remaining in it. "No," her voice now cracked, and it seemed as if she might cry, "I don't care if people read my story. I care that we save the lions. And," she looked at MJ accusingly, "I don't just mean mine; I mean all the lions. If I did another picture, I'd want to give it to save lions everywhere, not just my own." A drunk woman made this speech.

There was an awkward silence, Abe studied the ice in his drink. Shannon was pulling on a thread of her t-shirt. MJ and Annabeth made eye contact. Annabeth tried to convey in her expression that she didn't know what to say and that it was up to MJ. The silence remained for another few moments.

MJ sat up and moved close to Unina. She put her hands on the other woman's knees and spoke softly. Annabeth had to strain to hear, "Sweetheart, I'm sorry. You know I never want to upset you. And I know your heart is so big. I know you'd like to save the entire world. I will not tell you how to live your life. I only push because I care about you and the lions. But it's your life and your choice sweetie. I know you'll figure this out." Now she looked up, "And I know Annabeth, here, will write the best book and it will make so much money. Hopefully, you'll get to do everything you want with it."

Shannon and Annabeth shared uncomfortable looks. Both women knew that the finances of the place needed a miracle to keep it functioning. It would also need to be run by a stable proprietor. They'd be lucky if it survived another year or two at this rate.

# Chapter 11

The next morning, Annabeth woke to the sound of doors slamming and raised voices. Unina was shouting at MJ as they headed down the steps. The topic appeared to be alcohol. When she was certain they'd moved all the way down, the reporter in her had Annabeth sneaking a few steps closer to hear the conversation.

Unina was apparently angry at her own behavior the night before. She was attempting to declare the house be alcohol free. MJ used quiet soothing tones, words trying to convince Unina that no harm was done. Annabeth thought perhaps the other woman regretted revealing any of her old self to Annabeth.

Unina called Shannon into the room and told her to empty all the liquor bottles. Just then, Annabeth felt a hand on her back. It was Christian, coming from upstairs. She started to make an excuse for eavesdropping, but he paid no attention to her as he headed on down at a rapid pace.

"Enough! Calm down Unina." His voice was firm.

"There will be no more alcohol in this house. It is an unhealthy and foolish drug!"

"You can certainly give it up. Lord knows you overdo it when you drink, but you will not ban alcohol from all of us."

Unina's voice was outraged, "I can do what I want, this is my house!"

"It is our house."

"So now you're going to act like my husband?"

"As if you want me to," Christian's tone was dry. Annabeth could hear his voice directed elsewhere, "MJ, why don't you get Unina some water and aspirin."

Unina wasn't finished with him. "Oh, so suddenly, you wish to oversee me. I think your interests lie elsewhere."

From the staircase, Annabeth flushed. His voice was deadly low, "Don't embarrass yourself or anyone else in the room. I am as true to my commitment as you are."

Suddenly hearing footsteps moving in her direction, Annabeth raced to her room and shut the door. It was Christian, soon she heard another door slam in the right wing of the second floor.

****

She was happy to load her suitcase into the back of her car a day later. The weather returned to its sunny skies, and she was leaving. Her weekend getaway had come at last. Time with Unina exhausted her, as did the attempt to not be near her husband. Fortunately, Unina was her usual self the next day and allowed Annabeth a chance to come and photograph the lions.

Now, she decided a trip to the beach might be the perfect way to spend some time with Chase. He deserved it; he'd been very clear when they talked at night that he missed her. She could go home but her time was limited and three hours on the road was quicker than airport traffic. She didn't feel comfortable bringing him to the sanctuary. What if Christian said something or looked at her a certain way? She also didn't want Unina to think of her any less because she brought a stranger into the compound.

It'd taken some convincing, but Chase finally agreed to rent a small bungalow at the Outer Banks of North Carolina. In their brief relationship, they'd never been on a vacation. She thought this was just what she needed; a weekend away from the craziness of *Peaceful Pride*. The irony was not lost on her.

Within a short while, Annabeth cruised on the Coastal Highway, headed with other vacationers, over the bridge and to the peninsula that was the Outer Banks. She arrived at the little beach shack she'd rented from a vacation home rental app. The tiny place was appealing with cedar plank siding and a front door painted a raspberry pink. The back steps were just a few feet away from the sound. Two kayaks were available to use. Across the street, a view of the Atlantic peeked from between the houses.

After carrying in her bag and going to the small bathroom to freshen up a bit, she walked out to the back deck to see the sound. Behind her, she heard footsteps. Chase dropped his own bag and walked straight to her. His hands were on her shoulders. Annabeth turned in his arms and they kissed. Looking into his hazel eyes, it relieved her to still find him appealing.

"Hello stranger," he greeted when the kiss ended. "I've missed you."

"Missed you too."

He looked over her head and caught the view of the water. His hands dropped from her waist as he stepped out. "This is fantastic I can't believe you found this place."

Annabeth laughed, "Yes, there's nothing like a smartphone to get us everything we want."

Chase walked down the few steps to check out the kayaks. When he turned back, his expression resembled that of a small boy, "Do you kayak?"

Annabeth shrugged, "I can certainly learn."

Soon they were both seated in kayaks; hers green, his blue, making their way across the sound. They saw fish and turtles; happily, no snakes or alligators. The sun was rising, and it was getting warm, so she convinced him they should go back.

They decided they'd head over to the beach to cool off in the ocean, but when they were changing from their kayaking clothes to their swimsuits, they ended up in bed for an intimate reunion and a small nap.

A walk along the beach followed. They spread out a towel in the sand. Several bars had fabulous waterfront views, and they decided to come back in the evening. Annabeth was enjoying herself.

This time with Chase was what she needed. It served as a reminder of who should be with. Chase pretended to lift her up at the shore, threatening to drop her in. She almost called him Christian, but recovered, and he didn't notice. He was her romantic partner.

On Sunday afternoon they were sitting by the sound, dangling their feet in the water. Chase got a little moody, "So when are you going to be back in New York?"

Annabeth shrugged her shoulders, "I don't know. It's coming along, it really is, but I'm struggling with how it will end."

"It's not a novel, and she's not an old person who's near the end of her life, how is it supposed to end?"

"I don't know. I guess what I mean is that Unina and the sanctuary can't continue the way they're going. I feel like there's something bubbling under the surface and it's about to explode."

"What about her husband?" Chase asked.

"What do you mean?"

"Well, they're married. Can't he get it across to her what the situation is?"

"Their marriage is weird, to say the least. I don't think he has any more control over her than anyone. If her agent, MJ, can't talk her into anything, then no one can." Chase looked at her confused. "She's probably the only influence over Unina and even she can't get her to earn any money. You know my last assignment had such a great ending, which sounds bad. When Jack was hurt in his accident, it changed his whole life and it happened to be at the point when I was there writing. My other two subjects' books were about older people and so they were the living the after-career life. That was easy too. I'm uncertain what I will do with this one or how it will go."

Chase seemed to try to understand, but at the same time, she knew he was thinking selfishly about having her back in New York.

He turned to her, “There's only so much research you can do. Can't you get it done and come to New York to write it? If something changes, then you can return.”

Annabeth sighed. “I miss you too, Chase, and it's been great to see you this weekend. I promise you this isn't forever. It hasn't been that long. Do you know how many months I traveled for the other books? I’ll be back when I'm done.”

# Chapter 12

As she made the return trip to *Peaceful Pride* sanctuary on Sunday evening, she reflected on her time with Chase. He was a great guy, she genuinely cared about him. They were compatible. He made her feel younger and more active than she'd ever thought possible. She hardly recognized herself sometimes. But she also felt a pull or something deeper when she was around Christian. These thoughts were accompanied with shame. How had her thoughts of Chase turned to him?

She rolled into the compound just as dusk was coming on. It was a strange place. So much land, such a large house with extra buildings around it, but rarely any signs of life. Though there were people that were in and out daily and those who lived there full time, there was none of that family feel of someone coming to greet you at the door.

She no longer needed to buzz Shannon on the intercom because she had a code. She was certain be there. Though she did sometimes take weekends off, she hadn’t mentioned that she was

doing so. Annabeth pulled into the garage, grabbed her bag out of the back and on impulse headed out through the door she'd just driven in. She felt
like being outside for a while and not in the cavernous lonely house.

As she made her way to the front steps, she saw a silhouette of someone sitting by the watering hole. Was Abe here tonight? Annabeth placed her bag and purse on the step and moved toward the pond. As she got closer, she regretted that she had done so; it was Christian.

He didn't turn around, but said quietly, "How was your weekend?"

"It was nice."

"Come have a drink with me," he reached over and lit the candle in the lantern next to him. On the table was a bottle of wine with a few glasses. Was he expecting someone?

Annabeth should have said no. She should have remembered Chase, who just kissed her a few hours ago and once again said how much he wanted her back. But she walked in front of him and sat down, looking at the sunset; crimson and purple over the rippling blue water.

Christian poured a glass of red wine and handed it to her. He gave her a smile; the one she thought of more and more often. "I'm glad you had a nice time. It was lonely here without you."

She took two long drinks of her wine before she responded to him, "You shouldn't have said that."

"I know, but it was."

"Maybe I need to go to New York and write for a while."

"Are you done here?"

"Not completely, but I need to be." At this point she'd nervously gulped down the entire glass of wine. He reached over and refilled it.

"Tell me about Chase."

"He's a great guy, an IT engineer."

"And?"

"And what?"

"Is he the love of your life?"

"Well, I don't deserve to have him be, now do I?"

It was not quite dark, Christian looked at her. She could see his eyes and they bore into hers. "Yes, you do, you deserve to be loved like that."

She glanced away and then looked back at him, "You need to stay away from me."

He finished his glass of wine and set it down, "If only I could, Annabeth."

If she stayed a moment longer, she knew exactly where this moment in the moonlight, with the wine, would go. That wasn't acceptable. She stood and without looking back, walked to the house picked up her bag, her purse and went up to her room.

****

Rikki, her manager, called on Monday. "Just checking on your progress. Do you have pages for the editors?"

Annabeth was happy to talk to her. "I do. The outline and order are still a tad sketchy."

"It's progressing okay?" Rikki was a skeptic most of the time.

"Absolutely. I've taken so many photos. This book is going to need a big section for them. We can also use pictures of her when she was Celeste Barlow."

"When she was Celeste Barlow?"

"Wow," Annabeth chuckled, "We haven't talked for a while, have we?"

"No, but I think I want to."

Looking at the door, Annabeth hesitated. She felt uncomfortable saying things about Unina in her own home. After a moment she said, "Why don't I go somewhere and call you."

"Does she listen to your phone calls?"

"No, it just feels weird talking about this in her house."

"Okay, I'm dying to know. How soon can you call back?"

Annabeth turned down the lane and off the property when she used her Bluetooth to call her manager. Rikki picked up at the first ring. "Okay spill, what did you mean when you said she used to be Celeste Barlow?"

The answer was a long tale about Unina and even Udok. She tried to spin it in a positive light, but her manager wasn't fooled. "You're saying she's lost her mind?"

"No, that's not what I'm saying. She's devoted herself to the care of the cats, treating them like her children."

"She changed her name to be the mother of seven lions. That's nuts. Even made her husband, a college professor and veterinarian change his name. Is he as looney as she is?"

"Definitely no." *Had she defended him too quickly?*

"This sounds like it will be a hot book!" Rikki was most likely seeing dollar signs. "You definitely know how to pick them, Annabeth. Have you been back here?"

"I took a weekend away but went to the shore instead." She could hardly think of the OBX trip without also recalling the return and her conversation with Christian.

"Great idea. Did you meet your man from Chelsea there?"

"Yes, I did, we had a nice time."

"Good, because I'm sure that spending all these days and nights at a remote animal sanctuary is downright dull compared to the summer on the rock band tour bus."

*If only*, Annabeth thought. Instead, she just agreed.

"Okay my super writer, is there anything I can do to help you?" Annabeth said no. "Do you have any idea when I can tell the editors to expect some copy?"

She moved onto the highway, headed to Raleigh. "I'll try to hide in my room all day tomorrow and write like a madwoman."

"That's what I like to hear. I'll tell them that by the end of the week, you should be sending some. I'll also get someone to research photos of Celeste Barlow, when she still existed. I've got to tell you Annabeth, I'm pretty pumped about this."

When they hung up, Annabeth thought about it all. It would not be difficult to write the book, she just wondered where it was all going to end up. She'd learned from Abe that the average yearly cost per cat was $10,000. Where was that $70,000 coming from? She had to have drained most of her money on the construction of the place.

****

Back at the house, she stepped out of her vehicle, and heard Christian call her name. “Annabeth, where’d you go?”

She closed the back hatch and turned to him. He was in his standard work gear; cargo shorts, work boots and a *Peaceful Pride* shirt with the sleeves cut off. On his head was a battered cap. Her heart did a little flutter. “I had some errands to run and a call with my agent.”

“I sometimes forget you’re here to write about our crazy world.”

Annabeth was ashamed when his words stung. It was exactly what he needed to say to remind her that this was his life, his home. “That’s my job,” she attempted to sound flippant.

“I better watch my step.”

“It may be too late for that.” Her words had the wrong effect, he chuckled, those dark eyes sparkling.

“I was going down to check on the cats. Do you want to come along?”

Though instinct told her to avoid time with him, the invitation to be with the lions was the greater pull. She shoved her cell phone into the pocket of her shorts, “Let’s go.”

They rode in the flatbed vehicle, bouncing down the trail. Unlike his wife, he drove at a quick pace. Annabeth commented, “Unina said its best to approach slowly and quietly as to not upset the cats.”

“That’s bullshit. Ben drives a tractor around here all the time.”

It thrilled her to see the cats stirring at their arrival. Once again, the males approached the fence first. Unina was not down here, a rare thing. Annabeth wondered if that was why Christian wanted to come.

He stepped into the building and came out with a bag of dried pigs' ears; the kind given to dogs as treats. Apparently, this was also a lion treat. Beau stretched on his hind legs against the fence at his complete height, towering over Christian who approached him. "Hey big man!" He reached in and scratched the lion's belly, pulling his hand out fast as the cat moved back down to all fours, avoiding his claws.

Christian then pulled a pig's ear out of the bag and teased the lion. "Want one of these?" Beau moved like a house cat, jumping with his tail swishing. Christian handed one to Annabeth, "Give this one to Max."

The large cat knew immediately that it was for him. He began making the huffing noise and trying to reach his paw through the fence. The lion intimidated Annabeth, "How am I supposed to do that?"

"Like this," Christian took the one in his hand and slid it through a bottom link. Beau leaped at it as if it were alive. Grabbing it, he jogged away. Annabeth did the same for Max. Once he had it in his possession, he moved to the grass and began tossing it in the air. She laughed.

Together they moved to the area designated for the females to eat. Nova, Luna, and Duchess all behaved in a similar fashion.

Soon they moved away to chew on their treats. The youngsters were the most fun. Christian and Annabeth sat on the ground, knees touching, teasing the younger ones with the dried ears.

"Ouch!" Christian pulled his hand from the fence; Kyra snagged him with a claw as she pulled a treat from his hand.

Annabeth, without thought, grabbed his hand and looked at the slice. "That's pretty deep."

He reached over and wiped off the blood to look at it. "No, it's just a small scratch."

"How often does that happen?" She was trying to make light of the situation, aware that he was trying to entangle their fingers.

He seemed to get the hint, running his hand along the grass, to clean it, "A lot." He stood and reached his other hand to help her up.

Annabeth took it, rising as well. She forced her brain to keep talking. "Have you ever been hurt worse?"

"Yes. I've had some stitches, a broken clavicle," with that, he reached over and stroked her collarbone above her shirt. His hand was warm. Before she could respond, a force of great speed and weight was thrown against the pen facing them. It was Beau, looking for more treats. He roared impatiently.

Christian laughed, grabbing the bag off the ground, "Hey Beau, you're interrupting my moves."

"Thank God," Annabeth said. She reached into the bag and pulled out an ear. "Your timing saved me, big guy. Here." She tossed an ear through the fence a few feet from him, the lion pounced on it. Across the yard, Max saw and headed toward them.

"How long are you going to fight me on this?" Christian asked, his eyes on the lions as they each returned for more.

"Until you get the message. I will not fool around with you."

"But your eyes say you want to."

Annabeth turned to the man standing so close to her she could smell him, "I will not give in to my own selfish desires. You're married and I'm here to write a book about your wife. I also am in a relationship. Cheap sex and regrets aren't a part of my life plan anymore."

His eyebrows rose, "Oh, I see. You've made that mistake before?"

Annabeth turned her attention to the pen. The lions were now tired and finding spots for a nap. These big cats slept nineteen hours a day, they had just worn themselves out. "I made that mistake. It was embarrassing. No woman deserves another woman to do that to her. I will not be that person, especially to Unina when I'm here to write a book about her."

"Our relationship isn't what you think."

Annabeth held up her hand, "I don't want to hear any excuses. Christian, there will not be an us, not even as a fling." She looked at him, his dark eyes dropped, "I'm sorry."

They headed toward the house in silence. She was disappointed. They'd had the best time together. Her interaction with him and the cats had been the most fun out there yet. She'd loved seeing his affection for the animals. Why had it turned into something about them?

# Chapter 13

The next morning, Annabeth had coffee with Shannon. Abe arrived for the day and stopped in to fill his water jug. They were making casual conversation when Ben came in through the garage. He was a big man; as broad as he was tall. Already, his sleeveless tee was wet with sweat. He had a bandana in his hand, wiping his brow.

"Glad you're here, man. I've got a problem."

Abe was screwing the cap of his jug back on, "What's up?"

"It looks like one of the boys caught a bird, a big bird."

"Shit," Abe replied. Christian had explained to Annabeth that it was risky for the cats to eat animals from the wild. They could easily contract diseases from them.

"He's so amped about it that the bastard snarled at me and made a lunge as I got close to the fence. The ladies are staying away, on the other side of the enclosure. The other male is circling. I'm afraid they'll fight over it."

Now Abe was moving. He looked at Annabeth, "Will you call

up to Udok for help?" She nodded as he headed out of the house with Ben.

She climbed the stairs. It would be too awkward to knock on their bedroom door. Was Unina still in there with Christian? Why was she not down at the pen? Annabeth decided to just yell for him. What name did she use? Unina would be mad if she heard her call him Christian, but she felt stupid saying Udok. Taking the chance that Unina wasn't in the house, Annabeth yelled, "Christian, they need you!" She stood near the washstand where she could see the bedroom door but wasn't directly in front of it.

To her surprise, he came out of the door beyond Unina's. "What's up?" Was that his room? He was pulling on a shirt.

Trying to recover from the discovery of his possible separate bedroom, she shook her head, "One of the males has caught a bird."

"Damn," Christian headed briskly down the steps; Annabeth walked with him.

"Ben said the other male is circling, so I guess that makes two problems."

"It does." He moved through the kitchen, at the door he turned, "Are you coming?"

Annabeth nodded and moved rapidly to him. She learned on this assignment to always have her phone with her. This may be a time to video record for notes later.

Christian drove as fast as the utility vehicle would allow. They could hear two distinct roars. His mouth set in a grim line, neither spoke. He barely paused long enough to shut off the truck, before moving at a run toward the pen. Unina, was down there. Abe herded the females into the transfer pens. They were all being obedient to his commands.

Ben and Unina were on the other side of the enclosure where Annabeth could see the lion, she surmised was Beau, with a creature in his jaws. She could make out large brown wings. Was it a turkey buzzard? A hawk? Max was circling at a distance, bellowing a protest. He would occasionally lunge forward at which time; Beau would set down his catch and respond with a vicious roar.

Unina tried to call him away from it with training commands. Ben stood next to her, a large net in his hands. Annabeth didn't see how he would reach over a fifteen-foot fence to retrieve a dead bird.

Abe secured all the females and headed to where Annabeth and Christian stood. Unina gave up her commands and joined them. "Get the tranquilizer gun, Udok. I think that's the only way," Abe suggested.

"No, I don't want them unnecessarily drugged!" hissed Unina.

Looking annoyed, Abe responded, "It's safer than eating a wild bird or tearing each other to shreds in a fight."

"I agree with him," Ben chimed in as he approached.

Christian thought for a quick moment, then spoke. "Ben get them both turkey carcasses out of the fridge. Abe get the small pen open." He turned to his wife, "You will coax Beau to the food chute with one, after Abe gets Max into the pen with the other carcass. Then I'll go into the pen, grab the bird and get out."

Unina nodded, then stopped, "No, I'll get the bird. I'm fast, and he won't hurt me."

"Dammit, no. You're not going into the pen to take prey from an angry lion." Their eyes met in battle.

"Yes, I am. He trusts me more."

Christian raked his hands through his hair, "Ben, get the tranquilizer gun ready. You'll be along the fence near her at all times." Abe rolled out the turkey carcasses. Annabeth noticed that Max turned his head and sniffed the air toward the fresh meat.

It was easy for Abe to get the lion into the pen when he realized that on the built-in bench was the remains of a turkey. Soon he was safely locked in, tearing feathers off the bones.

Christian took the second turkey and moved to Beau's food chute. He began a clucking sound that they used to gain the attention of the cats at feeding time. When he rattled the chute that was Beau's, the cat lifted his head from the bird and looked up.

By now, Unina was at the gate nearest the wild bird. Next to her was Ben, tranquilizer gun in hand. Unbeknownst to her but through silent communication, Abe and Christian agreed that he should be next to Ben with an actual shot gun. A tranquilizer would not have an instant effect on the lion. If he turned from the chute and went for Unina, Abe may have to take him down to protect her.

Christian continued to cluck at the animal. Beau's life in captivity honed his instincts to count on eating at the chute. Though he could have an equal meal of the wild prey, he was more likely to respond to the meal given by the human. For a moment he stood looking at the offered carcass. Annabeth could see blood on his jaws.

At last, he dropped the catch and ambled towards Christian. Unina, across the way, tried to unlatch the gate as quietly as possible. The big cat was close to the chute as she stepped into the enclosure. The bird was fifteen yards from her.

Intentionally, Christian put the carcass only partially through the chute so that Beau had to work to get it out. This gave Unina more time. She reached the bird and gingerly picked it up. Annabeth could see her flinch as she lifted the bloody, mangled creature.

Beau had just pulled the carcass free of the chute and was preparing to bite into it, when suddenly his head went up. He froze for an instant when he caught sight of Unina headed to the open gate with the bird in her arms. Instinct took over, he stepped over the carcass and at lightning speed, headed to the other side of the field.

Annabeth screamed at Unina, as did Ben. Abe lifted his gun and set it towards his target. Christian tried to urge Beau back with his clucking sounds. Unina sprinted for all she was worth. As she arrived at the gate, she tossed the bird and fell into the transfer pad. Ben slid the door closed and was pulling the bolts when the 450-pound male lion lunged against it. Ben ignored the paws as they attempted to grab at him. Beau was roaring in fury.

Abe's hands were shaking as he returned the safety and laid

down the gun. He then went to Unina to help her up. By now Ben, whose arm was bloody, picked up the bird. The three of them headed to the front of the enclosure.

Annabeth felt faint. Unina was nearly killed, but she was smiling. Christian approached them, "Good job crew! Way to work as a team."

Unina looked at Ben, "How bad are you scratched?"

He looked at the slice, "I think it's fine." Then he tossed the bird in a trash can. "All that for a damn buzzard."

"Which of you thought we needed a gun?" Unina looked between Abe and Christian,

Christian faced her, "I did. Unina, you don't take chances like that."

"He wouldn't have hurt me."

"Bullshit! He would have destroyed you if he'd reached you." He spoke to the group, "We handled this fine, but we need to have a plan in place. There must be a better way to get something out of the pen."

Abe was looking at the other six cats in the pens. "How long do we need to leave him in there?"

By now Beau was back at the chute, intent on the turkey carcass. Unina walked over to him. "He's already forgotten."

"Give him two hours with the turkey carcass. Max will be finished by then too." Christian gave the orders. He looked at his wife, "You took a stupid risk. Next time we tranquilize the cat."

"No, I don't like them drugged."

"I don't care, that was dangerous." His frustration was clear.

Finally, he sighed, “Are you ready to go to the house?”

“No,” Unina said, “I’m staying here.” She turned as she answered and realized he was looking at Annabeth.

Annabeth wanted to close her eyes and not watch Unina’s reaction. “Of course.” She walked away from the group.

Christian tilted his head toward the flatbed. Without a word, Annabeth followed him.

****

She didn’t leave her room for the rest of the day. Her writing of the events was flowing out of her. Page after page sprung to life on the screen. Next to her, she kept her notebook, writing down questions she had. Would Abe have killed Beau? She made a note to look up others involved in deaths at  zoos or sanctuaries.

Unina had not been in the pens while she was down there. How often did she usually go in? Annabeth wondered if she should break the rules and try to sneak in a visit. It would be interesting to see what Unina did there by herself all day.

She also made a note to talk to Ben. Until today, she’d considered him just the groundskeeper. This morning, he’d been right in there with the action. He obviously interacted with the animals. What did he think about how the operation was being handled? What were his thoughts on Unina? Was she stable enough to run this place?

Annabeth got up from the laptop on her bed. She stretched her back, then paced. At the window, she looked out at the vast land between the compound and the road. She wondered what room Christian’s was. There was one more enlightening moment from this morning. She didn't want to think about. Sighing aloud, she looked at the ceiling. It was time to get her head in the game.

Outside, the moon was up. A million stars sprinkled the sky, unlike the city, no tall buildings obstructed the view. The change of scenery was nice. Like a stealthy child, she twisted her doorknob silently. Peering into the dark hallway she saw no one. Down the steps she went, slowly and quietly.

Shannon texted her for dinner, but she'd said she was too busy writing. She opened the fridge, looking for the plate she'd left for her. It was all cold food; slices of roast beef, fresh tomatoes, a berry mix. On the next shelf was an opened bottle of Cabernet Sauvignon, she picked it up too. Still trying to be quiet, she slid open a drawer for silverware, then softly opened a cupboard for a glass. Shannon had a tray on the counter. Annabeth placed her late-night meal on it.

Now she went to the foyer and looked at the front door. There was no alarm, she could get out fine. In just a few moments, she placed her tray on the table near the pond. The candle lantern was there, a lighter beside it. Everything was perfect.

Enjoying her solitary candlelight dinner, Annabeth sat in the near darkness. She wasn't sure anything had ever tasted more delicious than the cold roast and tomatoes with a glass of Cabernet. Soon her plate was empty. Filling her glass again, she leaned back in the chair.

The full moon reflected on the water. Cicadas and locusts filled the silence along with a chorus of bullfrogs. Annabeth breathed deeply. Christian handled today's near disaster smoothly. Everyone listened to his logic. He was the calming, authoritative voice. Unina may think she was the savior, but he was the one who made the important decisions.

*Peaceful Pride* needed Udok to function. How did his feelings for Annabeth play into it? She recalled the last married man she was involved with; Jack Corey's bass player, Trent Crosby. His interest in her had been strictly opportunistic sex. There was never a moment when she thought he cared for her. This wasn't how Christian acted. First, they hadn't had sex; he hadn't even tried. Well, perhaps that wasn't true. They'd kissed twice and the second time at the pond felt like it could've led to sex if she hadn't stopped it. He told her he had feelings for her. To what end? Not that she'd ever thought past her time here, but what if he did? He was obviously going to keep trying to get her to reciprocate whatever his feelings were.

She took another drink. Alone out in the dark, two glasses of wine in, Annabeth allowed herself to imagine what it would be like if she gave in to her desires. Her body flushed when she thought of touching him, feeling his skin against hers.

Then she took the thoughts to another level, pretended that they fell in love. Then what? Now her mood darkened. He couldn't leave *Peaceful Pride*; he was the driving force behind it. Sure, Unina could replace him with an employee if she had money, but she didn't!

Besides, he loved the lions; it was clear when they visited together and gave them treats. Today's near fiasco also proved that he was the one who was successfully running the sanctuary.

Romantic feelings toward Annabeth were petty compared to this.

"Well, dammit," she said to the darkness. This was exactly what she knew she would discover, but it didn't make it any easier. It was early. Her heart wasn't invested. Good Lord, she was still involved with Chase; more or less. It was time to be the grown up. No more stolen kisses, or hand touches, or even so much as sideways look at him.

Maybe she should leave, she could rent a place in Raleigh and just come onto the compound when she needed to. It would be the right thing to do. Annabeth stood and gathered up her dishes. She blew out the candle and moved toward the house. It was something to consider.

# Chapter 14

Annabeth remembered seeing bicycles in the garage when she and Christian rode the flatbed to the compound. She decided she'd bike down to the animals by herself the next morning. Unina would be there. It felt good riding the bike, stretching her muscles. It had always been this way when she wrote. She would feel lethargic and out of shape. This past year, she put a lot of effort into slimming down and building an exercise routine. This time it bothered her to not be more active.

Would Unina welcome her? The plan was to be quiet and check out a few things. Annabeth approached the buildings and the enclosure. She could hear some soft animal noises, fortunately nothing bad was going on. After the incident with the bird, she was sure she never wanted to witness that sort of danger again. The image of Beau charging Unina would be in her memory forever. Silently parking the bike against the back of the building, she made her way around the side.

What she saw shocked her. One of the male cats, she didn't

know if it was Beau or Max, was in the smaller pen and Unina was in there with him. It didn't seem to be an emergency. In fact, he was lying on the cement floor and Unina was standing above him leaning down, scratching his head. From her place at the corner of the building, Annabeth could hear Unina saying, "Come on, you're not still mad at me, are you? You know Mother was just protecting you from getting sick."

In response, the massive cat rubbed his large head against her shins. Unina stroked behind one ear. Annabeth froze in her spot, holding her breath. It was terrifying to see the thin woman with the lion that yesterday charged at her with the intent to possibly kill. Unina continued to talk to him, "You scared me, you, silly boy."

Annabeth heard a noise coming from the cat that sounded almost like purring. She stood, considering what she should do. Her unexpected presence might alarm the lion and he might hurt Unina. She glanced around the pen behind them, none of the other cats were paying attention to the two of them. Was this normal? Did Unina normally make contact in a cage with the cats?

She decided she couldn't risk causing the lion to react to her presence. Plus, until Unina told her she regularly entered the pen with the cats, she didn't want to be seen. Was this okay? Did Abe get in with the lions? Did Christian? Annabeth stepped backwards, quietly grabbed the bike and pedaled the way she'd come.

Returning the bike to the garage, she headed to her room. Once there, she got on her laptop and begin looking at YouTube videos of people and lions. There were quite a few examples of big cat owners who routinely climbed into pens and handled the felines. However, there were two things she noted; one, the responsible ones were never there alone, and two, the others looked like the people who owned cats they eventually had to give up to a sanctuary.

She closed the computer and thought for a moment. She wanted to know the truth about this. Who would tell her? Abe seemed a little too discreet. Just last night she told herself to stay away from Christian, but she wanted to know this information. Annabeth almost chuckled out loud, she wasn't one who would ever use feminine wiles to get what she wanted but today she may try it.

After a search of the downstairs, Annabeth didn't see Christian. Reluctantly, she pulled out her phone and text him. Everyone on the compound exchanged numbers except for Unina, who refused to carry a cell phone. On a property this size with so much responsibility, it was the wisest thing to do. Those who worked with the animals and Shannon had radios, but they also used phones.

Annabeth had never sent Christian a message, but now she asked a simple question, *Where are you today?*

He responded immediately, *Upstairs, what's up?*

*Can I ask you some questions?*

*Sure, come to my room.*

Annabeth didn't know what to do. It appeared the other day that his room wasn't Unina's room. How did she handle it? Did she say, "Which door?" or, "Yours and Unina's"? She must've hesitated too long because he texted again, *It's the second door on the right wing.*

*Okay.* A moment later she knocked on the closed door.

His voice sounded distant when he told her to come in. Opening the door, she was wondering if she'd find a room that mirrored Unina's; not even close. This room resembled hers with its old-fashioned decor and furniture. The only difference was that Christian's room also had a terrace.

Why was this his room? How long had he lived separately from his wife? Annabeth told herself these weren't the questions she came to have answered, though she was dying to know. If he offered the information on his own, that was fine.

His voice sounded distance because he was outside. His outdoor space was smaller with just two loungers and a table between them. Annabeth looked to the right expecting to see Unina's massive space and was surprised to see a wall constructed between the two balconies.

Christian was apparently not working today. Dressed in jeans and a black fitted tee, his long legs were stretched out on one lounger. He was barefoot. On the table next to him was a carafe of coffee and a mug. He had on sunglasses. When he turned and looked at her, she couldn't see his eyes, but he smiled. "Well, this is a nice surprise."

"Thank you for letting me talk to you," Annabeth attempted to be formal.

His response was a small frown, "I'd offer you coffee, but I just poured the last."

"That's okay."

"What did you need to see me about?" his voice had an edge, not appreciating her business-like tone.

"Well, I took a bike down to the enclosures this morning," she began.

"That's where you went, I saw you coming back," he said. Annabeth flushed. "Did you visit with Unina?"

"No. I was going to, that was my plan. But then I thought it was safest if I didn't interrupt her."

Her words made Christian pause a moment. Then he uttered a deep sigh. "She was in the pen, wasn't she? Please tell me she was at least not in the enclosure."

"No, she was just in one of the small pens."

"And who is she with?"

"I wasn't sure at first until I heard her talking to him about how he scared her with the bird. So, it was definitely Beau."

Christian slammed his mug down on the table and stood up, "Dammit Unina! She will get herself killed yet!"

"I suspected that it wasn't a good idea."

He walked to the rail and stood there. The view from his balcony was only the outer edge of the enclosure. The fronts of the buildings were not visible, he couldn't have seen Unina from here. Annabeth walked up next to him.

"Is that what you wanted to know about?" She nodded. "It's sanctuary policy that there must be two people down there before anyone can be with a lion. Unina thinks she's above the rules. It's her belief that her *children* won't hurt her."

"Even after yesterday?" This shocked Annabeth.

"That's the point." He turned to her, "You're a reasonable person, with little knowledge of these animals, yet you realized that if Beau reached her, he would have killed her. She has this insane belief that he would have recognized her at the last moment and stopped."

"You two talked about it?" Annabeth's mind was spinning. Celeste Barlow seemed to have lost any rational thought.

"No, I haven't talked to her since yesterday, but I know this is what she thinks." This comment came with an obvious admission. Christian and Annabeth made eye contact. "We aren't a couple of any sort. We barely converse." His voice was bitter.

"I'm sorry," Annabeth's voice was soft.

"Don't be. She's not the same woman I met here. Or maybe the woman I met was the consummate actress, and I fell for it." He turned back to Annabeth, "I'm fine with it. She lives her life as a human who thinks she's a lion. I love the sanctuary and get away from it when I need to have a real life." Now he looked into her eyes, "Your arrival here has thrown a monkey wrench into all of it."

She closed her eyes for a moment, trying hard to build up her resistance. What were those things she'd thought about last night? It was the crisis with the bird that made her realize she couldn't interfere with this. "Christian," she opened her eyes, he was staring intently at her, "I'm so sorry to hear that you're unhappy with your marriage. I allowed myself to be drawn to you."

"But?" his eyes were growing cold.

"But I'm here to write a book about Celeste Barlow and her life, not change the course of it. You can't leave this sanctuary; I know that and so do you. This is much bigger than you or her. I don't even register on the equation."

"What if?"

Before he could continue, she placed her hand lightly on his upper arm, "There's no what if that could ever occur. Besides, we don't know each other at all. I live in New York City. I love my life. I travel for months at a time with my job. You live at your job. I look like the perfect solution simply because I'm here in your world."

Christian Mendoza was a smart man. It took only a moment's consideration to see that she was right. His expression was now one of sadness. "It's not fair. I'd made peace with this until I discovered how much I was missing."

Annabeth let her hand drop and turned to go. "We needed to have this conversation. I'm not done with my work here, and I can't keep playing games with you."

Now, Christian moved next to her and placed his hand on the back of her neck. "It won't be easy. In fact, it will be damn hard, but I'll try to behave myself." He leaned in and kissed her cheek. Annabeth left the room.

****

Five minutes later, she was in the kitchen getting something to drink. Christian walked in, "I'm headed down to the enclosure."

Annabeth wanted to go. Was he still hurt by their conversation? “May I join you?”

“Grab whatever you need.” His tone was polite.

She thanked him and jogged upstairs for her camera and notebook. Once again, they rode in the flatbed utility vehicle, this time at a much slower pace. It could have been awkward, but he filled the quiet with information.

“All the cats were raised in captivity. Max came from a circus near Chicago and the cubs from one in Miami. He was treated poorly; whips and rods were used to control him. It’s still his nature to bond with his trainers so when we got him, he was submissive. His humans were the alphas.”

“He’s the alpha male now,” Annabeth guessed.

Christian nodded “Yes, he was the first male here. Beau and the three adult females came from so-called exotic farms. Humans raised them since birth. They were very used to people. It was a slow process adapting them back into a pride.” The vehicle arrived at the fence. He rushed his last words, “The purpose of the sanctuary is to give them a home closest to what they would have had in Africa. Part of that is teaching them to live in a structure of hierarchy within themselves.” The vehicle came to a stop, as he turned the ignition off, Christian said in a near whisper, “Constantly wanting to play with them negates some of that effort.”

Before he could say more, Unina appeared at the front of the vehicle. “Udok, is there anything we can do to see if Beau contracted something from that buzzard?” Her face was drawn in concern.

"No, I'm certain he'll be fine. He didn't even eat more than a third of it," Christian climbed out of the vehicle.

This answer didn't satisfy her, "But that's enough to have transferred germs." He strode purposefully toward the pens; she hurried to keep up. "What signs should we watch for?"

Now Christian stopped, and turned to his wife, "Make certain his appetite is regular. Check that he's drinking plenty and has a normal energy level." Unina was nodding her head, looking at the lion in question who was sleeping in the grass, belly up. Over her head, Christian caught Annabeth's eye and rolled his own. She gave a small smile as she approached the pen.

Kyra apparently remembered Annabeth from her time with the pig's ear. The young female, who was more legs than body, ran her back along the fence, requesting a scratch. Annabeth looked at the two owners of the sanctuary, they were still talking about Beau. She reached her hand out and touched the warm fur. Kyra's response was to push her back against Annabeth's fingers. "Okay, I get the hint," she scraped her fingernails against the young lion.

Close to her sister, Amra spotted the personal attention and ambled over. Before she could get to the fence, Kyra gave a playful growl and launched at her sibling. Soon the two were rolling on the ground. Annabeth grabbed her camera, sticking the lens through the fence for a good shot. The lens whirred as she took multiple pictures of the cubs.

Unina and Christian moved into the building. If she turned, she could see them working on vitamin prep. This was good for her book too, seeing the couple together. Annabeth switched to video mode and aimed the camera at the two of them. They were methodically pulling out a piece of meat and stuffing a supplement into it, then stabbing it with the skewer. At first it appeared that they were still talking about Beau. Her face was animated and concerned. His expression was one of frustration. Their conversation ended. As he needed different items, Christian would step around his wife, never touching her. This was intriguing to Annabeth. Her own experiences with him proved that he was a toucher; the kind of person who places his hand on your shoulder, or maybe your back when he moves by. He did none of this to his wife; she didn't touch him either. They also weren't conversing. Just working in silence.

Annabeth scolded herself. Was this observation for the book or satisfied judgement for her personal feelings? Suddenly she felt a massive force near her. She was still sitting on the ground near the cubs' wrestling spot but had quit looking at the cats and focused on the building.

She looked up from her spot on the cement, a male lion was at the fence. On four legs he towered over her. Her camera lens had been pushed through the links, so her position was extremely close to the fence. Now she backed up quickly, trying to maintain a calm tone, "Well, hello big boy. How'd you sneak up on me?"

The lion showed no malice toward her. His focus was on the food that would soon be arriving. When she spoke, he turned his eyes on her and sniffed. Annabeth stood up, a safe distance from him. There was no chance of a claw swiping her. Her timing was good because at that moment, the rest of the lions began moving toward the fence. She took the opportunity to film all seven as they moved near. They were making the huffing sound that lions do, eager for the treat that was coming their way.

Annabeth heard the squeaky wagon wheels and stepped back. As Unina and Christian rolled it past her to give the animals their vitamin filled treat, he lightly touched the back of her upper arm, "Getting some good shots?" he asked.

She smiled and nodded. Was the smile a response to the shots or from the fact that he'd touched her and not his wife?

# Chapter 15

They all gathered in front of the television. Abe was on the couch, his long legs on the coffee table. Unina was curled into a tight ball on a recliner. Shannon hovered near the kitchen; her comfort zone. Christian nervously stood close to the screen, pacing occasionally.

From her perch on the barstool at the counter, Annabeth watched not only the broadcast, but each person's reaction. The shores of North Carolina were preparing for Tropical Storm Mathias. All indicators were that it would not develop into a hurricane, but gale force winds and heavy downpours could still cause damage. *Peaceful Pride* was far enough from the sea as to avoid the full strength of the storm. Tonight's forecasters, however, were warning about the bad weather that would travel as far as the sanctuary.

Ben walked in from the garage; his mouth open to speak a greeting. When he saw all eyes were focused on the weather forecast, he closed it again. Instead, he moved across the kitchen. Annabeth noticed his work boots left a trail of dusty dirt on the wood floor.

The news went to a commercial. He took this opportunity to talk, his words directed at Christian. "I don't think we're prepared for this kind of storm."

Running his hand over his eyes, Christian responded, "I think it's safest to put them all in their pens."

Abe nodded. "They'll at least be covered."

"And we don't want limbs coming down on them," Christian added.

"Shit Udok, the kind of rain they're talking about will blow sideways into the pens," Ben wasn't satisfied with the solution.

Unina jumped up, a panicked edge to her voice, "That's why we need an indoor enclosure built."

Her husband looked at her, his face irritated, "That will not happen, it's well beyond our budget."

"But what can we do? They could drown!" her volume increased.

The room was momentarily silent as everyone thought.

"Do you have tarps?" Annabeth offered.

Ben grabbed onto the suggestion, "Yeah, we could wrap the pens so that rain wouldn't fill up the bottoms."

"Do we have enough?" Christian looked at Ben for the answer.

The big man thought a minute, "Yep, we have some here in the garage and a bunch in the storage building."

"How will they stay put?" Unina was still not calming down.

"Zip ties!" Abe had the answer.

She showed some relief. “Let’s do it now before the rain, so they won’t be frightened.”

Christian nodded, “Good idea. They’ll follow commands easier.”

Soon the group dispersed. Ben and Abe took the flat bed vehicle to load up the tarps. Christian, Unina, Shannon and Annabeth climbed into the other vehicle and headed to the enclosures.

Already, the sky was darkening. Ominous clouds could be seen in the distance. A strong breeze picked up. As they approached, Annabeth could see that the lions were restless. Beau was pacing at the fence. The females huddled near him. Max stood on the rock cliff, sniffing the air.

“They’re sensing the storm,” Unina spoke and leapt out of the vehicle before Christian came to a complete stop. When she reached the pen she spoke, “It’s okay, babies.” Two of the females approached her and leaned close for comfort. Max looked at her from the rock and issued a roar.

The flatbed arrived. The men began to pull out the tarps. Annabeth followed Christian into the storage building to retrieve the rest. Shannon searched for the zip tie tool. Soon they all stood facing the pens with the materials. The young lions walked over to the group.

“We must put the cats in first. They will not go into the pens we’ve already covered,” Christian was tugging on Kyra’s ear playfully as he considered the plan.

“How the hell are we supposed to cover fences with lions

inside?" Ben was unconvinced.

"I don't know," Christian shrugged his shoulders, "but we'll have to figure it out." He moved toward the building, "For starters, we all wear heavy gloves."

Abe had an idea, he turned to Unina, "Can you distract them with something. We can't put carcasses in their cage, they'll be aggressive."

Unina moved near him, "You're right, perhaps a special treat." Now she turned to Shannon, "Did you make those frozen lamb chop pops?" Freezing lamb chops served as a cool treat for lions in the summer heat.

Abe interjected, "She had me put them in the freezer yesterday." He and Shannon moved immediately to the building. When they returned, Christian and Unina were at the gate waiting. It was time to call the animals in. Annabeth moved away from the group. She put her camera on record mode. This was an important moment to catch on video.

As soon as Abe moved to the transfer pens, Unina and Christian entered the enclosures. Annabeth felt her heart squeeze; this was so very dangerous. As was protocol in the pride, the males stepped forward. Max was the oldest and therefore the first alpha. Beau trailed him closely. Max moved close to Unina and Annabeth did her best not to make a noise as her breath sucked in nervously.

Unina smiled at the lion, but her voice was strong and firm, "No, not now. Go!"

Several feet away from her, Christian was holding a training stick. He motioned with it and echoed, "Go!"

Max lifted his lip and gave a slight snarl but moved toward the gate. Abe opened the pen door, so it attached to one side of the enclosure. He then reached up and pulled a long rod on the enclosure gate, so it opened the gate and immediately fastened to the pen. Ben moved to the other side. When Max sauntered into the pen, he pulled a latch and the gate closed. The male lion was unconcerned. He leapt onto the attached bench and stretched out.

Once his pen was secured, they repeated the same procedure to get Beau in his pen. When he climbed in, he sprayed Ben. "You little bastard!" Ben yelled as he secured the pen and shook the lion's urine from his arm.

The females were very docile as they entered the pen they shared. The cubs, still learning commands, took longer to get in their pens. Annabeth at least felt she could breathe easier while she watched Christian push the flank of one of them to get her in the right direction.

As they locked the last pen, a light rain began. Annabeth helped Unina and Shannon with the lamb pops. The three men used the cubs as practice. They worked together to pull the tarps tight on three sides.

Ben insisted that the rain would blow from the east and the west side of the pens would remain dry. Christian agreed. He felt the lions would be spooked if they enclosed all four sides of the pen with a tarp. They could claw at them and rip them, so getting them tight at the bottom was crucial.

The job of zip tying the three sides of the pen was arduous. They had only completed the young lions' pen when the wind picked up and the rain increased. By now the females were nervous, pacing and making noise.

Annabeth and the other women took the lamb pops out of the buckets and lured the nervous lions from the tarps. Duchess was not easily distracted. The sound the plastic made when the wind slammed into the cage unnerved her. At one point she leaped at the side where Abe was pulling the bottom corner tight. He pulled his fingers away before they made contact with her claws, but it was close.

Finally, it was down to the male cages. Everyone was drenched. Annabeth securely locked up her camera in its weatherproof bag. Max and Beau were pacing in circles, the rain already soaking them.

"Hurry!" Unina shrieked.

The group moved to Max's pen; all with a sense of dread. This would not be easy. Unina dropped to a squat, a lamb pop in front of her. "Maximillian, look what Mother has brought you."

The male lion moved toward her, his nose inhaling the scent of lamb. Behind him, the men began with the bottom corners of the tarp. Max whirled around once at the noise, but Unina pulled out another pop. She teased him by holding it out of reach. This did the trick; he was focused on getting a claw close enough to snag it. Annabeth watched Unina, impressed. She was soaked to the bone, rain plastering her long hair to her face, just inches from a nervous lion, but her voice remained calm as she rewarded him with the treat.

The men secured all six bottom corners and were beginning the top ones. Max squatted down, eating the meat, but at one point snarled as they fastened a zip tie nearest his head. At last his pen was complete.

A full-blown storm now raged, and Beau was pacing in his cage. The water pooled at his paws. Unina once again grabbed a treat and stood at the front of his cage. At first it seemed they could not distract him. The men moved to the other side, and he snarled nervously.

"We don't have time to be cautious," Christian yelled, his voice carried away by the wind.

Annabeth left the front of the cage and joined the men. The increased wind was blowing the tarps. She helped Abe pull the first one tight. Ben snapped the zip tie. Christian was at the other corner and Annabeth moved to his side, reaching her hands below his to pull the plastic. Ben moved up behind them and fastened the tie.

She peeked in; Beau was eating another treat. Quickly the four of them finished the bottom of the pen. It was time for the top corners. The wind was whipping the ends out of their hands.

Ben climbed the ladder for the first corner. The other three held the side tight. Beau glanced their way and snarled again. Unina stuck a pop into the opposite corner. The cat moved to get it.

They were down to the last corner. Annabeth felt her hands shake with exhaustion as she helped pull the side tight. Ben climbed up and pulled out a tie from his pocket. As his fingers grabbed the chain link, lightning cracked overhead. Beau jumped in surprise, saw Ben's hand and pounced for it. Behind Ben, Christian and Abe grabbed him, pulling him from the ladder. He landed with a soft thud on the ground. Blood covered his hand, the glove shredded around it.

Christian knelt beside him, "How bad is it?"

Ben uncurled his fist, "I still have five fingers."

"Good," Christian grabbed the tie and climbed the ladder.

Annabeth bit her tongue to avoid yelling, "No."

Beau roared at him, but Christian's voice was equally strong when he shouted, "Go! Go!"

Unina stood at the other side and tossed in another treat. This distracted the cat long enough to get the last corner secured.

Ben moved to the front of each pen, "They're dry, and the water has poured out of the bottom of the male pens."

The group moved into the building. Christian took Ben over to his examining table. He cut away the glove and began to clean the sliced fingers.

"I knew I'd eventually need a vet, not a doctor," Ben joked when he was bandaged up.

Christian turned to the group, drying his hands, "I could use a drink, ready to make a run for the house?"

All but Unina eagerly voiced their agreement. "I'm staying with the cats."

Christian's look was resigned acceptance, "At least be smart enough to stay away from the metal cages in the lightning. She didn't respond and there was an awkward silence.

Shannon broke the ice, "If you need more clothes, I can bring them down."

Unina, who's attention was already back at the pens, shook her head, "I've got things down here."

****

Apparently, Ben kept clothes in an upstairs room, because when Annabeth emerged from her own into the corridor, he was stepping out of the door next to hers. He changed into dry jeans and a flannel shirt.

"Hey, did you film that?" he asked her.

"Until the rain got heavy."

"Can I watch it?"

"Sure, I'll grab my camera and bring it down."

When she joined the group, beers were passed out. Shannon spread the table with chips, bread, meat and cheeses. Everyone was making their own sandwiches.

Christian stood at the end of the table; his skin was a nice dark contrast to the bright white t-shirt he was wearing. Annabeth's admiration must have shown in her eyes, because he raised his eyebrows and grinned before putting his beer bottle to his lips.

She covered her embarrassment by asking, "Is there one of those for me?"

Abe twisted the top off a Corona before handing it to her. Christian reached over and put a lime in the bottle.

"I didn't know if you liked it that way," Abe explained.

Annabeth responded with, "I do," at the same moment that Christian said, "She does." Eyebrows raised, but no one commented.

Annabeth took a long drink. She then picked up her camera and adjusted the settings so that Ben could watch the video of their earlier escapade. The other three squeezed close to view it.

"We did the right thing for them," Abe said when it was over.

The group settled into the other room intending to watch a movie. Today's excitement and exhaustion followed by food and drink, had them all nodding off in their seats.

# Chapter 16

Annabeth wasn't sure how long she dozed. When she awoke in a corner of the couch, she no longer heard the wind or rain. The sun was out but fading. Her first thought was of Unina and what she was doing. She decided to go see.

Lifting herself slowly off the leather couch, Annabeth moved around the other sleeping bodies. The movie was over, another in its place.

She went up to her bedroom and packed her camera in its case, then slung it over her shoulder. In the kitchen Shannon was up, noiselessly putting away food. Annabeth stood close to her, her voice a whisper, "I thought I'd go check on Unina."

Shannon moved to the fridge, "Take a vehicle and I'll send her food." She pulled veggies, a container of hummus and cheese from the refrigerator and placed them in a canvas tote.

****

Driving the utility vehicle was fun. The small chunky tires splashed through the puddles left by the storm. Annabeth moved, enjoying the return of the North Carolina sunshine. Around her, the damage seemed minimal; a few branches down, flowers blown off their stems.

She slowed as much as was possible as she approached the enclosure. Uncertain if she was welcome and not wanting to disturb the animals, a quiet arrival was best. Annabeth turned off the vehicle, she heard no sounds from the lions. Grabbing the camera bag and food tote, she headed around the corner.

Unina was just stepping from the building, wire cutters in her hand. She jumped slightly in surprise. "Oh, I didn't hear you drive up."

"I brought you some dinner," Annabeth held up the tote.

"Good, I'm a little hungry." Unina's smile was welcoming. She moved toward the pens. "But first, you can help me. Put that in the building and grab another pair of these." Her hand held the wire cutters. "Let's get these tarps off the pens. They hate them."

Annabeth hesitated, was that a good idea? "Have you looked at the weather report?"

Unina sighed, as if tired of being doubted, "Yes. The radio report says it's passed completely."

"Okay, I'll be right out." As she dropped the things on the table and went to the tool bench to search for more cutters, Annabeth considered texting Christian about what they were doing. She decided against it. If he showed up, Unina would know she told him. Besides, this was more time for the two of them to talk. Annabeth had many questions.

When she joined her, Unina had already snipped off the zip ties at the bottom of Beau's pen. "Hold the ladder for me," she called. The lion seemed to understand what she was doing or simply trusted her more than Ben. He made no attempt to claw at her as she sliced off the plastic support. Soon she had all four sides free. He leaned his strong body into the chain link, Unina reached in with both hands, "You're welcome, big boy. My good man."

Max behaved equally well. The women went to opposite sides of his pen and the process quickened. When Unina was on the ladder, he swiped at her hand, but it was playful. She knew that his claws could still slice her and used her strong, "Go!" command. The big lion climbed on the bench and waited for her to finish. When the tarp was pulled away, Unina scratched along his spine.

"Was it frightening the first time that you went into the pen with them?" Annabeth asked as they moved to the females' cage.

"That would have been Nova and Luna, before the big enclosure was complete. They were in a pen that was about double the size of this small pen. I was somewhat nervous, but immediately they were friendly. All of these cats were born in captivity and are used to human handling."

"The day that Beau had the bird, it seemed he was a lion of the wild."

"They don't have all of the instincts that they should, but in that case, he was reacting possessively, which is natural."

Now they were at the young lions' cage, even Annabeth felt comfortable touching Amra's head that she pushed against the fence, looking for attention. Unina smiled at this.

"What would he have done if he'd reached you in the pen?"

The other woman frowned, "Beau knows me, who I am to him. I know Udok is convinced that he would have attacked me, but I don't think so." She had Kyra's face in her hands, rubbing the bridge of the lion's nose. "These are my children; I am their mother. He wouldn't have hurt me."

Annabeth wasn't so sure, but she kept quiet. She'd been there and watched Beau act like a wild beast. When he charged, she was certain that he wouldn't have stopped simply because it was Unina who was taking his prized bird.

"Let's walk the fence and see if there's been any damage to the enclosure." The two women moved along, looking in. As with the rest of the property, a few limbs were down, leaves scattered about. "The cubs will enjoy playing with the big branches."

They completed the long circle and returned to the pens, Unina patted the cages, "Let me get a bite to eat and then we can return the cats to the enclosure."

Annabeth considered the complicated maneuver of opening one gate, getting the lion in the next place and then closing the other. Could she do it? At least Unina wouldn't be in the enclosure this time.

They both munched on the hummus, carrots and cheese. Unina pulled a filled water bottle from the fridge as Annabeth continued her questions. "Did you have to visit a lot of other sanctuaries before building this one?"

"I traveled to six different states, making note of what I liked, and what I didn't. It was a difficult time for me. When I began this, I truly thought that I would be able to get cubs like those I saw left to die in Africa." She paused for a moment, her voice cracking.

Annabeth sat silently, reaching in her pocket, to turn her phone to record. Unina continued, "The laws of both this country and that one forbids it. I thought my dreams to save lions was pointless." She smiled, "Then MJ told me about a sanctuary in Colorado that she'd been to. We jumped on a plane to visit. Seeing the life they've given to animals, helped me plan this place." The discussion continued as she reminisced about the plans and construction of *Peaceful Pride*. Annabeth loved hearing about the arrival of the cats. Unina said, "I guess, for now we cannot add to the pride. It would take more land."

Annabeth asked the difficult question, "How are you going to continue to finance the sanctuary?"

The other woman's face darkened, "I'm not going to do a film and leave here."

Shrugging her shoulders, Annabeth offered, "Most places like this allow visitors in and make money that way."

"No, this is the lions' home, they're not on display. I don't want noisy children and cameras flashing around them. I don't want people throwing things in the pen. This is the first time that they can enjoy life the way it is supposed to be for them. I will not allow strangers in." Suddenly she stood up, "Let's let the lions out."

The process didn't take long. Unina was very adept at getting the latches and gates just right. Annabeth was able to follow her orders. The lions eagerly headed into the enclosure to sniff around and stretch out.

An hour passed, Unina was at the far end of the fence, chattering at the young cats who were playing with fallen branches. Seemingly unaware of the damp grass, she sat cross-legged, her hands in the fence.

On the bench near the feeding chutes, Annabeth pulled out her phone and was typed in notes of their conversation. She heard another vehicle pull up. Christian walked around the corner. He stopped, looking in surprise at the cats back in the enclosure. "Who did this?"

Annabeth put her phone in her pocket and stood up. "We did."

He moved next to her, "The two of you took off the tarps, put them away and let the lions into the enclosure?"

"Yep, and fed them dinner," she felt almost proud of her part in it.

"And the storm is definitely over?"

"I'm glad you asked me, I offended her by asking the same question."

Christian gave her a smile, "Thank you for being here to help her. I'm sure she would've done it herself otherwise."

"I'm not so altruistic, Christian. I was able to get more interviewing time in."

"Oh yes, your purpose for being here."

"Why else would I be here?" she regretted the words as soon as she said them.

He looked at her sideways, "A man could wish."

"Don't start it." She decided to change the subject, Unina

hadn't moved from the other side of the enclosure. "I asked her how she thought she could continue to finance this."

"And what did she say?"

"All she said was absolutely no film and then we quit talking and let the cats out. What do you think is going to happen?"

Christian was quiet a moment. His spoke with resignation, "Maybe next semester I can get another intern or two in here with Abe, and I can return to the university to teach."

"You're going back?"

"I don't know how else we're going to survive and even with my salary there isn't enough."

"It's admirable that you're willing to do that. I'm certain you prefer to spend your time here too."

Now he turned to completely face her, "Is that actually what you think? After the time you've spent here, you think I want to be trapped in this place?"

Annabeth met his eyes; his expression was one of sadness and frustration. She looked down, "You can't step away from the lions."

"No, but this isn't the life I wanted. I don't know what will happen to those seven lions."

Behind him came the shrill voice of Unina who apparently moved into hearing range, "What do you mean you don't know what will happen to them?" She stepped between them. "What are you planning?"

He shook his head, "Nothing, Unina. I was just explaining something to Annabeth,"

Annabeth interrupted, "I was asking him the same questions that I asked you earlier."

The other woman turned to her, a finger pointed at her face, "Your job is to write a book that will get people interested in our cause. They will learn to respect exotic animals and quit buying them as pets."

"Her purpose is to write a book that people will buy to save the sanctuary," Christian said.

"Whatever it is, it's not her business to ask us about our finances and how we're going to keep *Peaceful Pride* going." She looked at Annabeth, her eyes bright with anger, "I think you need to go away. I don't want you around the lions."

*What had brought that on?* Annabeth stepped back, "I'm sorry if I offended you. I was just asking questions that I thought were relevant."

"Please leave the sanctuary." Now she turned to her husband, "I don't want her here. You can take her back to the house."

"That's incredibly rude, Unina."

Annabeth touched Christian's arm, "It's okay. I'll make some arrangements for somewhere to stay." She turned and headed to the vehicle she'd driven.

He climbed into the passenger's side as she started it. They'd moved just a few feet from the building when he spoke, "I can't tell you how sorry I am for that."

She kept her eyes on the road, "It's okay. I'm accustomed to eccentric people. It'll be good to get some distance and time to write." Annabeth realized there was more than one reason to distance herself from this place. His words recently, had put thoughts in her head that were foolishly hopeful.

# Chapter 17

Annabeth moved her things into a hotel thirty miles from the sanctuary. It was a decent place; an in-ground pool, free breakfast, nice restaurant and bar. She set up her laptop on the table in her room and worked.

There was a lot to get written. She collected a good deal of material on how Celeste Barlow began the building of *Peaceful Pride*. The arrival of each set of lions would fascinate readers. The description of the sanctuary was easy to write, it was ingrained in her mind. Her hours there were filling pages. The photos and videos provided even more material as she turned them into words.

Annabeth had already written a good chunk of the book which described the celebrity, Celeste Barlow. Shannon helped provide information on her upbringing in North Carolina. She put together chapters on her successful television, film and even product sponsorship career. MJ had been helpful with this information.

Now she was beginning the chapters that showed the change

in Celeste. Much of it began with her name change; Unina was not the same woman. Annabeth rested her wrists on the edge of her keyboard. Along with Unina came Udok. She hadn't seen him for four days, and she hated herself for missing him.

Last night, she Facetimed with Chase. It was a good thing she did. It was obvious he wasn't feeling confident about their relationship. It had taken some work, but she was convincing him that another trip to the Outer Banks would be beneficial for them. This time she would get a house on the beach side. He said he would let her know within twenty-four hours, but Annabeth felt confident that she could get him to spend the weekend with her. She needed a break from thinking about everyone involved in the world of *Peaceful Pride.*

With that thought, she closed her file and stood up. After a brief stretch, she looked out the window. Sunlight was fading which meant evening had arrived. How long had it been since she'd eaten? She recalled nibbling on some crackers and peanut butter around eleven. It was time for a substantial meal. She'd freshen up a bit and head downstairs. The restaurant cooked a nice steak.

Annabeth twisted her hair into a thick braid, glad she'd chosen to let it grow. Her time in the sun added honey highlights to its natural chestnut color. She applied her makeup, amazed at the woman she'd become. After pulling on skinny denim jeans and a black cotton V-neck, she slipped into black sandals and headed out of her room.

In the restaurant, there was a decent crowd. It was a nice

atmosphere; good music, candlelight and a gorgeous lit bar on the right side of the room. A habit from days gone by, Annabeth opted to sit at the bar instead of at a table alone. Overhead a baseball game was playing. To her left, three men watched the game; drinking and eating. To her right was a couple sharing an appetizer and a bottle of wine.

She ordered the filet and a glass of Pinot Noir. While she enjoyed the tender cut and the wine, Annabeth watched the game on television. It was just the relaxation she needed after her mind was bogged down with the book. A few times she checked to see if Chase responded about the weekend, not yet.

It wasn't long before she was full, and her plate empty. Turning down the suggestion of dessert, she signed the receipt with her room number and slid off the barstool. Just as she got to the hostess stand, she saw him. Christian was walking towards her, looking decidedly handsome in all black; jeans and a button shirt. He flipped his sunglasses up on his head.

"Perfect timing" he spoke, a smile splitting his face.

Part of her thrilled at the familiar face of the attractive man. Another part of her cringed; what was he up to? Christian approached and pulled her in for a hug. She responded in kind; inhaling the scent of spicy cologne that was uniquely him.

"Perfect timing? Are you here to see me?"

"Were you leaving? Come and have a drink with me."

Annabeth gave a small sigh but turned back into the restaurant. The hostess led them to a table. She ordered a bottle of the Pinot Noir she'd had with dinner.

"Excellent idea," Christian grinned again.

"So, what are you doing here?"

"Checking on you."

"I didn't tell you where I was staying."

"I know, I saw your car in the lot."

"Were you driving to all the hotels or was this by accident?"

A server appeared and opened the wine, then filled two glasses. Christian used this as a chance to ignore the question and instead held up his glass, "Cheers, Annabeth. I've missed you."

She couldn't help it; she clinked the rim of her glass to his and smiled. "What's new?"

He shrugged, "Nothing at all, same old, same old. How's the writing?"

"I've done a lot."

"Well good, I guess that makes your absence worthwhile."

She looked at him, "How'd you explain my sudden departure to everyone?"

"Annabeth, no one is surprised when Unina has an outburst."

"How is she doing?"

"I don't know, I've barely seen her. Since the storm, I don't know if she's even been inside the house." Annabeth didn't comment on how strange their marriage was, but she thought it. He read her expression. "I don't want to talk about it. I wanted to apologize. I thought maybe you'd just left the sanctuary forever."

"Then you don't know how seriously I take my job. This book is important to me. It will be an interesting read."

Now he frowned, "A tell-all book about how crazy we are?"

"No, I wouldn't do that. Give me some credit. I've been around long enough to understand how important the pride is. It takes a lot of devotion to make their lives so complete."

He gave her a long look, finally his hand rested on hers, his voice was quiet, "Thank you for saying that. You truly understand why I stay."

She hadn't meant it to be about just him. She wanted to wrestle her hand from under his, but that would be rude. Instead, Annabeth nodded, "I do. I understand the commitment it takes all of you. I don't intend to write about Celeste Barlow becoming Unina in a disparaging way."

Caressing his fingers lightly over the top of her hand, before removing them to pick up his wineglass, Christian smiled, "Thank you."

Damn if his touch didn't send shock waves shooting through her. She thought perhaps it was the wine but drained her glass anyway. Christian refilled it immediately. Annabeth gave up on the idea that she wouldn't be at least slightly drunk soon and took a swig.

The server came back and asked if they wanted food. He refused without even asking her, then refilled his own glass. He turned to her, "So when you're not on assignment writing a book, what do you do? You know that my life is nailed down to one location, but yours isn't."

It was a sad truth, this was a man clearly unhappy with his life, but what could he do? He married a woman who only cared about seven lions. Annabeth was certain that they never slept together, ate together, even talked to one another unless it was necessary information about the cats. Now, he would be forced to return to work and maintain the business part of their financially unstable world.

"I haven't taken too many vacations, because my job seems to always involve travel. I love New York. I eat out, go to the gym, hang out with friends." As a guilty afterthought she added, "And Chase."

"And how is Chase?" Christian's tone revealed that his third glass of wine was setting in.

"He's just fine," she answered defensively. "In fact, we're going to spend the weekend together." She hoped her voice was more confident than she felt about it. From his grin, she suspected not.

"Another beach romp?"

"That's not your business," Annabeth tried to be annoyed, but couldn't help enjoying the building flirtation. Was she ever going to have any self-control around this man? She turned the tables on him. "How's your wife?"

This cooled things off, Christian's face was deadly serious, "She's not my wife."

The wine that she'd just poured into her mouth, threatened to spill out, as she opened it in shock. "What are you talking about?" After a coughed swallow, Annabeth continued, "You told me all about your wedding."

"I know," now he downed his glass, and looked at her. "Dammit, I wasn't going to do this. I promised myself."

"What?"

"Is there anywhere to walk around here, I don't like the crowded room," Christian was glancing at the other tables.

"Sure, there's a small yard by the pool." She waved at the server and signed for the wine, despite his attempt to fling his credit card at the young woman. With that taken care of, they stood. She led him toward the backdoor adjacent to the lobby.

Outside, it was dark. The only light was the glow of the moon and lights surrounding the pool. They walked in silence for a moment until they were past the few swimmers. "Okay, explain what you said," Annabeth held in her curiosity as long as she could. She turned to face him; his eyes looked everywhere but at her.

Ahead of them was a set of chairs around a table. He moved toward that and leaned on the table. Now he made eye contact, "Remember the story about Mable's death and when I proposed?"

"Of course, and at the ceremony she announced your new names."

"Right. Well, by the time we got to the wedding part, Celeste wasn't spending any nights in the house." This was the first time he referred to her as her former name. "I made the room in the storage building more of a joke than a gift. She misunderstood."

"Okay," Annabeth filled the silence when he paused.

"After the ceremony, the Justice of the Peace informed us that we hadn't got the proper paperwork done for a license. Neither of us even thought about it. He said to come to his office during the next week and he would get it signed."

Now Christian turned away from her, toward the pool,

unseeing. "It was our wedding night, and Unina went down to the enclosure during the reception. I followed her later and tried to urge her to come to the house. She refused. I was drunk, got mad and slept alone in our room. The next day when she returned to the house, we had a big fight. Unina said she'd already put me down as her legal partner in *Peaceful Pride*, so we didn't need to bother with the marriage license."

Annabeth sat down in a chair as he'd told his story. Now she looked up at him, "So you never married?"

"No, and I moved into the room next door." He looked at her, then squatted on the ground facing her, his hands on her knees, "See Annabeth, I'm not trying to cheat on my wife. I don't have one. We haven't even slept together or had any kind of relationship for years."

She knew it was unwise to have this conversation after they'd split a bottle of wine, but she placed her hands on his, "You've only stayed because of the animals?"

"Yes," Christian tried to reach for her face, attempting to kiss her."

"Where do you see this going?" She moved her head away, avoiding his lips.

He stood, and reached to pull her up, "Upstairs."

Annabeth pushed him back and moved a few feet away, "That's what I mean. I'm no longer in the 'other woman' business, and even if you two aren't married or romantically involved, that's all this would be. No, thank you." She moved even further away. "Did you think revealing your unmarried status would win me over?"

He was suddenly angry, "I was never going to tell you that. It's not why I came here!"

She was equally annoyed, "Then why did you?"

Christian looked at the ground, then back up, "Because I miss you. The sanctuary has been interesting with you there. The rest of the crew enjoys your company. We've all been more sociable with you around. Even as much as you push me away, at least you were there to see."

"I'm here for a job. My time spent with all of you is to research the book. When I'm done in a few weeks, I'll head to New York."

His tone was scornful, "Well, good for you. Get away from the sickness that's our situation. Glad you got to play with the animals and the humans."

"I never intended to play with you or get at all involved. I've tried to avoid it from that very first night."

"Have you?" he looked doubtful, "You mean like tonight? I don't think I forced drinks on you. I didn't see you pulling your hand away from mine or refusing my embrace."

Annabeth rubbed her eyes, "I've got to go."

"What?"

"I'm done with this conversation." Before she walked away from him, she spoke slowly, "Christian, another time and place I would have been thrilled to meet you. Your attention has been flattering. But, your place here and my purpose here prevent it from going any further." With those words she left.

As Annabeth leaned against the mirrored wall in the elevator, she realized she'd said the same thing to him more than once. Christian was proving to be the most stubborn of the alpha males at *Peaceful Pride.* Once again, the name of the wretched place was horribly ironic.

This time, things were different. He wasn't married. The words caused her head to spin for a moment. What if he'd told her that the very first night? Would it have made a difference?

It didn't change things. He still lived here. She had a life in New York. Annabeth also had a boyfriend there. Why hadn't he text her back. The newly discovered status of Christian's marriage was threatening something deep inside of her to bubble to the surface; hope.

# Chapter 18

It was a complete surprise when she was summoned to the sanctuary less than a day later. MJ called her on the way from the airport. "Celeste is having a slight meltdown and I guess it's about something she heard you saying?"

"No, it was Christian. He was discussing his need to resume his teaching schedule at the university to earn money. It offended her because I know of the financial issues."

MJ snorted in response, "She knows that's why the book's being written."

"Regardless, she sent me away. I've been staying in Raleigh now for a week and a half."

"Are you done with your work there? Do you have everything you need to finish the book?"

Annabeth wanted to say; *How can I? How would I possibly end this story with it in crisis mode*? Instead, she just said, "No."

"Let me make peace with her, then I'll have you come and together we can sit down and get you the information you need for the book."

She would have waited to hear from MJ, but later that afternoon, Shannon phoned. She'd been cleaning out the office and found some photos of the early construction of the sanctuary. The photos even included Celeste when she was still a star who wished to save the lions. Annabeth headed to the house. It would be easy to stay out of Unina's way. She could avoid the enclosure.

Driving into the opening gates felt somewhat like coming home. How easily she'd become acclimated to this life. Her spot was available in the garage, from there, Annabeth walked into the kitchen. Shannon greeted her with a cup of coffee and a fresh brownie. "I've missed you."

Annabeth bit into the still warm treat, "I've missed your cooking, this beats cellophane wrapped goodies in the lobby."

The two women walked to the office that sat between the television room and the formal living room. In the office were file cabinets and a large desk. Apparently in earlier days, Celeste Barlow had been involved in the business, before she took on a fake husband to handle that part.

Shannon sat in the swivel desk chair and motioned for Annabeth to pull up another chair beside her. In her hands were a stack of photos. A photo of the original farmhouse was on the top, a large but very normal looking residence on a farm. Beyond it were several outbuildings. The next photos captured the destruction of the original buildings. In those to follow were the construction progress of the current house and the buildings at the enclosure.

Along with workers and most likely architects, was Celeste Barlow. Whether in shorts and a sleeveless top or jeans and a tee shirt, this was the gorgeous and sexy starlet that Annabeth remembered from the movies. Her face was shining, her arms and leg muscles toned. Even her hair looked thicker and healthier. The shine of her eyes and brilliance of her smile could no longer be found on Unina, not even when she was talking to her lions.

"Wow," Annabeth breathed, "she's really changed."

Shannon nodded, "This was the woman who hired me. Her excitement over the project was contagious. We all felt she would change the world." She picked up a photo that showed Celeste sitting in an open cage in the back of a truck, a female lion resting her giant paws on her lap. Celeste was laughing. "She transformed the world for the cats." The woman's voice was filled with loyal admiration.

"So, what happened?"

"She lost part of herself, believes she's one of them and not a human caretaker. This morning she and Udok had a big row. Ben told me about it."

"Oh?"

"Yes, I guess Udok found her alone in the enclosure. She didn't even have a training stick with her. Max or Beau was on the ground with her." Now she was staring at a photo of one of the male lions, being led out of a trailer. "She's let herself get so thin; it would take nothing more than one paw to kill her."

"Did anything happen to her?"

"No, I guess he threatened to come in and get her, so she got out. Ben said they were screaming at each other once she stepped out of the pen."

"Are they still down there?" Annabeth wondered if her own fight with Christian the night before caused his anger.

"No, he flew off the property a while later. Ben's out mowing in back. MJ's been down there with her for an hour or so."

"I knew she was here. She wants the three of us to sit down together today." Annabeth packed up the photos in her case. "Do you think I should go there now?"

Shannon stood, "I'm certain it would be fine. If MJ wants you there, she'll smooth things over with Unina. You can take one of the vehicles."

"I think I'll just take a bike. It feels presumptuous to use the equipment; besides I've been cooped up in a hotel room, writing for days. I could use the exercise."

****

The trail was dusty, they'd seen no more rain after the tropical storm. The bike moved smoothly down the worn path. Annabeth could smell the cats as she approached the enclosure but didn't hear the lions. It was late afternoon; they were certain to be napping in the sun.

As she passed the small side window of the building, Annabeth heard soft laughter. Without a thought, she peered in. The bed, that Christian put in for Unina, was directly across the room from the window. At first, it looked as if a single person was moving on the bed. On closer inspection, she could see that there were two people. MJ was curled against Unina's back. Unina's face was upturned, pressed into MJ's shoulder. Her gauzy white top was lifted, her bare breasts showing. MJ's hand slid into the waistband of the other woman's pants. Unina was moaning softly.

Annabeth put a hand over her mouth and stepped back. Once again, she climbed on her bike and pedaled toward the house as fast as she could. What had she seen? Were the women lovers? Wouldn't Christian have told her that, if he'd known? It made little sense. When she spoke to MJ about revealing anything unpleasant in the book, she didn't seem to care. How could that be if they had a relationship?

Ben was parking the mower in the garage as she rolled in on the bike. He looked pleased, "Are you back?"

"No, Shannon had some pictures for me, and MJ wanted to meet with me."

"How'd that go?"

She fumbled for words, "Unina was sleeping, so I didn't bother her."

His face darkened, "Creepy, huh?"

Annabeth's eyes widened, "You know?" Ben nodded. "Does everyone know?"

"I sure as hell have never said a word about it."

"Are they a couple?"

He shook his head, "Not exactly, I walked in on them once. Unina didn't see me, but MJ did. She told me to keep my mouth shut, she was just comforting her."

Her mind was reeling, "Comforting her? So, they aren't together?"

"What I saw looked like a one-sided thing."

"Me too."

"Are you going to tell Udok?"

"Nope, I'm not telling anyone about that." The two walked toward the kitchen together.

"I'm kind of glad I'm not the only one who knows. It feels like MJ's controlling Unina that way."

"There are managers that will do anything to keep their clients happy," Annabeth said as they headed up the steps.

He turned to her, "Don't you have a manager?"

She punched him in the arm, "Not that kind of manager, smart ass!"

They were keeping Shannon company in the kitchen when Annabeth's phone buzzed. She read the text and looked at the other two. "They must be headed to the house. She asked me to meet them. Will it be a problem that I'm already here?"

"No," Shannon responded, "I asked you to come."

****

The three women met on the terrace. The view below revealed sleeping lions. Unina was cordial when Annabeth stepped into the room. She felt it was her responsibility to make the peace, after all she needed to finish the book. "Unina, I'm glad we could meet again. I'm sorry that I upset you on my last visit to the enclosure."

Unina accepted the apology and invited her to a chair near the railing. She sat on the couch near MJ. The smile she gave her manager was endearing.

"So, how's the manuscript coming along?" MJ got right to the point.

"Very well. It'll be a great book with the collection of photos I've gathered."

Unina looked at her sharply, "Photos of what?"

"The sanctuary. Shannon found several from the initial construction and the arrival of the lions. Those combined with the photos I took with you at the enclosure. The readers will love them." Annabeth knew mentioning the photos of the actress, Celeste Barlow, would be a bad idea.

"Can I see the lion photos you've taken?" Unina perked up.

"Sure, I've got new ones I picked up this morning." Annabeth reached in her bag and pulled out an envelope. She took the photos on days when Unina allowed her to spend the day with her. She'd captured the playfulness of the youngsters. Abe and Unina were pictured in the pen with the three females, the males were on their usual rock cliffs. There were even a few of the cats receiving checkups or vaccines from Christian in the building.

Unina made appreciative noises and sometimes even laughed. When she finished, she handed them back, and smiled, "I love these. I like the fact that the world can see how lions should live. I want them to know that my cats are being cared for by a mother who loves them."

Annabeth wrote Unina's words in her notebook. What a great quote for the book. MJ was watching her. If she knew what she was thinking, it didn't bother her. In fact, she gave a conspiratorial grin to Annabeth.

"What other information can I give you for the book?" these words from Unina came as a surprise.

Annabeth pulled out her notebook, "I'm glad you asked. I was thinking about your success at this. Are you hoping that others could do the same thing?"

Unina frowned at the possibility, "Maybe for different animals?" She made a dismissive motion with her hand, "No one can give their animals what I do, become their family."

Annabeth knew this was good stuff. So did MJ, she had a satisfied expression on her face. So, she would serve Celeste Barlow in any way she needed to if the end game was going her way. It would be impossible not to write this book without the readers being aware of how one of their beloved movie star thinks of herself as a mother to seven lions; to the extreme. People would read this; the press would talk about. MJ's expression told Annabeth that she was seeing this too.

Unina continued, "I mean maybe bears, or something like that; people could be inspired to build shelters where animals weren't forced to perform or be neglected. This book might help with that. I'm not expecting someone else to," she paused searching for the word, "transform herself to be what her animals need."

"And you've transformed yourself?"

Unina gave her a look of disappointment, "I'm surprised you haven't seen this in all the time you've spent with us." The "us" being the lions, which she indicated by tilting her head toward the visible enclosure. "I understand them, and they understand me. I can now sense their feelings."

She felt she had no other choice but agree so Annabeth nodded deeply as she scribbled notes, "They certainly are drawn to you."

"It's more than that, they look to me as their mother."

"Do you consider yourself the alpha of the pride?"

Now Unina's face broke into a smile; the look a teacher gives a student when they have retained something they've learned. "You've been doing good research. Yes, I guess that is true. I am the alpha of the pride."

MJ appeared bored with the conversation; she was sliding her finger along her phone screen. Annabeth wrote furiously. "I didn't know males normally permitted females to be alpha."

"Well, that's where the fact that I am not an actual lion is to my advantage." *Did she just say an 'actual lion'?* "Because then my gender is a non-issue. I am the one who protects them, makes certain they have food and shelter. I am their Unina."

"And what role then is Udok?"

Unina's smile faded slightly, her voice taking on a dismissive tone, "Just as the name suggests, the doctor; medical care giver."

"And what about Abe or any other interns?"

"Because I accept them around me, the cats know to accept them as well." She picked up one of Annabeth's photos, "That is how you've been able to capture these. I have shown my acceptance of your presence." Unina rifled through the stack, "Maybe we could do some shots of the pride without the fences showing." She walked to the edge of the terrace, "Views like this, unobstructed by the wires." Annabeth joined her and they looked at the inside of the pen surrounded by trees, rocks and with the watering hole in the center. It looked like they were in their natural habitat. Unina sighed deeply, “How I wish they could be free.”

Annabeth attempted to offer her solace, “I think it feels like freedom to them.”

The other woman turned to her, offering her a gracious smile. In this moment, Annabeth could see that she was still the lovely face that won over millions on the silver screen. Certainly, Christian was still in love with her. All this talk of not caring for her was to cover up the fact that she broke his heart with her rejection. She felt a pang of sympathy for him that was edged with guilt. It was unfair of her to play with him, even the small amount she had.

“Why don’t you come down at sunset. They’re active. Maybe we can get Ben to pull out the big truck and you can climb on it, for some good pictures.”

# Chapter 19

"Absolutely not!" Christian's voice was steely. "She will not hang over the fence." He stood at the side of the truck with Unina, Ben and Annabeth. Ben showed up an hour earlier with a cherry picker truck from a neighboring farm. The bucket attached to the hydraulic arm was a perfect spot for Annabeth to get better photos than the fence allowed her. Unina thought it would be ideal to move the bucket over the fence to assist with the shots.

"Udok, this is made to be safe," Ben patted the side of the truck. "It lifts workers up to skyscrapers."

"The pictures will be perfect," Unina's voice was pleading.

"I don't care, we aren't taking that kind of risk," Christian folded his arms over his chest.

Annabeth stepped forward, "The risk is mine, and I trust Ben's knowledge of the machine." Christian opened his mouth to disagree, but she said, "I'm doing it. Ben, help me up."

Christian raised his arms in the air, "I'm only trying to protect you. There's no reason to put yourself in a dangerous position for photos."

She appreciated his concern, and without thought said softly, "Christian, I know, but it will be fine." In her peripheral vision, she saw Unina's head snap at the use of his name. To avoid any confrontation, Annabeth took Ben's hand and climbed into the large steel bucket.

Minutes later, she hovered above the lions. Their initial curiosity prevented her from getting any good shots. Max roared at her, his ears flattened back as he stood on the tallest rock ledge and stared at her. The young ones, Amra and Kyra, went as far as trying to leap in her direction. She realized her best action, was to sit down in the bucket for a few minutes so they would lose interest in her presence. This worked. Soon they all resumed their normal activity.

Annabeth was thrilled when she stood again. With her long lens she could catch them all. Beau was belly up, rolling in a patch of grass. The three older females curled together near the watering hole. Max lounged on the rock.

With the change of a lens, Annabeth could capture shots of the entire group looking for all the world as if they were home in Africa. She spent a good half hour getting shots. Finally, she turned to the cab of the truck and gave Ben a thumbs up. The cherry picker began to move slowly away from the enclosure and lowered back down to the truck.

Christian jumped up and reached out a hand to assist her exit. Annabeth turned, smiling, to thank him. To her surprise, he was scowling, "Yep, you're right, you're not for me." His voice was a hissing whisper, "One more woman who takes stupid chances for the damn lions." With those words, he let go of her hand and jumped off the truck. Soon he disappeared into the building.

Ben and Unina circled around Annabeth, eager to see the first glimpse of her photos. They were excellent. Unina oozed compliments. She was pleased with the effort.

****

Back at the hotel, it was already dark. Annabeth was exhausted. This day was more eventful than she could ever have imagined. First Shannon shared good photos of the past, then she'd seen MJ and Unina in some sort of strange sex act. The best part was when she got to hang over the lion pen and take photos. She couldn't forget the tantrum that Christian had.

Annabeth took a long swig from a water bottle and stretched out on her bed. She needed to separate herself from this unhealthy situation. It was time to Facetime Chase and convince him to join her. He had not answered her all day.

Fortunately, when she attempted to contact him, his face came into view immediately. He was out on the street, she could hear the noises of traffic, but he smiled at her. "See what you're missing?" he asked and held out his own phone to scan the scene.

"It looks blissfully chaotic." Annabeth could use some time around anonymous strangers. "Are you going to meet me this weekend?"

Chase frowned, "I hoped that you'd come back here to see me."

"I would, but it's been crazy here."

He looked at the bed and wall behind her, "Are you in a hotel?"

"Yes, Unina kicked me out a week ago."

"Annabeth, you don't need this shit."

"Yes, I do. This will be an interesting biography. Anyway, she had me come today, and it went exceedingly well."

He sighed, "Really? Then why do you suddenly want to get away?"

"Maybe I just miss you!" She offered him a flirty smile and was disappointed that he didn't return the look.

"I guess I could come. When are you going to be done down there?"

Now it was her turn to frown, "I'm working on that. It's a big project. Come on, say you'll meet me. I can tell you all the sordid details then."

He smiled, "That sounds interesting. I guess I could. Send me the info."

Annabeth hung up awhile later, relieved to have made plans to spend the weekend with Chase. She was resolute in her feelings to not have any more personal contact with Christian. In another day, she'd be at the beach house, snuggling with Chase.

# Chapter 20

Annabeth came awake slowly; her face pressed against a strong, cool shoulder. Her arm was slung across the chest of the same body, her fingers were entwined with his fingers. Overhead a ceiling fan dropped a slight breeze. She slept so well. A tiny smile played on her lips as she opened her eyes. She loved waking up with a man, savoring the moment.

As her head cleared, she remembered the night before. "Oh shit," were the words she nearly spoke aloud.

Outside, she could make out the sound of waves crashing and gulls calling from above. This was the beach house she'd rented to meet Chase, but he'd cancelled on her. After he'd agreed just a couple of nights ago. Things seemed fine. Then out of the blue last night he'd called as she'd arrived at the beach. He couldn't be gone for the entire weekend; she should fly up to New York. Unlike him, she wasn't required to be back first thing Monday morning.

She'd tried to explain that this was a crucial time. With the story looking as if it may be stagnant, she didn't want to leave now. It seemed nearly complete. If he would come to the beach, then she would try for New York in a week or two.

Annabeth was hurt by his accusatory words, "You're so caught up in the story that you won't give any time to our relationship." He sounded like a petulant child.

Her frustrated sigh was followed by her justification, "But this is what I do. My career involves immersing myself in a subject's life for a brief period and then returning home to write the story."

"A brief period? It's been seven weeks."

She couldn't believe him. "The last two books took six months of research."

"I'm not willing to be in a part-time relationship."

And there it was. An excuse to end it. The old "out of sight, out of mind" cliché? "You don't think we're worth waiting for?"

"That's the problem, Annabeth, we're not together enough to be a 'we'."

"Maybe my next book will be about someone in New York City." Who was she kidding? Annabeth Muldoon was at the top of her career. Now was not the time to slow down or pick only local assignments. There was a pained silence. This was the part she was never good at. Her instinct of fight or flight was the latter. "I've got to go. Guess I'll take advantage of the beach alone."

His own sigh sounded guilty, "Annabeth, I'm sorry. Maybe..."

"It's okay, goodbye Chase," she hung up. In another minute she'd slammed out the door and headed to the shore.

Annabeth didn't know how to be the woman who sat in the sand, letting her tears mingle with the waves. Instead, when she saw a beachfront bar, she went in. Soon, she was seated at a table, frosty beer in her hand. Watching surfers trying to stand against the waves was a good distraction.

Across the deck, a man with a gray-flecked beard sat in front of a microphone, a guitar in his hand and belted out *Brown-Eyed Girl.* Three ladies in their sixties, wearing bathing suits and sarongs, danced in front of him. Annabeth switched to Crown and an order of tacos. Her barefoot kept time to the song on the sandy floor. At the table next to her glass, her phone buzzed. The text read, *I'm sorry I was a jackass.*

She sighed and tapped a response, *Don't worry about it, you were right.*

*What are you doing?*

*Getting drunk alone at a beach bar.* After that, she turned her phone off. She didn't want to hear Chase's excuses. Instead, she ordered another drink, deciding that the guy with the guitar did a hell of a Jack Johnson, as he was now singing *Upside Down.* One more drink and maybe she could go cry into the waves.

When she'd paid her tab, Annabeth headed back out to the beach. It wasn't long before she decided that the booze and the effort it took to walk in the sand wore her out. Her air-conditioned cottage and bed sounded like a better option. She almost walked by her place because she didn't see her SUV, it was blocked from her vision by another vehicle; a Range Rover. Christian sat on her front steps, his eyes on his cell phone.

"What the hell are you doing here?"

He looked up and saw her, "Thank God, do you know how

many beach bars there are here?"

Annabeth pulled open her own phone, the texts she'd exchanged earlier were with him, not Chase.

Christian stood, shoved his phone into his shorts' pocket and grinned. Those white teeth and bright eyes warmed her in places she couldn't control.

****

Now it was morning, and the strong shoulder she had her face pressed against was not Chase's, it was Dr. Christian Mendoza's. Crap.

She breathed against his shoulder, then attempted to extricate her fingers from his. His hand held hers in place. "Don't even try it," his voice was soft but firm. Christian moved his face to kiss the top of her head. "Good morning, sweetheart."

"I'm not your sweetheart," Annabeth pulled her hand from his and rolled to the side of the bed. She looked at the floor next to her. Once a chubby girl, always a chubby girl. She would not strut naked to the bathroom. On the floor was a damp beach towel; a reminder of their late-night playtime in the ocean. Annabeth grabbed it and carefully wrapped herself in it as she stood.

Lifting her bag off the floor, she didn't even glance at the bed before she locked herself in the bathroom. She emerged twenty minutes later; showered, minimal makeup on and dressed.

The bedroom was empty. She walked hesitantly into the living area; no sign of Christian. Had he gone home? Did he realize how stupid they had been?

Annabeth opened the front door to see if his car was gone. No, in fact he was climbing out of it with coffees and a pastry bag in hand. Sunglasses covered his eyes, but the rest of him from that luscious black hair down to his bare tan legs looked perfectly groomed. How had he managed that? She looked back in the house. On the counter near the kitchen sink were a toothbrush and shaving kit. On the floor was a duffle. Dr. Mendoza intended to stay.

"Good morning, Annabeth," he was now next to her.

"Christian, last night."

Before she could continue, he waved her off, "So how long are you planning on playing this game? You reject me, you accept me. Last night we let ourselves go and didn't let anything come between us. It was wonderful."

Annabeth reflected on the night. He'd convinced her to put on her bathing suit, and he did the same. They'd crossed the street, heading to the beach. Christian insisted that he needed to catch up with her.

She was drunk. While he got himself something to drink, she spread out the beach blanket and laid down on it. The sun felt marvelous on her skin. When he returned, he stretched out next to her.

"I'm sorry that we fought before you left. And I'm sorry that you were here alone this afternoon." With that he kissed her. She could already taste the sweetness of the liquor on his lips.

The beach, the ocean, the sun and the drinks were too much. Annabeth let go of all her inhibitions, she pulled his face towards her and kissed him back. When it became clear that things were heating up to a dangerous point, she stood and jogged to the water. "Time to cool down."

He laughed as he stood and moved quickly to her. "Then we're both going in." He grabbed her hands and pulled her into the waves while she shrieked. They both bobbed in and out of the water, kissing once again.

Annabeth knew that they'd ended up back at the beach bar. Slow dancing was followed by more drinks, and tacos while the gray-bearded singer did his own renditions of Jimmy Buffett and Kenny Chesney. She recalled some incredible moments in bed. The desire that had been building up between them was not dampened by any drink. She must have fallen asleep or passed out immediately afterwards, because she truly was surprised when she awoke in his arms this morning.

And now in the light of day, he was telling her to quit denying the feelings growing between them. Annabeth took the offered coffee. After a slow sip, using the time to organize her thoughts, she spoke, "Let's get this out of our system."

He laughed out loud, "Is that what you think we were doing last night?"

"It's all we can do. Tomorrow, I must return to the sanctuary and finish my work. I'm under contract. If I wasn't, I'd resign from the position now."

"But you know my marriage is a farce."

She looked at him incredulously, "Then why are you still living there?"

Christian ran his hand through his hair, quiet for a moment. "I can't just leave."

"Unina?" her heart froze as she waited for his answer.

He looked her in the eyes, "The lions. Seriously, if I leave, she must pay someone to replace me. There's no money to do it."

Annabeth nodded her understanding of that, then remembered the woman who'd stood on the terrace, still so beautiful. "But don't you love her?'

"No, I don't even know her. The woman I became infatuated with has completely disappeared."

So, he saddled himself in this life because of the animals? Annabeth was just beginning to understand this. The last weeks, when she spent time out there, she realized the sense of commitment. Those beautiful felines had lived horrible lives and deserved the world they were now in. He couldn't leave *Peaceful Pride*.

He was looking at her, waiting for a response. At length, she gave a half-hearted shrug, "I'm single, so I'm not cheating on my boyfriend and I know you're not a married man. Soon enough, I will be done in North Carolina and will return to my own life."

Now it was Christian's turn to look miserable, "That's not the sentiment that I wanted to hear."

"That's all I've got."

After a moment, he mustered a small smile. "You've also got this cottage for another day, let's make the most of it." He leaned in and kissed her softly. Annabeth didn't fight him.

****

They walked along the shore; hand in hand, strolled ankle deep in the Atlantic. Christian occasionally scooped up a rock, skipping it back into the sea. He named each of the sea birds that scurried out of their way or flew overhead.

"How'd you get into veterinary medicine?" she asked him.

"I grew up in Texas. At sixteen, I got a job at a cattle farm. I found myself interested in the steer's health. When I witnessed my first calf birth, I was sold. I wanted to care for animals."

"You came to North Carolina because of the university?"

"Yep, to finish my program and I stayed. I like the east coast better than Texas. Have you always been a city girl?"

"Nope, my dad was military. I was an army brat who moved all over. When I chose a college, I wanted to be in the big city. Then *Rolling Stones Magazine* hired me. I settled in New York City and was in heaven. It was my dream job."

"But you left it?"

"I saw the change in my line of work. Technology has transformed everything. Besides, like every writer, I wanted to try my hand at a book."

"And you've been incredibly successful."

"Were you ever a vet in an office?"

They'd reached the end of the large pier that jutted out in the ocean and sat on one of the built-in benches, watching the waves roll up to the shore.

"During my training. Even as a professor, I still got to deal with animals. The local zoo called us in for any major issues."

"Then there was the sanctuary."

"Yep, that was unexpected."

"All of it, I'd imagine."

He looked uncomfortable, as if he hadn't wanted the conversation to return to that subject.

Annabeth understood, today was too nice. "Are you teaching at the college again?"

Christian showed his appreciation on the change of topic by squeezing her hand, "I am. I met with them on Wednesday. My position as director is being covered by another. I can't expect them to simply push that person out. I did, however, agree to teach a few classes at the start of the semester. Annabeth, I've gotten myself into a position that I don't know how to get out of."

She turned toward him, both of their expressions forlorn, "It seems hopeless."

Christian pushed a stray curl from her cheek and pulled her in for a kiss. "Not today. This is a gift."

Though inside, she felt deep sadness, Annabeth kissed him back then smiled.

He stood, "Let's go crash into those waves." As she rose next to him, he put his hand on her waist, "Unless you have a better idea."

They spent the day swimming, dozing on the beach and ending up back in the cottage for a shower and some precious time in bed together. In the evening, they returned to the beach bar, a place Annabeth knew she would always remember as their place.

Once again, they ate, drank and danced. Tonight's entertainment was a band who played current country hits. Annabeth had been certain that what she was building with

Chase was what she wanted. There was something, however, about the magnetism of Christian that made her feel everything stronger. His touch was electric, his eyes were only for her. She wanted to bask in those looks forever. When they found themselves in bed late that night, Annabeth held onto him with all her might and dozed off.

# Chapter 21

A phone was buzzing on the nightstand. Annabeth climbed over Christian's bare chest to reach for it. It wasn't hers; it was his. The screen read Abe. She shook him lightly, "Christian, it's Abe on the phone."

He came awake slowly, "What does he want?"

"I'm not answering!"

Christian remembered where they were and took it from her, sitting up. With his free hand, he reached over and ran his fingers through her hair that was now fanned out on the pillow. "Hello?" She couldn't hear Abe.

Suddenly Christian's hand stilled, and he sat up straighter, "What's wrong?" He waited. "What happened? How long ago?" He swung his legs off the bed, "I'll be there as quick as I can, it's going to be a few hours. Here's what you need to do," he stepped into the bathroom and Annabeth couldn't hear the instructions.

She also leapt out of bed and pulled on her shorts and a T-shirt. Christian returned to the bedroom. "Bad news. I've got to go now."

"What's wrong?"

"It looks like one of the other cats has attacked Duchess. Abe went down to feed them and she was against the fence, bleeding badly."

"Where was Unina?" Annabeth couldn't believe that she hadn't been at the pens.

"I guess she stayed in the house last night. MJ is still there."

Annabeth thought about that, did Christian understand the meaning of that statement? He showed no signs of it. "She must be devastated."

"I don't even have time to think about that, I've got to get back." He was pulling on his clothes from the evening before. Suddenly, he stopped and looked at Annabeth. His expression was forlorn, "I'm leaving."

"I'll be right behind you," she said hoping to placate him.

"That's not the point. I know what it'll be like when we get there." He stepped close, "Not like this." Christian pulled her to him and gave her a long kiss. Her hands wrapped around his neck. When the kiss ended, he whispered, "What can we do, Annabeth?"

She laid a hand on his chest, "Don't think about that now. We'll find another time to talk." She hoped her words convinced him because they didn't make her feel one bit better. His need to race to the sanctuary was a reminder that the weekend they spent together was a one-time thing.

After his departure, it took Annabeth another hour and a half to get the cabin cleaned according to the rental agreement. She wanted to rush to the sanctuary also, but there'd be no time to come back here. It may have been for the better. This time in the place alone gave her a chance to adjust her thinking.

While she took the sheets off the bed and tossed them in the washer, she had time to recall the twenty-four plus hours that they'd spent together. It was fun, passionate and the worst thing was that it had also felt natural. Alone here in the Outer Banks, Christian and Annabeth responded to one another as a couple.

As she washed and dried the dishes they'd used, she let a few tears drip down her cheeks. It wasn't meant to be. Typical, Annabeth always fell for the wrong guy. The added complication was that she couldn't just run away from this one. When she returned to New York, there was no reason she had to cross paths with Chase again. She could even join another gym if she chose to. After her affair with Trent Crosby, from The Jack Corey Band, ended it was pretty much a guarantee they'd never see one another again.

This time, though, she wasn't done with *Peaceful Pride* or its human members. She closed her car door, in fact, in just a few hours she'd see them all again. It would be difficult to be around Dr. Christian Mendoza. Yesterday, he'd stolen her heart.

****

Annabeth called MJ as she traveled from the Outer Banks. The call went straight to voicemail, so she texted her. MJ responded that she knew of the accident but left this morning before they found Duchess. Now, she was with another client in LA. She'd only just arrived and needed to be there at least until tomorrow.

Unina's agent said she'd join her at *Peaceful Pride* as soon as she could. Annabeth snidely wondered if MJ "took care" of all her clients in quite the same way. Then she chided herself, wasn't she once again inappropriately getting involved with someone from her book subject's life? Was she any better?

****

Annabeth broke the rules and drove her car down the path to the enclosure. As she got closer, she could see she was not the only one who had done so. The Range Rover was there as well as Ben's pickup. Both utility vehicles were also parked behind the building. She grabbed her camera and rushed out of the car.

Inside the building, many voices were speaking at once. Instinctively she aimed her camera and hit record. Duchess was on the examining table, a spotlight focused on her from overhead. Unina had her back to Annabeth, she was hunched over the cat, her hands stroking the flank of the leg closest to her. Abe was next to her, but up closer to the cat's head. He was wearing gloves. Ben stood across from Unina, his hands at his sides, looking uncomfortable and helpless.

At the head of the table was the man in charge; Christian. He was now in a white coat and gloves. He was performing some procedure on the cat, from her angle it looked to Annabeth as if he was stitching her. "What's her BP?" he looked at Abe. Out of the corner of his eye, he saw Annabeth. His expression softened into a sad smile. It was obvious enough that the other three people turned and looked at the door.

She lowered the camera, "Can I help?"

"No," Christian responded as he continued to pull a needle through the flesh of the lion. Abe's hands were near his, washing the blood away as it seeped through. "She's out, which is the best thing, she's not fighting us."

"But it's not good for a cat her age to be under anesthesia," Unina's voice was anguished.

"I know," Christian sighed, not looking up, "but we have to repair what we can of her wounds. Bleeding out would guarantee an instant death." He ignored her sob.

Annabeth wanted to help, "Unina, could you come out here and tell me what happened?"

Abe gave a slight nod to indicate this was a good idea, "Get a drink and sit for a while. I'll call you if anything changes. You have a long night ahead of you. Go sit with Annabeth."

Though she looked as if she would protest, Unina moved, virtually too weak to stand. The two women sat on the bench nearest the pen. The other two female lions were pacing nervously at the gate. Unina got up and placed herself on the ground in front of them. Annabeth joined her.

The felines welcomed the reassuring scratches. This also allowed Unina to calm slightly. Focusing on the cats, she spoke, "I think it was Max."

"Max attacked Duchess?" Annabeth worked to keep her voice quiet and neutral.

"It was just one bite, but it was to the neck. If it happened any sooner in the night, she would've been dead when Abe came down." Unina choked on the sentence and cried for a moment.

"Do you know why he would have done that?" Annabeth saw very little interaction between the males and the females. One advantage of spaying and neutering the cats was that it prevented the normal acceptance and refusals of males desiring to mate.

"Duchess is the only female who ever tried to take any of his food. Occasionally when treats were offered, she would step a little too close to him when he got one. He growled and even swatted at her before."

Annabeth considered this, it made sense. A thought occurred, "Did anyone feed them a treat last night?"

Unina was gazing out at the pasture. Max was on his rock cliff, asleep, his tail flicking away flies. "No, he may have found a bird or a mouse."

"Maybe she did, and he tried to take it away."

Unina spun to Annabeth, "You're right, that sounds like the most plausible thing. Duchess wouldn't have given up her food easily." She slumped her shoulders and looked at the massive beast, "He's not a vicious boy."

"How bad are her injuries?"

"Her neck is punctured. Udok is uncertain if her jugular is sliced. There's also a concern of the bones being broken there."

Annabeth sat back and stared out at the field. This lion may not survive. She realized the gravity of the situation; the woman next to her considered herself a mother who may lose a child.

Unina stretched out along the fence, so that her body was almost spooning a female lion. Any part of her that could press

through
the chain link was touching the big cat. The other feline was settled so that its head rested on the hips of the one nearest Unina. Annabeth could see that Unina was crying, her shoulders heaved.

After some time, the movement stopped. Unina fell asleep. As much as the other woman's proximity of the cats worried her, Annabeth knew that at least she was getting some rest. She stood up and headed back into the building.

Ben and Abe were at the large metal utility sink. Christian still stood at the table next to the lion, though his hands were at his sides. Annabeth approached him. To her relief, she could see the cat's chest was moving, albeit in an uneven manner. Duchess was alive.

Sweat ran down Christian's forehead, he had a bloody smudge on his cheek. Annabeth moved until she was directly next to him. "How is she?" she asked in a near whisper.

"I don't know if she'll make it," his voice was hoarse. "I've done everything I can." They both stared at the cat. Her neck was a combination of raw skin, sutures, gauze and blood.

Annabeth moved closer, so that her shoulder was against his, an attempt at comfort. Christian laid his head on her shoulder. "I just don't know if it's enough."

Annabeth's hands itched with the desire to pull him into a hug, she felt the same energy in his arms. After a long moment, he lifted his head. Abe was moving toward the table.

The younger man must have seen their sideways touch but didn't mention it. "Are we going to leave her here?"

"No," Christian glanced around the room, "Let's roll the small travel pen in." Ben also returned to the table. "Pad it with sheets. Abe, we'll have to keep her out long enough for the IV tube to fill her with antibiotics."

"It's a real strain on her heart."

"I know, but infection will also kill her."

Ben left the building to get the pen. Abe was checking the IV. Christian walked over to the sink; Annabeth followed him.

"What's Unina doing?"

"She's pressed up against the fence sleeping with the females."

He shook his head as hot water cascaded down his forearms, "Not the safest position but at least she's resting. We'll have our hands doubly full with her. Maybe I could slip her a sedative too."

"Not a bad idea."

As Christian was drying off, he looked at her as if remembering for the first time where she'd come from. "Did you get everything closed up in the cabin?" Annabeth nodded. "I'm sorry I left so suddenly."

Abe was across the room; Annabeth didn't know if he could hear. Apparently Christian wasn't concerned. "Don't even think about it. I'm glad you made it here on time."

This refocused him back to the matter at hand, Christian was moving to the table, "I hope I did. I'm not feeling very confident.

# Chapter 22

The tragedy of Duchess' attack didn't stop the routine of the other six cats. When dinnertime rolled around, they began their orderly procession to the food chutes.

Unina was not outside to assist. She was in the building, on a blanket, next to Duchess' infirmary pen. It was a battle to keep her out of it. When she first walked in as they were transferring the cat off the table and onto the padded floor of the pen, Unina entered the cage and sat down at the cat's head.

"Absolutely not," Christian voice held no sympathy for the heartbroken woman. "This is an injured animal. When she wakes up, she could well be vicious. She will not know where she is, and she'll be in pain."

"That's exactly why I need to be with her!" protested Unina. She tried to disengage her arm from his strong grip as he dragged her out of the pen.

"Then getting a fucking blanket and sit next to the cage. You will not get in there! I'll padlock the pen and take the key, if I must. The last thing I need to deal with is treating your injuries as well."

Unina began to cry, which had no effect on Christian. Abe went to a cupboard, pulled out blankets, and placed them closest to

Duchess' head. She collapsed into a heap, her fingers reaching in to stroke the feline's whiskers. "Don't give up, sweet girl."

Annabeth watched as Christian and Abe fed the others. When Max moved to his chute to eagerly take the meaty mixture, Christian spoke to him, "Did you do this, you greedy bastard?" The male cat grabbed his meal and moved away, uninterested in the scolding.

Nova and Luna were currently not concerned for their fellow pride mate. They both readily took their meals. Even the young ones were undisturbed. Christian and Annabeth stood against the fence watching the animals eat. Abe rolled the wagon back into the building.

Christian rested his forehead against the fence in exhaustion. "If I'd known this would be such a hellish day, I'd have gotten more sleep."

She turned to him, prepared to hush him. He was looking at her, a small smile on his face. Annabeth couldn't resist the smile. "I'm very sorry, that will never happen again."

His smile dropped away, "Don't say that."

She felt bad, she'd meant it as a joke about not letting him sleep. He'd taken it wrong. Though, she wanted to appease him; it was futile to make an empty promise. All she had to do was review the last three hours. This was his life. The cats and Unina were a package deal. With this in mind, Annabeth spoke quietly, "I'm sorry, now's not the right time to have this conversation."

Before he could respond, Unina began urgently calling for him. Ben jogged into the building right behind Christian and Annabeth. It was unclear if Duchess was completely conscious, but she was snarling, and her paws were attempting to rip at the IV tube and the dressing on her neck.

"Shit, Abe get a sedative."

Unina rushed over, "We can't drug her anymore. It will kill her!"

Christian pushed her arm away as she grabbed at him. He knelt to the cat, trying to talk to her softly. When Unina moved next to him, he spoke, "We have to get her calm enough to shackle her paws, so she doesn't tear out her stitches."

"Shackle her?" Unina was horrified.

He turned to her, "Get out of the way, so Abe and I can take care of her."

Unina moved back, and Abe knelt beside him. They were talking to each other, but Annabeth couldn't hear their words over the sounds of the cat. Her cries were hoarse and high pitched. Behind the closed door, she could hear roars from the enclosure. The other lions were responding to the stress calls.

Abe added a syringe of liquid into the IV, in less than a minute, the lioness calmed. When her eyes rolled back, Unina cried out. Ben approached her, "Come on, let's get out of their way." The big man led the frail woman to her blanket on the other side of the pen. She knelt and began stroking the cat's fur.

Ben moved beside Annabeth. "Good job," she whispered.

He looked at Christian, "How are we going to keep her paws off of her injuries?"

Christian monitored her vitals for a moment, then stood, "She's very weak. I think ropes will do the trick."

"That sounds awful!" Unina spoke from the floor.

"Just until the IV bag is empty. We can construct a sort E collar to keep her from hurting her sutures." The group stood and watched the lion fall back into a medicated sleep.

Annabeth knew there wasn't much to do. Shannon texted her a few times asking for updates. She must have seen her drive by earlier. Now, she stepped quietly out of the building and to her car. Shannon ran out the front door of the house as she pulled up.

"It's been killing me not knowing what's going on!" She led Annabeth to the kitchen and fixed her a glass of lemonade.

After a long drink, Annabeth set her glass on the table and shared the events with Shannon. She told it in as much detail as she could. While she shared the story, the other woman heated a piece of chicken and a serving of potatoes.

Between bites of food, Annabeth continued the story. When she finished, she took a deep breath. "So, as far as I know, there's no guarantee Duchess will pull through."

****

It wasn't long before Christian returned to the house. Annabeth went to her former room intending to rest, but instead was writing copious notes on a tablet that Shannon gave her from the downstairs office. She was using her recording of the events as a reference.

He popped his head in the door. "Hey." Christian looked exhausted. The combination of sweat, most likely blood and who knew what other substance was causing bits of his hair to stick up in odd places. There were dark circles under his eyes.

Annabeth stood, "Any changes?"

He motioned for her to sit back down, "No, not at all. She's resting, most likely because of the drugs. Her breathing is weak. Abe is monitoring her. I need to make some calls." He turned to leave the room.

She moved toward him, "Take a shower first." It felt right to place a comforting hand on his back. "How about something to eat or drink?"

Despite the exhausted expression in his eyes, Christian smiled, "Are you trying to take care of me?"

Boldly, Annabeth kissed his cheek, "I'm beginning to understand that here, you hold everything together. Go get in the shower, I'll bring you some food."

He turned so that their lips met, "Or you could join me."

"Go," was all she said as she slipped past him and headed downstairs.

When she knocked, then entered his room, he was just pulling on a clean shirt, over his shorts. His hair was still damp. Annabeth set a tray of food and drink on the desk. Christian moved toward her and pulled her in for an embrace. She could feel his fatigue in the way he leaned his head on her shoulder.

"I've got to make some calls," he said in a moment, around bites of a sandwich.

"I'll be in my room."

"Don't be ridiculous. Let's go out on the terrace. Monitoring the other cats would be wise."

She agreed. Anyone down at the enclosure would be watching Duchess. As he scrolled through his phone looking for numbers, she picked up a pair of binoculars on the table and looked out at the pen. The six cats were doing what they did best, sleeping. She could see no human movement, Unina and Abe must still be in the building.

Christian was on his phone. She listened to his side of the conversation. "Kurt, it's Christian, well we've had an accident." He relayed the discovery of Duchess, what probably happened, then he described the treatment and her condition. "Thanks, I would really appreciate another set of eyes." He moved into the bedroom.

Annabeth followed him in to get a drink off the tray. She was exhausted. The bed looked irresistible, and she sat down on it, the pillow felt like a magnet trying to pull her head to it. She resisted.

"I'm afraid she'll drown in her own blood. I know. Yes. I would be so grateful. Yes, if you could bring Ava too, that would be great. I would welcome any advice." He moved toward the bed and sat next to Annabeth. "An hour will be fine. Thanks so much."

"Other vets?" she asked as he ended the call.

"Yes, colleagues from the university." He then searched for another number and pressed the call button.

"Dr. Tomas, this is Dr. Christian Mendoza, I'm sorry to bother you. Thank you. We've had a serious lion injury. It's not looking good. Yes, she's in pretty rough shape. No, I guarantee she'll be unable to eat. Sleep? I'm uncertain. I'm concerned because of the seriousness of the situation. Shannon knows?"

Annabeth gave up the pretense of not listening. She'd thought he was talking to another vet, but what would Shannon know?

He continued, "A milkshake? Oh, I see. She knows the correct mixture. Okay. I'll try to get her to drink it. No, I think that will help. Yes, I'll let you know. Thanks so much."

He ended the second call. Annabeth was looking at him expectantly. "That was Unina's doctor. I wasn't completely honest with you before." She waited for more. "Unina was suicidal after the death of Mable."

Annabeth's mind sorted through what he'd previously told her about that time. She fleetingly wondered if that was the reason for his proposal. This explained quite a lot.

"I just want to make certain we keep her calm and safe as we deal with Duchess." While he spoke, Christian stretched out on the bed, pulling Annabeth down with him. She didn't fight him. Soon her head was on his chest, his arm wrapped around her shoulders. "I don't know if I'm doing everything I can."

Lightly scratching his chest, she spoke, "From what I can see, you've done amazing work saving Duchess's life." *And perhaps Unina's*, she didn't say this aloud.

"I'm uncertain Duchess will survive." Christian kissed the top of her head, then relaxed back on the pillow. Within moments she could feel his steady breathing. Annabeth allowed herself to doze off too.

****

Ever the light sleeper, Annabeth checked her phone after she disentangled herself from the sleeping man. It had only been a twenty-minute nap for her. She scooped up the tray and headed down to the kitchen.

"Thank you," said Shannon, who was watching television, but joined her in the kitchen.

"He's asleep, but he's got some other vets coming from the university."

"It's terrible," it wasn't a question.

"Yes, I think it's the damage to her windpipe. He mentioned something about drowning in her own blood."

"Oh no, Unina," was Shannon's response.

"And speaking of her, he called a Dr. Tomas." The other woman nodded. "I'm sure Christian will tell you all of this, but they were discussing a milkshake you make?"

Shannon opened a cupboard and drew out some items, a protein powder, another powder. Then she went to a second cupboard and picked out bottles. One looked to be a prescription, a couple of others perhaps vitamin supplements. "Yes, this is a healthy mix to keep her nourished and calm. I make it for her frequently." She held up the prescription bottle, "But I've rarely added this."

Annabeth began fixing a pot of coffee, busyness helped her so she could gather information in an informal manner. "Christian also told me about her being suicidal after the death of Mabel."

Shannon turned to her in surprise, "We agreed not to discuss it with you."

So, they'd apparently had a conversation about what she should and shouldn't know. This was never good for a story. "I see," her tone was short.

"I'm sorry Annabeth, we didn't know what you would be like before you got here. We were concerned that you'd see that Celeste Barlow doesn't live here anymore and be determined to write her story in an unkind manner."

The coffee was pouring into her mug, and Annabeth went to the refrigerator for creamer. "I understand."

"But we don't feel that way now. You seem to genuinely care about Unina. As you have come to discover, she is a very fragile woman."

Annabeth nodded, then took a sip of her coffee. "Things are very different here than I expected when I arrived."

Shannon took a deep breath, "Perhaps you should also know, their marriage isn't what you think."

With a raised eyebrow, Annabeth responded, "You mean their fake marriage?" Shannon returned the eyebrow raise. "I know, he told me."

"Udok or Christian," she said the word as if it was unfamiliar to her, "confides in you a lot." It was a question without being one.

Annabeth rolled the warm mug between her hands, "It can't be that way. He is as much of the lifeblood of this place as you are."

"And you are a writer from New York," Shannon nodded.

"Exactly." She placed the mug on the counter, "Why don't I take that shake to Unina and if Ben is still down there, send him here for a break. I'd like to send Abe too, but I don't know if he'll let Duchess be there without a doctor."

Before she could move, Shannon placed a hand on her arm, "Udok is a good man, one of the best." She hesitated and Annabeth wondered if she was about to get a scolding for her obvious time spent with him. "When Mabel died, he committed his life to Unina's dream. I know she didn't and still doesn't appreciate the sacrifices he's made for her and the sanctuary." Now she gave Annabeth a stern look, "He deserves some happiness. Please don't trifle with his heart."

Annabeth should have known how well-loved Christian was by the others in the house. He was the lifeblood of the entire place. Her face flushed, and she mumbled a heated, "Okay," to Shannon. What else could she say?

# Chapter 23

Three veterinarians and one in training placed Duchess back on the table to examine her. Unina drank her shake. Expecting her to be sleepy, Annabeth spread out a blanket for her near the enclosure. When the two young lions came close for attention, Unina could barely scratch them, her eyes heavy with sleep. Finally, she gave in and stretched out on the blanket.

By the time the moon pushed its way past the sun, the other vets had left the sanctuary. The prognosis wasn't good. Christian and Abe were doing everything they could. The damage seemed too great for her to recover.

They all agreed that keeping her comfortable was their best course of action. She was no longer in her cage. There was little chance of her rousing at all. With Unina in a medicated sleep, they could decide to keep the lion sedated. The benefits outweighed the risks.

The big cat looked weak, laid out on the padding in the middle of the room. She was in some form of sleep, ignoring the IV in her flank. The bandages at her throat still revealed fresh blood.

Unina staggered in from the pens, in a haze, and curled herself around the cat. The men exchanged exasperated looks but left her there. At Christian's urging, Abe was stretched out on a fold out lounge chair near the cat. It was obvious he would be there for the night.

Annabeth was in a position common in her profession; she felt like an awkward third wheel. Her job as an observer was out of place. She headed to the door, "I'll go up to the house. If anything happens, let us know." Her eyes focused on Christian, "Climb into that bed and get some sleep."

He followed her out, "I hate that this happened today."

"It's hard to believe that yesterday we were on the beach," Annabeth agreed.

"We awoke in the same bed this morning. I wanted to say things to you." Things that would not make a difference in their situation, Annabeth thought. "We didn't even get a good kiss goodbye."

She looked around them. Not a soul in sight. It was guaranteed that Abe was as dead to the world as Unina. Annabeth laced her hands around his neck, her face moved close to his. He wrapped his arms around her waist, his mouth drinking hers in. The kiss was soft, sweet and went on for a moment. When they pulled away, she felt a lump in her throat. Right now, with all this tragedy and his obligation surrounding them, a goodbye kiss held much more meaning. "Get some sleep, Christian. I'll be back down here in a few hours."

As she rolled along the trail in the utility vehicle, Annabeth was glad it was dark. She didn't want anyone to see the selfish tears she shed. Once they were out of her system, she knew she had a big story to write.

Back in the room that she'd lived in for over a month, she dug out her laptop and clicked it on. She could give up a night's sleep to work on this material. It was best to do it while it was still fresh in her memory. It wasn't long though, before the words were blurring on the screen. Annabeth was exhausted. She would have to give in and sleep.

****

Duchess held on for another three days. They were difficult for everyone involved, but especially Unina. She was constantly weeping, but only moved from the cat when they dragged her away to check her neck or perform any other medical procedures.

Annabeth was the one who could usually lure her out to the other lions. At desperate times she would remind her that all six of her children needed her or that Luna and Nova were missing their counterpart. Sadly, this worked. Annabeth was now accustomed to gathering the meal supplies from the large refrigerator and cupboards in the building and loading it all into the wagon. She would roll it out and convince Unina to do the feedings.

This was when Unina was at her best. Like a real mother, she wanted her other children to also feel loved. She would talk to each one as they were eating. After they'd completed a meal, most would come over for a scratch.

On the second evening, she was still inconsolable. Annabeth

convinced Abe to get in the enclosure with Unina so she could visit with the lions. The two young ones were the most attentive. When Unina laughed aloud at the antics of Amra with a big limb, Annabeth knew it had been a good call.

The other vets stopped by daily. The prognosis was bleak. Not only was there little hope of her throat healing, Duchess was not regaining consciousness. The final night before she passed, the four from UNC; Christian, Abe, Ava and Kurt sat down with Unina and discussed the situation.

Annabeth chose a seat out of sight with Ben, virtually hidden behind the counter for food prep. They sat together on folding chairs. It seemed too cruel to record their conversation, but Annabeth knew she had to at least take notes. Ben didn't appear to disapprove of her writing.

The woman, who was her biography subject, wailed, yelled, argued and eventually wept quietly. Annabeth wondered if anyone was holding her to comfort her but decided that she didn't want to see. When the meeting was over, the chairs scraped back.

Unina must have returned to Duchess' side because Annabeth could hear the woman cooing words of love, broken occasionally by a sob. She felt near tears herself and closed her notebook. She and Ben stood; the others left the building. They both silently followed out.

Christian and Abe were shaking hands with Kurt and Ava as they climbed into the University Jeep. Apparently, it was agreed that Abe would stay with Unina. He moved to the bench. The two older females approached the fence. He knelt to pet them.

Ben gave Christian a hug and climbed into his own pickup and headed up the dusty trail. Annabeth approached Christian as he watched the truck disappear in the twilight. When she got close, she touched his arm lightly.

He turned to her; tears spiked his lashes. Without a thought about Abe, Annabeth wrapped her arms around him. Christian silently held on to her for a few minutes. "Let's go to the house. I can't do anything else here tonight."

She pulled back, nodding her head. "Do you want to drive, or would you like me to," with her head she indicated the utility vehicle nearby.

"Can we walk?" Her response was to move toward the trail. Christian took her hand.

Together they moved at first in silence; only the sound of cicadas and night birds intruding the peace. Annabeth considered the ramifications of what they'd said tonight to Unina. Duchess would die. They could not save her. In her mind, she was losing one of her children. Could she get through this? How many times in the last two days did she drink a "special" milkshake? There'd been no food eaten. She was already frighteningly thin; she couldn't go without eating for much longer.

Christian's classes were to start in a week, would Abe and Ben be able to handle the workload? Would she snap out of it enough to care for the cats? Would she snap out of it at all?

His thoughts must have been running along similar lines, he asked, "Why didn't MJ stay and help?"

Annabeth considered how to answer. She'd been out by the

enclosure when MJ zoomed straight down the trail in her latest rental car yesterday. Unina was in the building with Duchess. MJ walked in the open door. "My darling, what happened?" she heard the woman gush.

The response was a surprise. "Get away!" were the first words Unina spoke to her manager.

"Sweetheart, I'm sorry. I was in California. I came as soon as I could get a flight."

"I need you to go." Annabeth then heard choked sobs. "Please leave me alone."

MJ's voice was a whisper, Annabeth strained to hear what the woman was saying.

Unina was not whispering, "I wasn't down here the night it happened. I was in bed with you. How incredibly selfish and careless of me."

"Oh honey, you couldn't have stopped it. Come on, let me hold you," Annabeth admired her persistence.

"Not now, I just can't. I must focus on my baby. Please MJ, I'm not upset with you. It's just that seeing you reminds me of just how much I messed up. Please go."

Guessing that the other woman would soon be outside, Annabeth moved further toward the cement pad, out of earshot for the rest of their conversation. As she expected, MJ came out shortly.

She approached Annabeth and asked quietly, "How's it looking?"

"Not good at all."

"Well shit, shit! She won't let me in there with her."

Choosing to feign complete ignorance, Annabeth said, "She doesn't want to be around anyone but Duchess."

"Is she eating?"

"No, Shannon is giving her protein shakes. She's had just a few of those."

MJ gave a strangled laugh, attempting to hide her real concern, "We can't have the star of your book dying on us."

****

Now as they walked to the house, Annabeth answered Christian, "Unina sent her away."

"Why?"

"She'd hung out with her at the house the night that Duchess was bitten."

He was quiet for a moment. Annabeth wondered if he knew what went on between the two women. He gave no sign. On the porch, he turned to her, "Any chance I could convince you to come sleep with me?"

She sighed, "You've had such a terrible week. I wish I could keep you company. But Christian, I can't. If anything happens down there, someone will come to your room to tell you."

"I know," he let go of her hand as they climbed the front steps.

****

It was Shannon who awoke Annabeth with the news. At three a.m., Duchess died. Apparently, she did just what Christian feared she would do. A suture opened in her throat and she drowned in her own blood. Unina, at her side, was woken by gurgling sounds.

Abe was there to help, but in less than a minute she passed. Christian had been at the enclosure since.

# Chapter 24

The press got word of Duchess. Shannon said the phone rang off the hook for hours. At the gate, the camera and television vans clogged the road. The worst was when a drone flew over the enclosure to capture footage. The buzz of the flying object disturbed both Max and Beau; they roared and attempted to leap to it.

Unina was livid. Ben held her back from storming the gate and yelling at the press. They would have loved that. She also accused Annabeth of contacting the press. Apparently, she'd called MJ in a rage and told her that the book deal was off. She said that Annabeth broke their confidence just to get a story.

MJ called Annabeth, who reassured her she'd never said a word to anyone. The two of them considered how the story got out. They realized it may have been the vets from the college. Unina's agent called the two doctors. Kurt Johnson, the man that Christian first contacted for advice, reluctantly admitted that he'd told his wife. She, in turn, posted a statement about how sad she was about the lion. Once again, social media spread the news like wildfire.

The only good to come of it, was that Unina accepted this. Annabeth could finish her book. She returned to her hotel the day that Duchess died. Her things were still there, and she felt this was not the time for her to be hovering around, asking questions. She spent four days typing her manuscript. Once again, she felt guilty that the story was developing on its own. As when Jack Corey was critically injured, Annabeth was right there capturing the big story for her biography.

That evening, she ate at the hotel restaurant. Though the book was full of good material, she was still uncertain of its ending. She couldn't leave it this way, there had to be some sort of conclusion; good or bad. Annabeth hoped for good but didn't know how it could be.

As she finished a glass of wine, she looked at the television above her. She was sad to see the gates on the screen. A reporter was standing outside of *Peaceful Pride* talking about the rumored death of one of the cats. The brief story included information and photos of Celeste Barlow who was now a recluse lion owner. The piece ended with brief drone footage of the lions.

It was time for her to go back to the sanctuary and see how things were. As she thought this, her phone buzzed, it was her manager, Rikki. Annabeth signed her tab and headed toward the elevator.

"Tell me you're knee deep in all of this publicity. Why haven't you sent me something to go out on the wire?"

"I'm back at the hotel."

"Did you miss all the action?"

She slid her key over the lock and clicked back into her room, "No, I stayed at the sanctuary for days after the lion was injured. I left after her death to give them some privacy and to write."

"So sad, what happened?"

"Just a bite from another cat."

"How's Celeste?"

"Rough. I may not even get to interview her again. She's in bad shape."

"Medicated?" Annabeth liked her agent, but she couldn't trust that Rikki wouldn't let some insider information slip out.

"Just incredibly sad. I'll go back out tomorrow and check on everyone."

"Good to hear. Keep writing! Send our editors more pages."

****

Shannon suggested she try to come in before six a.m., the press seemed to be late sleepers. Annabeth cruised through the gates without incident. It felt familiar, and she hoped she would still be welcome here.

After a brief chat with Shannon, who informed her that Unina and Ben were at the enclosure, Annabeth walked the trail. The cool morning breeze made it a pleasant form of exercise. She also wanted some time to mentally prepare herself to face the grieving woman.

Ben was nowhere to be seen; perhaps in one of the buildings. Unina was on the ground playing with the youngest lions. When the two cats saw Annabeth, they responded eagerly as it meant more hands to scratch them. The other woman turned to see who arrived. For a moment she didn't speak, Annabeth could read nothing in her expression. When she was turning toward the cats, she said simply, "The girls are glad to see you."

Annabeth took this and ran with it. She placed her bag on the bench and knelt next to Unina. Her fingers reached in and scratched the fur of the lion behind the fence. The four adults lounging in various places in the pen, showed no interest in her arrival.

Facing the cats and speaking in a soft voice, Annabeth spoke, "Unina, I have not had a chance to say how sorry I am over the loss of Duchess."

Next to her, she could see Unina nod a few times before her voice cracked out, "Thank you. It hurts so bad." Her hands dropped from the pen.

Annabeth turned and pulled the crying woman to her shoulder. They both wept for a moment. Unina pulled away and wiped her tears. She looked at Annabeth with a weak smile, "I thought maybe you wouldn't come back."

"I didn't want to intrude; I've heard that the press has hounded you. But, when you're up to it, I'd like to discuss her with you. She deserves some space in your book. And," she stood and went to her bag, reached in and pulled out a large envelope, "I had these printed for you."

Unina sat on the bench, for a moment. She held the envelope to her chest. "I hope these are what I think they are."

"I had some photos of her printed that I took that day in the cherry picker." Annabeth sat down as well.

Slowly, Unina slid the prints out. They sat in silence as she looked at them. One photo displayed the three older females curled on one another, sleeping. "Oh," her voice was anguished. "They're doing pretty well, but I know they miss her." Tears dripped on the prints, and she used the hem of her shirt to wipe them away. When she finished looking at the stack, she carefully slid them back into the envelope. "Thank you for these, it helps blot out those images in my mind of how she looked on her last day."

"Would you like to talk about her and let me take some notes for the book?" Annabeth removed her notebook from her bag, opening it to a blank page.

For an hour, the two women sat side by side on the bench and Unina talked about when Duchess arrived at *Peaceful Pride*. There were more tears, partly because she had been brought to them with Mable, the first lion to die here. She also shared the story of how Luna and Nova accepted her and eventually Max accepted both she and Beau. Annabeth wrote until her hand ached.

At one point, Max wandered over to the fence. He made a snuffling noise. Unina moved to him and reached into touch him, she pressed her cheek next to his. "I don't blame him for any of this. It's their nature to protect their food and sometimes play hard."

"Do you know for certain it was him?"

"Yes, Abe found blood on his mouth that wasn't his."

Annabeth knew that if Unina could share this information without an emotional break, then her state of mind was improved.

Soon after, she bid Unina goodbye and headed back up the trail. It was after twelve, and the sun blazed hot. She felt sweat dripping down her back. When she heard a vehicle behind her, she was pleased.

Ben pulled up in the flatbed, "Why didn't you come get me out of the building. It's too damn hot to walk."

"I didn't know you were there; you saw me?" She climbed in and they moved on.

"Yep, I came out a while ago, but I could see the two of you talking. I didn't want to interrupt."

"It was a good talk. She shared a lot about Duchess."

"Then you've been good for her. Wasn't sure she was up for that yet."

"Me either, I took a chance coming. I brought her some prints of the lioness. She really liked that, though she cried a lot."

"She's always crying."

"Where are your vets today?" Annabeth included Abe; it was too much to ask after Christian.

"Udok started his classes today. Abe has his own class to take. He should be here real soon. Udok will be gone several days a week."

"How's that going to work?"

"Well, the deal is that someone has to be with her. Since we lost Duchess, she wants to be in the enclosure even more. Abe is getting extra graduate students to serve as volunteer interns. I guess Udok can sign their college credit papers now that he's a professor again. Their job will be just to keep her out of the pen and help with feeding."

"That already sounds like a big job. Are you worried that you left her alone?"

"No, you seemed to make her happy and Abe should be pulling in right now."

****

She didn't stay long at the sanctuary after that. Abe spoke with her for a while then she popped into the house to say goodbye to Shannon. As she drove out, there were news vans, but the number had decreased. Her face was unrecognizable, and therefore, no one asked her any questions. She passed them and headed toward the highway. In the car, Annabeth told herself she was glad Christian wasn't there. She didn't need to see him and stir up any emotions. If only her heart agreed.

# Chapter 25

He stayed away from her and she was grateful. The night after she'd been to visit Unina, he'd texted to say thank you for cheering her up. If he thought this would make Annabeth feel better, he was wrong. His text was a reminder that his world existed within the fence line of *Peaceful Pride*. Even his time at UNC was to financially support the sanctuary. Everything in his life circled around the cats, their well-being and ultimately their "mother."

Though she was unsatisfied with the ending, Annabeth felt it was time to complete the book. Her background on Celeste Barlow followed by her conversion to Unina and all the way to the loss of Duchess and recovery seemed to be the conclusion of the biography. After all, what would change? Unina would do nothing to earn more money, losing the lioness just instilled her belief even deeper that she must be with the cats always.

Christian proved that he would continue to desperately search for ways to keep the place afloat. It didn't matter how he felt about Unina or his own happiness. His heart was tied up in it all, as well.

It felt to Annabeth as if they couldn't continue to survive like this. She had some inkling of the finances. Though she'd never ask, she was curious to know when the last time Shannon or Ben received a paycheck.

These were things she brought up when she called MJ yesterday. The woman was elusive and refused to give actual numbers, but it was clear that things were relatively dire. Her own defensiveness, Annabeth thought, may have been because of the personal relationship the agent had with her client. At one point in the conversation, MJ stated that Celeste was not capable of any human relationship.

Annabeth responded without thinking, "I thought you two had something going on between you." There was an awkward moment of silence on the line. She wished she could bite her tongue and take back the insinuation.

When MJ spoke, her tone was a matter of fact, "I know what my clients need. Celeste will be in the spotlight again when this book comes out. My greatest hope is that it may inspire her to appear on screen again. In the meantime, I will do anything a client needs to keep her going."

Annabeth got the message.

The other woman added, "You have an agent, you must understand."

Though her thought was; *Rikki doesn't take care of me that way*, she appropriately responded, "You are good to her." That seemed to be the thing to say. When the call ended, MJ offered to help with any additional information she needed.

****

Annabeth set a deadline for herself that she would be out of the hotel on Friday and on a plane back to New York. If anything came up, she could come back down immediately. It was now Tuesday, and she would return to the sanctuary tomorrow to let Unina know that she was done with her research.

Her phone rang, it was Christian. "Are you ever coming back out here?" His voice was slightly whiny, but she liked hearing it.

"I'll probably be there tomorrow."

"I have class most of the morning and early afternoon."

Resolutely she responded, "I guess I'll miss you then."

After a beat, his tone was serious and quiet, "No, I miss you."

Ignoring the race in her pulse, Annabeth said, "I just want to tie up loose ends. I think I have everything I need here."

"Just like that?"

"I've been here for almost two months. It's definitely not been just like that."

"You know what I mean."

"Yes, I do. But there's no reason to talk about it."

He sighed into the phone, his voice now bitter, "I guess that's where we disagree." With that he clicked off the call.

Two hours later there was a knock on her hotel door. Annabeth was wearing pajama shorts and a tank top. She pulled her hair behind her ears and peeked out of the peephole; it was Christian. She knew it would be.

As soon as she turned the knob, he pushed in. His eyes traveled over her body and he smiled. He appeared to have been drinking.

"I think this is a bad idea," Annabeth said as she closed the door behind him.

"You can't just leave."

She moved to the small couch in the room and sat down. "I'm not. I was here for a job that's done."

Christian sat down next to her, too close. "I'm not done with you."

"I have a life in New York. And Christian, your life here is even bigger."

He placed a hand on her leg, "But it was all better when you were out there with me."

She stood and moved to the mini fridge. Pulling out a water bottle, she handed it to him, "You need to drink this."

He obeyed, and for a moment they were silent as he guzzled over half of the bottle. When he set it on the table, he turned back to her. "I have strong feelings for you."

"I'm sorry about that," Annabeth was fighting to stay firm.

"Don't you have similar feelings for me?" his eyes searched hers. She shook her head, but he smiled again, "Then why have you avoided me?"

He took her hand, Annabeth let him. "I'm avoiding you, because I have to leave, and you have to stay."

"Dammit, I want to be with you." Before she could say anything, he pulled her in for a kiss. She responded.

His fingers traced down her bare shoulder to her collarbone. Goosebumps popped up on her flesh. It was with a conscious effort when she closed her mind and let her physical feelings take over.

Soon they were on her bed. Her shorts and tank were scattered on the floor with the clothes he'd showed up in. Under the sheets, they kissed each other's bodies, their hands roaming everywhere. Together, they tried to make love as slowly as they could.

At last, they lay naked and sweating side by side. The room was dark, the only light was the glow coming from the hall. They were on their backs, eyes staring unseeing at the ceiling.

"I guess we needed a proper goodbye," Annabeth offered.

"Is that what you think this is?" his voice was laced with irritation.

"It has to be."

Now he turned toward her face, though their features were just outlines to one another. "There has to be a way. You can finish your book at the house; in my office, in my room."

"That sounds perfect. I'll move into your room with you, next door to the woman that the world thinks you're married to."

"Then tell them I'm not."

"I was already doing that, but it doesn't make it okay for me to move in."

Christian sat up and hastily turned on the light, "You're going to reveal that we aren't married in the book?" His tone was accusatory.

She covered herself with a sheet, and sat up, "Yes."

"How? Like it's a joke or dirty secret?"

"No, simply the fact that after the death of Mable, she was

devoted to nothing but the lions."

"What an imbecile that makes me, pretending I was her husband."

"That's what bothers you? Or is it because you want to be her real husband?"

Now he leapt out of bed and paced the room, "You'd ask that when we just made love?" She remained silent, and he continued, "I'm part owner, and so it made little sense to announce that we weren't married." He sat back down on the bed, "I want you. Since you've been around, I've felt like a new person. I know there isn't any easy answer, but I can't imagine you could just walk away and never see me again."

Annabeth knew that allowing herself to respond to his touches had been a mistake. This was because she also felt that in another time and place, he could be the man for her. She hadn't felt like this about anyone, ever.

Hadn't she thought she felt the same way about Chase before she arrived in North Carolina? Not exactly, if she was being honest with herself. This thing between her and Christian was stronger than anything she'd had before. There had been nights when she'd fallen asleep fantasizing that he was the one she'd met at the gym.

Now, he was looking at her. "I'm not walking away. I must finish my book. It's the reason I came here, I've done all I can at the sanctuary."

Christian calmed down and sat next to her. His voice was still pleading, "Finish the book, then you can come back here."

If only it would work that well. She considered how quickly

things went south with Chase when she was out of sight. This was probably what would happen again. She reached over and touched his cheek. "Let's see how it goes."

He smiled, encouraged by this. "I know how it will go. I can't believe you're starting to admit that you don't want to walk away."

She pulled him close and kissed him. "I've given up fighting myself." He laughed and pulled her down with him. Annabeth ignored the ache in her heart. She felt certain that this was only temporary.

# Chapter 26

Rikki called a day later; Annabeth wasn't headed out of North Carolina just yet. The editors read the pages she'd sent. There needed to be more about Celeste Barlow. The request was to get the woman to talk about her life as an actress. Third party accounts weren't enough. Readers wanted to hear her voice in the pages.

Annabeth walked the trail to the enclosures. In her head, she was practicing ways to approach Unina on this matter. She finally decided the best tact was to remind her of the purpose of the book; the need for the book to sell well. "Sell" was a poor word to choose, Unina did not wish to be reminded of money. She would focus on the book having readers understand her purpose.

The woman in her thoughts was standing in the middle of the lion pride enclosure. She was surrounded by two male lions. The largest, Max, was circling her legs like a house cat, his spine bending to get close to her. Beau was lying next to her, belly up. There was no one else in sight.

Her heart faltered slightly when Annabeth thought Unina was alone in the pen. Though the lions' mother was smiling, it was a daunting scene. Her size resembled that of a weak gazelle. In the wild these two cats could take one down with a swipe of their immense paws. She leaned over to scratch Beau's belly and Max practically sent her toppling on the other lion as he leaned on her.

Unina's laugh was audible as she recovered her balance and pushed at the big beast. From near the food chute, inside the enclosure, Annabeth heard a strong voice, "Maximillian, no!"

Christian was also in the pen. It looked as if he was repairing a spring on the lid. The big cat perked at the sound of his name and jogged to the man. Annabeth's heart rate sped up. Was it fear for Christian or the thrill of seeing him? She took a deep breath; this would be tricky.

The older females spotted her and made their way to the front of the enclosure. This drew the attention of both proprietors. Unina smiled at her. Annabeth hoped she could not see the equally big grin from her pseudo-spouse. His look was one of satisfaction; she was still here.

Christian turned to Unina, "All right, it's time to get out." He focused on her as she moved toward the gate. The younger lions approached her, and she gave them a kiss goodbye before she joined him to exit the enclosure. It impressed Annabeth that none of the lions attempted to get near the gate for an escape. Her research taught her that animals only wanted to be in the safety of their familiar environment.

She hoped to look like the professional writer today. Over her shoulder, was her camera bag and her laptop bag. If the interview must take place down here, perhaps she could convince Unina to go into the building. Annabeth had some online biographical information about Celeste Barlow that she wanted to compare with the woman's actual story.

"Udok said you were done with us," Unina said as she approached her.

She gave him a look that was questioning. How had he explained a private conversation with her? Or perhaps he was right, Unina didn't care what he was up to. Her eyes focused on the woman, "My agent called. The editors requested that I talk to you more."

Unina nodded, "Sure. What about?"

"Well, when we've talked before it's been about your life here, the lions, and your decision to live this life. That will be the bulk of the book, but they would like to hear it in your words about your early life."

Unina frowned, Christian jumped in, "That's a good idea. You don't want Annabeth to rely on other accounts of your life. You should tell your own story."

She seemed to consider it but was momentarily distracted when the two younger lions gave a half-hearted roar and pounced one another.

"Maybe we could go inside? There are some stories I've read. I'd like to compare them with your memories."

Once again, Christian spoke up, "Why don't you two go up to the house. Sit on the terrace, have some lunch and relax. I will be here all day. I don't have any classes." Over Unina's head, he gave Annabeth a meaningful look. She felt a tingle, was he hoping for alone time?

To her surprise, Unina nodded, "I think that would be nice. Let's take the vehicle and go to the house."

Annabeth shot Christian a gracious look. To her horror, he pursed his lips in an air kiss. Her surprised smile gave her away before she turned her back on him and followed Unina.

****

"My Uncle Thad was the theater nut. He'd been in community theater since high school. I think he'd always imagined making it big on Broadway, but instead he settled in the Sonoma area." Unina paused to sip her ice water. On her plate, was an array of fresh fruit and vegetables, untouched. Annabeth found it interesting that the only thing she would eat was roast beef. Perhaps she indeed was considering herself a feline. "As soon as I was old enough to read a script, he had me audition for shows with him. Mother indulged him in this; he never married or had his own children."

Annabeth nodded, "Was he gay?"

Unina shrugged her shoulders, "It wasn't something that mattered at all to me. I knew he had friends. I'm sure that's why he left this area and moved to the west coast. Grandma and Grandpa said nothing around me, but I'm guessing he and my farming grandfather didn't see eye to eye."

"How'd your parents end up in California?"

"Mom used to spend summers with him. She met my dad there

and never came back."

Writing things down, Annabeth asked, "So how did you go from child actor in community theater to a star?"

"My big breakthrough was playing Harper Lee's character Scout in a production of *To Kill A Mockingbird*."

"That is a good role."

"Thad invited some agents to see me. I had no idea. He'd sent letters to several. It was his belief that I was very good."

"He was right," this wasn't pandering, Annabeth knew that Celeste Barlow had been quite a good actress.

"Before I was in middle school, they signed me on with the Andrews Talent Agency." She then summarized her first roles in television and eventually film. Annabeth had her laptop open on the table at the terrace. She was comparing Unina's list to the one she found online. It was the same; good, less rewrite.

After some great anecdotes and quotes about her acting career, Annabeth asked, "So tell me about your marriage to Tate O'Rourke."

The other woman frowned then waved her hand dismissively. "It started as a publicity stunt while we were in Barcelona. MJ and his agent cooked it up. We went to restaurants and theaters together. During the filming of a love scene, I realized he was really into it. That night, I decided we might as well sleep together. Being out of the country was getting boring. He was the perfect distraction. It just sort of happened from that."

Bringing up painful memories was always difficult for a reporter, "And then you tried to have a baby?"

Unina took a long gulp of water, she looked into the glass and said, "I guess I shot myself in the foot with the alcohol ban." She eyed Annabeth, "There is still alcohol in the house isn't there?"

"Yes." Annabeth hesitated only a moment, "Would you like Shannon to bring some up?"

Unina broke into a grin, "Why the hell not? Should I go down there?"

"No, I can text her."

"Ah yes, cell phones. Another thing I gave up."

Later, both women were sipping large glasses of Pinot Grigio. Annabeth was worried, Unina was so thin. She'd only eaten deli meat for lunch. This would hit her fast. Then again, she had her pen and recorder ready. The interview was about to get much better.

As expected, after half of her glass was empty, Unina spilled out the story of her miscarriages. She admitted that Tate tried to be understanding, but he had a new film to shoot in Canada. When he left on location, Unina walked away from him.

Her heartbreak was not about the man, it was because she'd never have her own children. "My friends were well intended when they convinced me to join them on the safari. I, too, thought seeing animals and staying in a wild country would get my mind off my sorrow. I never imagined that my heart would break anew over two tiny lion cubs." At this part of the story, her voice broke. She refilled her glass and took a long swig. "I believe things happen for a reason. I was meant to see those cubs. If I hadn't, then I wouldn't have realized that lions were suffering. It was a long road to end up here. Look," Unina stepped into her room and pulled an iPad off her nightstand, she slid it open and handed it to Annabeth.

It was the video of the mother lion being shot trying to get food to her cubs. Annabeth gasped, covering her mouth with her hands. When it ended, she returned it to Unina.

"I was recording the mother, when this happened."

"That must have been terrible," it explained a lot.

Unina emptied her wineglass for the second time and stood at the terrace. Her eyes were on the lions in the grass. From her seat at the table, Annabeth couldn't see any. After a moment, Unina turned and looked at her, "This was what I was always meant to do. My job as an actress came about so I could earn a lot of money. My grandparents farming this land was so that someday I could turn it into *Peaceful Pride*. I am here," with this she placed her hand on her chest, "to be Unina; mother of lions."

A sob escaped her throat, and tears filled the corners of her eyes. "I lost a daughter; it still hurts so terribly."

Annabeth realized that two glasses of wine made Unina quite intoxicated. She was, as she'd seen before, an emotional drunk. The interview was over. That was fine, the information she'd given was perfect.

Now her biography subject stretched out in a lounger next to the wicker couch and wept. Annabeth moved to her and squatting down placed a hand on the woman's arm, "You have done a fine thing here. Those cats are living a wonderful life. Even Duchess' death was one that would have occurred in the wild, but she was not suffering in captivity."

Unina looked up at her with tear-stained cheeks, "You truly are a kind person. I'm glad you're doing my story." With that, she leaned back and closed her eyes. In a moment, she was somewhere between passed out and sleeping.

Annabeth walked to the table, finished her own second glass of wine and packed up her stuff. There was something she'd rather do with a wine buzz than babysit an unconscious woman.

****

She found him in the building. He sat at the desk, his back to the door. In front of him was a ledger and receipts. The perfect time for a distraction. Annabeth moved quietly behind him and placed her hands on his shoulders. Before he could turn around, she leaned in and kissed Christian's temple.

He clamped his hands on hers and pivoted in the chair. The wheels spun fast enough that Annabeth lost her balance and landed in his lap. "Perfect!" he laughed as he put his arms around her waist.

Their lips met for a kiss and afterwards he pulled back, his tongue tasted his own lips, "Have you been drinking wine?"

"Maybe," Annabeth smiled at him.

Now his eyes lit up brighter, "Did you get Unina drunk?"

She held her hands up in innocence, "She passed out after two glasses of wine."

Now he stood up, still holding her in his arms. "That's wonderful." As he moved toward the bed, his mouth sought hers again.

They landed with a thud onto the mattress. For a moment, it reminded Annabeth of the last rendezvous on the bed. Oh well, there were many secrets at this sanctuary. Soon they were both naked, as he positioned his body over hers. Christian grinned, "I was afraid I'd never get to do this again."

Annabeth pulled him into her, "Surprise," was all she said.

Afterwards, she refused to allow them to snuggle under the covers. She remembered Ben admitting that he'd seen Unina and MJ. She'd also peeked in that window. There was no way she wanted to be the subject of anyone's voyeurism.

Christian complained and complied at the same time. When they were back in their clothes, he sat next to her on the edge of the bed. With his hand, he stroked the back of her hair, "I know now."

Annabeth turned her head sideways to look at him, "You know what now?"

"You feel the same as I do."

Her tone was flirtatious, "Maybe."

"Just so you know, if I have to, I can do a long-distance relationship for a while." He emphasized the word "I" and she knew he was referring to Chase's excuses for ending their relationship.

A voice in the back of her head reminded her that their chance of survival was minimal, but Annabeth gave him a sweet smile and spoke, "That's good to hear."

# Chapter 27

It came as a complete surprise when Unina asked to see what she was writing about her past. Annabeth almost chuckled, the past wasn't the problem. She should be more concerned with what she was writing about her in the present.

Annabeth gave up her hotel room and was back in the guest room in the house. She spent the next afternoon rewriting the chapters on Celeste Barlow's beginnings and endings as an actress. The editors had been right; it was much better with Celeste's own telling of the story.

That evening, she met Unina in the kitchen before dinner and handed her a copy of the pages she'd just printed in the deserted office. The other woman thanked her. She was headed down to the enclosures and would take them with her.

Next to her stood Erika, a new intern from UNC. This was her first week at the sanctuary. She looked nervous in her pressed cargo shorts and bright, new *Peaceful Pride* polo shirt. Annabeth hoped she had enough backbone to keep Unina out of the enclosure.

She knew that three new interns were taking on shifts at the sanctuary. Besides Ben, Abe and Christian they served as guards for Unina. Poor Erika volunteered for third shift. Could she stay awake and monitor the owner? Abe insisted that at night, Unina usually slept. But the word "usually" was not too reassuring.

Her phone buzzed as she watched the two women leave the house. It was Christian. His last class was over in half an hour. Would she like to meet for dinner? He thought it would be fun to go back to the Carolina Cantina, where they'd first met.

This seemed like a good idea. Annabeth felt like celebrating the completion of a chunk of her book. Things were going well with the members of *Peaceful Pride*. Perhaps she would find a way to end the book on a positive note. She knew one thing for certain; she was looking forward to seeing Christian.

****

It felt like a date. They greeted each other with a hug and kiss in the parking lot. Annabeth dressed up in dark, sleek jeans, and cream colored, off the shoulder top and wedge sandals. Her hair flowed in loose curls at her shoulders.

They were beyond the point of pretending away from the others. He held her hand in his as they headed into the restaurant. Annabeth refused to think about the time soon when she was leaving. For now, she would enjoy this man that she cared deeply about.

After a dinner, that included a few drinks, food that wasn't overly spicy and great conversation, Christian asked her what she wanted to do next. Annabeth gave him a shy smile, "That night at the beach bar, we danced. I would love to do that again."

He broke into a grin and grabbed her hand across the table, "Lovely Annabeth, it would be my pleasure to hold you on the dance floor."

"You're so smooth, Dr. Mendoza."

"Now, where is there a dance floor around here?" He thought a moment, then his eyes lit up, "I know just the place."

They left her car in the lot and climbed into his Range Rover. She had no idea where they were headed but didn't care. It was so fun just to be with him and not attempting to pretend she didn't want his affection.

The sun was dipping down; the music coming from his speakers was a nice mix of country and rock. Soon they were winding through the downtown streets of Raleigh. Christian parked across the street from an old brick building, the sign above it promoting cocktails and live music.

He took her hand, and they crossed the street. Inside, she enjoyed the exposed brick walls, tall leather booths and the stage at the far end. On the small stage was a four-piece band. The lead-singer clad in jeans and boots was singing into the microphone.

Before they'd even found a table, Christian took her hand and pulled her to the small space where others were dancing. They moved slowly as the musician crooned Kenny Chesney's *Me and You.* Christian sang the lyrics softly in Annabeth's ear as they swayed, "We're a dream come true... Me and You." She tightened her grip on his neck. "There's no way I could ever let you go, even if I wanted to."

The sound of his voice so near and the strum of the guitar were magical, she felt the moment was perfect. Annabeth rested her cheek next to his, savoring the warmth of his skin so close.

When the song ended, he whispered, "Me and you," and kissed her. Her eyes were shining when they stepped apart. Christian's tone was serious, but a smile played on his lips, "You do feel the same about me." It wasn't a question; it was a realization.

"Yes," Annabeth breathed. It was a relief to admit it.

They continued dancing. When the singer announced a short break, hand in hand they stepped off the dance floor and sat in a booth. Annabeth picked up a menu.

"Let me go up to the bar and get us a drink," Christian stood then turned back. "What would you like?"

"I don't care." Annabeth was so completely consumed with this moment. She was out with a man who cared about her, she felt the same about him. They had just been dancing in each other's arms, he was singing words of love to her. It was perfect. Her smile toward him revealed her feelings.

Christian sat back down and pulled her close. "You, my dear, are an open book. I think I'd better stay near. This is a rare thing."

She kissed him, letting her hand caress his cheek. "It's just such a wonderful night."

When the band returned, they danced through the entire next set. At last, the band played the final number. The couple stepped out onto the street for some fresh, cooling air. Hand in hand, Christian and Annabeth moved along the sidewalk.

They walked in silence for a moment, simply enjoying each other's company. At last, Christian spoke, "If we lived in a perfect world, would tonight be the beginning of forever for us?"

Annabeth took in a deep breath and smiled. She loved the sound of that statement. The darkness allowed them to have this conversation. "In a perfect world, I think that may well be what was happening. I have feelings for you, I'm not certain I've ever had before." He squeezed her hand, and she continued, "If I could have this be the beginning of what I wanted, then when I finished this assignment, we could be together away from the things that force us apart."

"We could live wherever we wanted."

"You could open your own practice; dogs and cats would be your patients."

"And we'd build you a lovely office in our home for your writing. Since it's a perfect world, you would become a novelist and not need to travel for months at a time."

Annabeth laughed at this. "I think I might enjoy the break from reality and create happy endings."

Christian stopped walking and moved toward her, he placed his hands on her waist, "We'd be the happy ending."

They kissed. Annabeth didn't say her thoughts aloud, "If only."

****

He drove her back to her car. They kept up their good spirits on the trip; holding hands and singing with the radio. When she got out, he did too. Leaning against his Rover, he pulled Annabeth into his arms. "Tonight meant everything."

Their kiss was slow. "It did," Annabeth was breathless.

She pulled into the garage first, Christian's vehicle was not in sight behind her. To her surprise, when she opened the door to the kitchen, Unina was standing at the counter.

Both women jumped. "Unina, I'm surprised to see you up here." Most nights since losing Duchess, she'd been down at the enclosure.

Unina nodded, as she got a pitcher of water from the fridge and poured a glass. "The new intern starts tomorrow. I think his name is Shaun. I figured that I better be well rested to train another one. The lions are calm. I've got my radio and Erika is doing well."

Before Annabeth could respond, the door flew open. There was laughter in Christian's voice as he asked, "How fast were you going?" He stopped when he saw Unina.

She looked at the two of them and gave a knowing, "Hmm."

Annabeth realized she didn't owe this woman an explanation, instead she walked out of the kitchen and up to her room.

She'd just slipped out of her sandals when her door opened. Christian looked at her, his expression a mixture of disappointment and determination. He shook his head as he spoke, "We don't have that kind of evening together then climb into separate beds in the same house." Before she could protest, he continued, "Either you come to my room or I stay here. I will make love to you tonight."

Heat shot through Annabeth's body. There would be no refusing that statement. Instead, she grabbed his hand and pulled him close. "You're not leaving this room," she whispered as she reached for the buttons of his shirt.

****

An alarm beeped in her ear. A man's arm reached over her and turned off the cell phone sound. Before she could even open her eyes, she felt lips pressed against her forehead. "Good morning, mi Amor."

She peered over at Christian's smiling face. Now he kissed her lips. "Good morning," her voice was still rough with sleep.

"I must get ready for class. You stay here and sleep in. This is how we should wake up every day; together."

Annabeth sat up, combing her hair with her fingers. Trying to tame her unruly waves after a long night was futile. She swiped at what was certain to be stray mascara remnants under her eyes. Christian laughed, "You're beautiful."

Now she laid her hand against his chest, "That's a lie, but you're right; last night was perfect. Was your conversation with Unina in the kitchen awkward?"

He stood, waving his hand, "No. She doesn't care."

Annabeth raised an eyebrow in doubt but made no response to the statement. "Time to teach brilliant young minds?"

"Yes, but I'll be back this evening." He climbed out of her bed and pulled on his jeans then gathered the rest of his stuff.

She couldn't help herself, she grinned, "Good. Me too."

He gave her a final kiss and left.

****

Annabeth received a call from Rikki and headed to the

enclosure to talk to Unina. She biked down the path, her mood decidedly good after a terrific night and a sweet greeting early this morning.

Luna and Nova were stretched out against the fence. Unina was on the ground beside them, her fingers issuing welcomed scratches. Annabeth approached hesitantly, hoping that Christian was correct; Unina wasn't bothered by the fact that they'd returned together from a night out. Nova noticed Annabeth first and flicked her tail, this got Unina's attention. She looked up. Her expression gave no indication of any malice or irritation. Annabeth took that as a good sign and joined her in the grass.

"Hello. I've had a request, and I wanted to run it by you." Unina said nothing but looked at her waiting. "The publishers want to send a professional photographer here for the cover photo."

The other woman was skeptical, "Can't you take the picture?"

"No, I'm not adept at portrait photography."

Now Unina was shaking her head, "I will not get dressed up and pose for portraits."

"No, no. The cover will feature you and the lions."

This received a positive reaction. "Yes, that's exactly what I wanted."

"Do you think it would be okay if a stranger came for that purpose?"

"I think the cats would be fine with it. They're used to you and your camera."

"They're eager to get this going. I guess there's someone good here in North Carolina, so this could happen as soon as tomorrow."

Unina nodded, "Good.  This might even be fun."

# Chapter 28

Jocelyn Crane arrived the next morning. She was a tall blonde, probably in her mid-40s. Her hair was cut in a short, spiky style; one that Annabeth wished she could have. It would save so much time. She was wearing jeans and a khaki vest full of pockets over a white shirt. “I’m not trying to fit in with the jungle vibe,” she confided in Annabeth as she climbed out of her jeep, “This is just an easy way to hold all my gadgets.”

Annabeth liked her immediately. “That’s so smart, I hate lugging around my awkward camera bag.” She pulled up beside Jocelyn in the four-seater utility vehicle. “Climb in and we’ll head down to the enclosure.”

“Thanks for calling me. I’ve heard about this place. I’m excited to get to photograph not only Celeste Barlow but also actual lions. How many are there? Seven?”

Annabeth slowed the speed of the vehicle, she realized there was a lot of information she needed to give Jocelyn before they got to the pens. She told her that Celeste went by the name of Unina but did not offer an explanation. “Also, there are only six cats. We lost one just a few weeks ago,” Had she just said “we”? Jocelyn didn’t seem to notice. Annabeth continued with a description of each cat; the age, gender, and name.

By now they’d arrived behind the building. Ben, Abe and Christian were down at the pen today. They knew of the event and that Unina would want to be in the enclosure for the photos.

Once again, Christian slept in her room last night. It had been awkward when he’d returned from the university. She and Shannon were making dinner together. He hung out in the kitchen talking. It was difficult not to make any personal references to one another with the other woman in the room.

They must have done a poor job of it, because when the meal was complete, Shannon practically ordered the two of them to take their plates outside and eat by the pond. Annabeth was embarrassed, this was compounded by Christian suddenly placing his hand at her waist as she picked up plates. How was this going to work?

Now Annabeth looked at the man who climbed out of her bed this morning. She didn’t want to give off a couple’s vibe to Unina or Jocelyn. She had a feeling the other men already guessed that something was going on between them.

Jocelyn gushed about getting to meet Unina, and she even used the correct name. Annabeth was pleased to see Unina respond in kind. She must certainly have been the type of celebrity that was benevolent to her fans. The lions approached the fence, curious about the stranger. Unina proudly stood near them, introducing them to Jocelyn as she rubbed their fur.

The entire group joined in on the discussion of the photos. Unina, of course, wished to go into the enclosure. She wanted Christian and Abe to help her get all six cats around her. Christian scoffed at the notion. "There's no way you can force them all in a close space without some sort of squabble breaking out."

"They'd do it for me." She looked around the area, "I think the best pictures will happen if Jocelyn is inside the enclosure."

Now Christian roared, sounding like Max, "Absolutely not! We're not risking that. She will have to be on the outside."

"But then she has to get photos through the fence," Unina argued.

"Why don't we use the cherry picker again?" Annabeth suggested.

"Yes!" Christian jumped on the idea. Ben pulled his phone out, contacting his friend who owned the truck.

Unina scowled, "I didn't think the two of you were in charge."

Annabeth turned to Jocelyn, an obvious move to ignore Unina, "I got to use it for some pictures earlier. From up there, it's an unobstructed view. Are you okay with heights?"

"Absolutely," Jocelyn nodded. She turned to Unina, "I have very powerful lenses, it will look like I'm right in there with you." This seemed to placate the other woman.

Within thirty minutes, the two veterinarians and Unina were inside the enclosure. Jocelyn and Annabeth were positioned in the steel bucket overhead.

Jocelyn was good at what she did. She was able to place Unina in so many ideal positions. For a few, she was perched on the rock cliff with one male lion on each side. Annabeth's favorite was when Beau laid down and placed his front paws on her lap. Next to her, Max stood like a sentinel.

There was another set with the two older females. They were more than happy to include her in a cuddle or sit with her. Annabeth appreciated the radiant smiles that Unina gave the camera. The readers would recognize Celeste Barlow in these photos.

The youngsters were their ornery selves, but it made for some good photos. Unina stood between them, a hand on each. This evolved into them swatting at one another. Soon, she was on the ground with them. At one point they both had their faces against hers as if kissing her cheeks. Another time, they squabbled, wanting to climb on her lap.

As Jocelyn shot photos, she laughed. "These will be incredible to look at." Annabeth recorded this on her own camera. The videos she kept were great help in writing.

Finally, she felt she'd gotten everything she needed. The three in the pen left the enclosure before Ben moved the cherry picker. The noise irritated the lions a tad; it was wisest to remove the humans first.

Unina eagerly approached Jocelyn as she and Annabeth climbed out of the truck. "Did you get some good ones? How do you think they turned out?"

"Yes, definitely. I'll go right back to my studio and work on them."

"When can I see them? I want just the right one."

Annabeth stepped forward, "Ultimately the publisher chooses the cover."

"That doesn't seem fair."

"I'll be happy to give Annabeth prints when I'm done," Jocelyn offered.

Annabeth turned to the group, "Thank you everyone for your help. I'm going to take Jocelyn back to her car now."

Christian spoke up, "I'll ride with you."

The three of them were soon moving up the trail. Jocelyn was looking at the screen of her camera. "This was amazing. I can't wait to get on my computer."

Annabeth stood at her door, as she prepared to leave. "Thanks again for coming out on such short notice."

"Are you kidding? This is big for me; a national book cover. Plus, I got to meet Celeste Barlow and photograph lions. Thank you."

They watched the dusty cloud that followed her Jeep to the gate. When she drove onto the outside road, Christian pulled Annabeth close, "That was fun!"

She pressed her lips to his, "Yes it was. It will be a beautiful cover!"

He frowned, "One more step to you being done here."

"Who knows, the editors have my latest pages. It depends on if they like them or not."

"Of course, they will, you're a brilliant writer and this is a fascinating story."

Touching his cheek, she smiled, "I especially like the veterinarian, the true hero of the story."

"So, what are the chances that a beautiful heroine can ride in and save him from his wretched life?"

Annabeth chose to kiss him rather than offer fruitless promises. She remembered him saying that in their dream life she could write novels, this seemed like a good idea. Just once she'd like to create a perfect conclusion for herself.

They were close enough that she felt his phone buzz in his pocket. Christian pulled it out and looked at the screen. He frowned, "The antagonist wants me to come back down and look at a scratch on Kyra's leg." As he moved back to the utility vehicle, he added, "I'm certain it's nothing."

Annabeth stepped toward the house, "I'll go up to my room. I want to call Rikki about the cover photos and check on any edits to my pages."

Christian moved purposefully toward her, and spoke, "Annabeth, if your time here is indeed close to being over, promise me you'll quit making me sneak in and out of your room. Spend the remaining nights in mine."

She thought about Shannon's words; he deserved happiness. This was only temporary, but it seemed kinder than a refusal. "I'll pack my toothbrush."

After a quick kiss, Christian laughed joyfully, "That's all you need."

# Chapter 29

Two days had gone by, it was morning and Annabeth was sitting at a table on Christian's deck, checking her email. He'd left an hour ago to teach a class, promising to be back before noon.

She'd spent the last couple of nights in his room. When it seemed that no one knew of her presence in his quarters, or perhaps didn't care, she'd agreed to move her own things into it. Working on the terrace, with a view of the enclosure, was quite inspiring. Annabeth had been productive. She was now working on what she thought were the final chapters of the book.

Her last book, the rock biography of Jack Corey, concluded with a near fairy tale ending after a tragic accident. This book would not have a satisfying conclusion. Her outlined plans were to finish up the continuation of life here after the death of Duchess. Those chapters had been easy to write. The last portion would show that, as in nature, the world of *Peaceful Pride* continued to thrive.

There was an email from Jocelyn. She'd finished her work on

the portraits. The message expressed her extreme satisfaction with four or five of them. She felt they were better seen as prints then slides on the computer; therefore, she was sending them out this afternoon by messenger.

Annabeth responded with a thank you response, then stood up. She moved to the rail and looked out toward the lions. Using the binoculars, she could see that Max was on his usual rock. Beau was being the lazy old man, sleeping by the water. The females were stretched out near him. It took her a minute to find the young ones. Just then a bush rustled and one of them leaped out, followed by the other who pounced. They rolled across the grass.

She laughed aloud and her heart pulled just a bit. She would miss those cats when she left. They held a special place in her heart, not too distant from that which Christian held. Never would she have imagined that. When she took the assignment, Annabeth just thought of the lions as an interesting extra to the subject; Celeste Barlow. She'd always liked animals and thought they were a bonus for the story. Annabeth realized she was wrong. The lions, seven when she'd arrived, became the core of the story. Every action and thought made by the people at this sanctuary was because of them.

Her own fondness grew as the lions became accustomed to her. Annabeth suddenly felt tearful at the thought of leaving *Peaceful Pride* and never feeling lion fur on her fingertips. She wished she could see how big Amra and Kyra grew to be. Would the older females add them to their quiet group when they outgrew their playful cub stage? She shook her head to chase away the melancholy. If she let it sink in, she'd soon be a puddle of tears because it would lead to the thought of also leaving Christian here.

Instead, she would go downstairs to hang out with Shannon while waiting for the messenger. Annabeth opened the bedroom door and stepped into the hallway. The next door opened, and Unina stepped out at the same moment. There was an awkward silence.

She shrugged, "I'm aware that you're keeping Udok company. I don't care one way or the other."

"Okay," Annabeth mumbled, she could think of no other appropriate response.

"When will you be going back to New York?" The question was pointed, not a polite inquiry.

"I think the conclusion is more or less done."

Unina couldn't help changing her tone to one of intrigue, "How's it going to end?" Together they were descending the stairs.

"I think it's best to show how *Peaceful Pride* and all of its inhabitants, both feline and human, continues life after the loss of one of the family."

"It's what we have to do," Unina was nodding.

"Exactly."

They'd reached the kitchen where Shannon was working at the sink. She turned, "Can I send you with food or drink?"

"No," Unina responded, "I just came to get a shower." She walked into the garage.

Annabeth reached for a coffee mug, "That was awkward."

Shannon grinned. "Did she catch you walking out of your

boyfriend's bedroom?" she teased.

"Boyfriend?" Annabeth rolled her eyes, "I think we're a little too old for that term." After she poured coffee and sipped it, she confessed, "But yes, she did." They both laughed.

"She doesn't care."

"That's exactly what she told me." Then Annabeth considered Shannon's words, "How do you know she doesn't care? Let me guess, Dr. Mendoza has had overnight guests before."

"Very few." Shannon poured herself a cup of coffee, and they sat at the counter. "It's been a few years. I think he did it just to spite her for not marrying him but trapping him in this life."

"I'm surprised that in the first year he didn't walk away."

"I thought he would." Shannon was quiet. "But that's when Duchess and Beau were new. The joining of the new members to the pride was a big undertaking. He got caught up in it. Soon it was his life too."

The garage door opened, and the subject of their conversation appeared. Annabeth couldn't help but notice how handsome he looked in his khaki slacks and a white dress shirt. The coeds in the veterinary department of UNC must have their eyes on him.

His lit up at the sight of her. In his hand was a large manila envelope. "I pulled in and a guy was right behind me. He said this was from Jocelyn, so I signed for them. Are they the photos?"

Annabeth jumped off her stool and took them out of his hand. "Yes. She said they were so good that she wanted us to see them in print." She unfastened the metal clip and carefully slid out the photos.

They were incredible. The three of them "oohed" and "aahed" at each one. She had thoroughly captured the personality of the lions. The camera showed the spark of orneriness in the cubs' eyes. Max's appearance was dignified, while Beau looked like a giant baby with his paws on Unina's lap. The females were both tranquil, their position of cuddling with Unina expressed well the comfort that her sanctuary gave them.

The most remarkable thing to Annabeth was the beauty and sheer joy present in the face of Celeste "Unina" Barlow. She was every inch the lovely star that millions admired. Her expression glowed as she sat, stood or laid down with her "children". These pictures were the perfect representation of both the celebrity that readers were interested in and the woman who transformed herself to save the lions.

Annabeth couldn't help but grin triumphantly. This cover would sell the book in a large way. She gathered them and placed them back in the envelope. "Let's take these to the pens. Unina will love them."

****

Christian was quiet as they bounced down in the flatbed. Annabeth, on the other hand, was chattering excitedly about the great work that Jocelyn had done. When she realized his responses were lacking in enthusiasm, she laid a hand on his leg. "Hey, what's wrong?"

"These are proof that your time here is over. The story is written, the cover is done."

"The story isn't completely written."

He eyed her, “How much is left? Be honest.”

Annabeth sighed, “Maybe three or four chapters.”

“How much time?”

“I could finish it in a week, if I worked hard enough.”

Christian was silent, staring straight ahead.

Now she combed her fingers through the back of his hair, “Sweetheart, let’s save this conversation for tonight. We can sit out in the moonlight on the terrace or go for a late-night swim and talk about it, not now. Let’s go down to the enclosure and be happy with Unina when she sees the photos.”

Her words had the desired effect, Christian pulled her hand to his mouth and kissed her fingers. “That’s what we’ll do.”

****

Unina adored the photos. She laughed and cried at each one. After they finished looking at them, Annabeth started to put them in the envelope, Unina’s hand closed over hers with a surprisingly strong grip, “Don’t take them away. I want to keep them here tonight and look at them closer when I’m alone.”

“Okay,” Annabeth nodded slowly, “that’s fine. Jocelyn has already sent them to my publisher.”

“But I get to pick the cover,” Unina sounded like a child.

“No, I’m sorry. Neither you nor I have that power. They make the final decision.” When Unina looked crestfallen she added, “Tell you what, you look at them overnight. Tomorrow you can tell me your favorite and I’ll let the publisher know your preference.”

That seemed to satisfy Unina. She moved into the building with her envelope of photos.

****

It was a warm night, so they opted to swim. Annabeth gathered candles and lit them around the pond. It felt strange, knowing that Unina was just a quarter of a mile away with the lions. There was no need to worry about her coming this way, she was with the new intern, Shaun, for the night. Plus, Christian had the radio with him, they'd have fair warning. Ben had gone home tonight. Shannon knew of their plans; she'd not be walking outside.

While Annabeth lit the candles, Christian found a station that played soft 90's music. He also unloaded a basket that contained a bottle of Pinot Noir, two glasses and some crackers. The only items that were comically out of place were the swim floats shaped like a slice of pizza and a bottle of wine.

Was this real? Annabeth couldn't imagine that she was out here on a balmy North Carolina night, setting a romantic scene around a sandy pond. The man who was enjoying this evening with her was the most handsome man to have ever even glanced her way. And, he truly cared about her and desired her. Perhaps Unina wasn't the only one who'd transformed her life.

She slipped out of her cover up and stepped into the pond. Behind her she heard the movement of water; a hand touched her shoulder. "A glass of wine, sweetheart?"

Annabeth turned and there stood Christian with two glasses of wine. In the fading glow of sunset, his eyes sparkled as he smiled at her. "Thank you, handsome." She took the glass with her right hand. With her left hand, she pulled his chin toward her, until their lips were touching. They kissed.

Together, they pushed her swim raft out further into the pond. They waded until the water was above their waists. He held the wine glasses as she maneuvered herself to a sitting position on the raft. What followed was more hilarious than romantic. The love song crooning from the surrounding speakers and the near darkness were the only things that saved the moment as she now held the glasses and he attempted to join her on the raft without upsetting their drinks. Finally, they both straddled the inflated wine bottle, facing one another, holding their still full, glasses of Pinot Noir. He clinked his against hers. "To the most interesting and intelligent woman that I have ever met," his words warmed her. Together they took a drink.

"Thank you. You too are the most intelligent and interesting man that I've ever met. And to add to that, I must say that I admire the care and dedication you give the six precious cats down in the field."

After another soft kiss, he spoke, "If only I'd met you before I met them."

She wagged her finger at him, "None of that. Nothing good ever came out of saying, 'if only'".

They floated in silence for a moment, drinking their wine as Richard Marx sang out, *Now and Forever* on the speakers. The yard was in complete darkness, except for the candles lit on the tables and the low lights surrounding the pond.

Christian tipped his glass up for one final drop of wine. Annabeth quickly swallowed the last bit of hers. "Let's paddle over to the side and drop off our glasses," Christian suggested.

Together they used one hand to move toward the side of the pond. It was another laughable moment as they realized they were moving their hands in opposite directions. After some practice, they figured out the pattern and together edged to the shallow end.

Christian took her glass and stood up to deposit both on the shore. His movement caused the raft to rock. Annabeth was unceremoniously dumped from the raft. Her backside was planted in the sandy bottom of the pond, her feet still on the wine bottle shaped mattress.

Christian hooted. After he set their drinkware on the grass, he reached toward her and held out his hand. His intent was for her to grab it and use it as a support to pull herself up. Annabeth had other ideas. She clasped his hand and with her own strength, pulled him down to the pond bottom with her.

*Baby Doll* by Mariah Carey came on the speakers. Christian pushed himself next to her, then surprised her when he wrapped his arms around her waist and pulled her onto his lap. Annabeth eagerly snaked her arms around his neck. Their lips met. The kiss grew hot. The cool water of the evening turned warm as their bodies pressed against one another. His hand ran along the length of her bathing suit, finding its way under the fabric to touch her bare skin. Annabeth gave a sound of pleasure and her hand moved down below his waist. The raft floated away from them.

In no time, they shed their swimwear and were rolling around in the shallow part of the pond. Annabeth tilted her head as his mouth moved down her neck. "Have you ever made love in the water?" he asked against her skin.

"No, how about you?"

"Not successfully," as he spoke, Christian stood up and moved to deeper water. He wrapped her legs around his waist. The water gave her buoyancy and together they moved. Their sounds were appropriately primal as they found satisfaction in each other's body just a quarter mile away from the grassy field where African lions roamed the night.

Soon after, they were both softly kicking their feet out, their elbows resting on the wine float. In their hands, were refilled glasses. Christian smiled. Annabeth tilted her head, "What's the grin for?"

"I can't help it. I love this."

"Me too."

He gave a contented sigh and looked up at the stars, "This feels like perfection. I haven't enjoyed myself so much in many years."

"Thank you. It's magical out here," Annabeth was looking at their surroundings.

He reached over and touched her cheek, "I'm not talking about the night, my love."

Annabeth turned her mouth, so it was in his hand and kissed his fingers, "Thank you. This is a perfect night."

"Every moment I spend with you makes me feel even more certain. This is something important."

Her heart leapt. She understood exactly what he was saying, felt the same way, but she also knew of the reality. Annabeth

Muldoon had no permanent place in this world. *Peaceful Pride* belonged to Celeste Barlow and Christian Mendoza. Inevitably, she would walk away from here; very soon.

He sensed her hesitancy. She watched him take another sip of wine. Was he trying to talk himself in or out of something? His chest rose and fell in a deep breath, then he looked into her eyes, "I know this is crazy. I never dreamed that your arrival to write this book would be a good thing for me. I was very wary of you even coming. I know how she is, and it didn't seem possible that you could write about this place without making it seem like a looney bin. That's all I thought until you got here. As soon as I met you, I was drawn to you. That very first night in the Cantina, I knew who you were, I just didn't admit who I was, because I wanted to enjoy the anonymity of our first encounter."

Annabeth raised an eyebrow and gave a slight nod at this information but didn't speak. He obviously had more to say. "I imagined that next morning it would all have just been a pleasant conversation with some light flirtation. However, with each day that you've been here, my feelings have grown. When you went to the hotel, I was missing you so much. I guess you know that, I showed up twice. I can't believe you've finally reciprocated my feelings."

Christian laid his glass down on the raft, so it wouldn't fall in. Annabeth followed suit. They were no longer floating, but stood in the chest deep water, facing one another. "I need to tell you, tonight, that I have fallen in love with you, Annabeth." He let his hand run down the side of her face, "I love you." His words were slow, each syllable accented, then he pulled her close for a kiss.

She thought he must feel the pounding of her heart; it had to have been beating nearly out of her chest. Her feelings were a dangerous mix of joy and panic. She loved him too, there was no question. This man, standing deep in the dark water with her, was everything she'd ever wanted. That was the joyous part. Reality, however, was causing her to panic. Christian Mendoza was tied to *Peaceful Pride*. Annabeth knew she couldn't stay here. There was no room for her. With this in mind, she kissed him back with all her heart, but when they pulled away, she was silent.

He seemed to sense that she would not respond in kind. Sadly, perhaps this was just the latest of his unrequited love relationships. Christian pulled her into a hug. Against her ear he whispered, "Are you ready to get warm in our bed."

Now she spoke quietly, "Yes."

They wrapped themselves in the dry towels they'd left on the lounge chairs. He blew out the candles and turned the music off his phone. She collected the empty wine bottle and glasses. Together they moved toward the front steps.

****

He wasn't in the bed when Annabeth awoke the next morning. She stretched out on his massive king-size bed and stared at the ceiling. How could one of the best nights of her life also feel like one of the saddest?

She grabbed her phone and opened the airline app. It was time to go. How fast could she grab a plane back to New York? As

Annabeth hit confirm for her flight, a text buzzed in. She waited for her flight confirmation before checking it. It was from Christian. She lay in bed and read it. Her eyes teared up. After another half a dozen rereads, she got up. It was time to say goodbye to Unina and the lions.

****

Unina's greeting was at first curt. Perhaps she knew of their time at the pond last night? Or was this her normal uninterested response to the humans at the sanctuary? Annabeth informed her she was heading to New York tonight.

"You're done?" Unina's voice was friendly.

"I think I have everything I need. Thank you so much for allowing me to move in here and become a part of it all. You've given me a feel of the entire place."

"I believe you truly understand us here."

As they talked, the two women moved to the fence. Amra and Kyra approached. Annabeth's eyes burned as she rubbed the ears of one of the young lions. "I'll miss these guys." Her voice cracked slightly.

To her surprise, she felt the thin arm of the other woman wrapped around her waist. "You have learned what it's like. They steal your hearts."

They stood in companionable silence for a few minutes. Annabeth moved back. "I think it will be a good book. You have an incredible story."

Unina nodded, "I hope it sells well. We need it to." Together, they walked along the fence. Annabeth scratched the necks of Luna and Nova. She let Beau slide his whiskers along her palm. Her life had intersected with theirs for a small time and she felt blessed because of it.

Ben and Abe arrived in the flatbed vehicle. Shaun's shift was over. Unina told the group of Annabeth's departure. Abe hugged her lightly. "Don't forget, if I'm in the book make certain I sound incredibly handsome."

She laughed, "No problem, you already are." After promising to let Unina know what the cover would be, Annabeth turned to Ben. He was taking Shaun back up to the house. "Room for one more?"

"Of course, Shaun jump in the back." The young man did as he was told.

They bounced along the trail. Annabeth tried to get her emotions under control. She hadn't expected to feel so forlorn.

"Udok isn't here," Ben stated the fact, but his eyes were questioning as he glanced her way.

Well, nothing was a secret around here. "Yes, I know. I said goodbye to him, yesterday."

"So that's it. Back to New York?"

She felt she had to defend herself, "Yep. It's where I live. My job is there. My time here may be done, but the book isn't."

They parked in the garage. Shaun climbed out and headed to his car. Ben came around to Annabeth's side and pulled her into a bear hug. "It's been fun having you around."

"I've loved it here. You take care of yourself." They pulled apart. Annabeth looked at him meaningfully, "And everyone else."

Her farewell with Shannon was understandably tearful. The women had built a fast friendship. She also felt guilty leaving Shannon with the lone responsibility of keeping not only the place but all its residents in line.

# Chapter 30

The plane touched down right on schedule. As Annabeth stepped outside to find a taxi, it surprised her that the humidity in New York matched that in North Carolina. One positive to heading back to the city was that she'd hoped for a break from the late August heat. The city mocked her.

Her apartment was cool, the air musty. She opened the patio door. The air on the balcony was warm, but fresh. Annabeth rolled her luggage into her room and dropped it beside the bed. She lacked the motivation to unpack now.

Instead, she wandered into the kitchen and opened her fridge. It was empty, except for condiments, a half full bottle of vodka, a tub of butter and two bottles of Corona. Perfect. She pulled one beer out and twisted the cap off. Out on her balcony she swiped webs off her deck chair and sat down. Around her were tall buildings, below her the sounds of constant traffic and dogs barking. Annabeth hoped these would distract her from the sights and sounds she was already missing; green grass blowing in the breeze, cicadas' constant cadence, birds squawking or the sight of a thick golden tail with a brown tuft of fur at the end, swatting a fly.

She took a long swallow of beer and sighed. It would not be easy, but she could move forward. She'd most often lived as a solitary person. Being in a quiet place alone was what she'd done for a decade. "I don't need anyone," Annabeth said the words aloud, but even to her own ears they were unconvincing. Her eyes filled with tears and a sob escaped from her lips. Now she leaned her head back and closed her eyes. For just a moment she permitted herself to remember her final moments at *Peaceful Pride.*

The night at the pond was a memory she would allow herself to recall whenever she was feeling alone and unloved. Dr. Christian Mendoza said he loved her. She believed it to be true; he loved her. That night she choked on the words, not wanting to confess her feelings to a man she must leave.

The next morning, when she woke up, he was gone. He'd sent a text; today's version of a love note.

*I decided that I can't be there when you leave. From what I've learned about you, I am guessing that will be happening very soon. You may think not voicing your feelings kept me from knowing what they were. You're wrong. I love you, Annabeth. Christian.*

Now she closed the house, changed into an oversized t-shirt and climbed into bed. She thought it would be comforting to be home in this familiar place. She was wrong. The bed seemed cold and lonely. Clicking on her phone, she reread the message. Tears flowed easily.

****

After hours of staring at the ceiling, then sleep that included dreams of lions running with the traffic in New York City, Annabeth was awake again. It was still dark outside her window, but she gave up the pretense of sleep.

This would be as good a time as any to start working on her new pages. The sooner the manuscript for Celeste's book was completed, the quicker she could focus on another project and not what she left behind in North Carolina.

The words flowed easily. Her last interviews and general recollection of the entire experience seemed to appear on the page. By the time the sun was peeking above the tall building across the street, Annabeth felt accomplished.

She got up from her table and went into the kitchen. The sad contents of the refrigerator reminded her that there was nothing for breakfast. Creamer was absent from the shelves. A quick mental scan of what she'd written told her that this was a good stopping place. A shower and run to the market would be ideal.

Soon she stepped out of her building. The city of Chelsea, New York had not undergone any changes during her weeks in the south. The traffic crawled along, people hurried to their next destination, and dogs continued to bark at passing walkers.

The coffee shop on the corner lured her in before she reached the grocer. Annabeth took in the familiar aroma of over- cooked coffee beans. The bitter brew which required two shots of caramel and a generous shot of milk welcomed her back to her city life.

The barista at the counter, a woman in her twenties whom Annabeth remembered was working on her first science fiction novel, greeted her as if she'd only been here yesterday. "I bet you want your usual tall."

"How's the book coming along?" Annabeth asked after she nodded in response.

While her hands moved around the espresso machine with quick speed, the woman answered, "I think I completed the first draft. Now it's time for edits."

"Good for you," Annabeth smiled sincerely, then pointed to an egg and cheese sandwich beneath the glass of the counter. "One of those too, please."

Just as she paid for her breakfast, her phone buzzed. Annabeth sat at a corner table and answered her phone. It was Rikki. "Welcome back!"

"Thanks." She bit into her sandwich, wanting to enjoy it while it was warm.

"Are you settled in?"

"Yes, and I've already written a dozen pages."

"Well then, I'm glad you're back. Do you want to meet and catch up?"

"No," Annabeth may be pretending that life was going to get back to normal immediately, but in truth she needed time to adjust to the change of scenery and the absence of faces she had grown accustomed to. "I'm going to spend the next few days writing like a madwoman."

"That's what I like to hear. Call me if anything comes up or when you're ready to send things to the editors." The two women ended the call. Annabeth continued down the block to the corner market, she needed to fill the fridge.

****

Another day and night had gone by. Her only focus had been the book. At one point, Christian had text checking on her safe arrival and how she was. Though she cried when she read his affectionate words, Annabeth response was friendly yet polite. Afterwards, she turned her phone off. No more distractions, it was time to put this book to bed and move on with her life.

The following morning, Annabeth was discouraged. Everything that was written was good, but it was missing something. Celeste had filled her in on her past; her start in acting and the many things she'd accomplished as an actress. However, the chapters were lacking.

She walked out on her balcony and surveyed her surroundings. What more did she need? Annabeth prided herself and her method of biography writing. The readers felt they really knew the celebrity after they read the book. Celeste's history felt one dimensional. That was it.

MJ answered on the second ring. "Are you calling me to tell me you've finished our book?"

*Our?* "Not quite, but I'm close. I need your help."

"Anything," the other woman was being very charitable now

that they're business together was close to being complete.

"I would like to talk to someone about Celeste as an early actress."

"Well, I know those details."

"No offense, but I was wondering about family."

The refusal was swift, "Her parents will not talk to anyone about their daughter. They insist on staying private."

That was disappointing. "Is there anyone else? A relative?" Annabeth's mind searched the information she had gained. "Is her uncle still alive?"

"Thad?"

"Yes," he was the one who got Celeste started in the business.

"He's, still in California." MJ added, "I have his number somewhere, he would be just the person to talk to."

Thaddeus Emery, now 72, answered on the second ring. When Annabeth introduced herself, his response was, "I wondered when you would get around to calling me."

"You were expecting me?"

"I am the one person who knows the accomplished actress, Celeste Barlow, the best."

Annabeth hoped her smile was conveyed in her voice, "Then you are correct, I need to talk to you. Do you have some time right now?"

"Oh, my dear, this is not a phone conversation. If you want to get the true picture of Celeste, then you must come to my home and see my collection of all things her. I cannot even begin to do it justice over the phone. Let's plan a visit."

****

Just like that, Annabeth found herself on a plane once again. She had rented a loft apartment above a wine room on the plaza in Sonoma for a night. Thad had told her this was where they would meet for lunch before heading to his home that was just a block away in the historic town.

The plane ride was longer than the one she'd recently made from the Carolinas. Annabeth opened her laptop and perused social media. She wasn't in the mood to work on her manuscript. Across the aisle and one row up from her were a couple who looked to be in their fifties. He was watching a movie on his phone and she was reading a book. The flight attendant asked for their orders, the woman spoke for both when he didn't notice. At one point he patted her arm to show her something he was watching, the woman laid her head on his shoulder and they watched together, her ear pressed to his so they could share the set of earbuds.

Annabeth felt a stab in her chest. It would be lovely to be taking a trip out west with a partner. She could imagine she and Christian traveling together. Like the man in front, Christian would probably watch a movie, maybe they'd watch one together. Would they have cocktails on the plane or the standard canned sodas?

As she thought this, the attendant served the couple plastic tumblers of alcohol. They touched the rim of their cups together and the man said something that made the woman smile. She leaned in and gave him a quick kiss before they drank. Yes, that would be wonderful. It was time to shake off Christian Mendoza.

How would the owner of six lions ever be free for a vacation?

The couple nearby depressed her. She laid her head back against the seat. Her eyes began to drift shut and her thoughts as she moved into a dream state were of the times that the two of them swam in the pond. Imaginary scenes of large waves tossing them in the small pond while they clung desperately together took over her sleep.

A nudge from the woman next to her awoke her. The attendant handed her the diet soda and a cup of ice she ordered. Just as well, she didn't want to wallow in moments with Christian, whether memories or dreams. After a sip of the drink, Annabeth looked again at her laptop on the pull-down tray.

She checked her email. Rikki had sent her one titled, "Hot idea". It was a copy of an email to her agent from an agent located in Los Angeles. This was the agent of a long-time television reporter who had anchored a major network morning show, followed by the evening news and an investigative program. Now, this reporter was slowing down a bit by taking on a travel series, exploring unique locations and interesting people around the world. The agent felt this was the ideal time to have a biography written of the broadcast journalist.

Apparently, word had gotten out that she was on her fourth biography and that the subject was another famous person with a story that was certain to sell. The agent said his client was interested in meeting with her to discuss the possible project.

Rikki had included her own message. "This won't be until you have the Barlow book printed and done the proper book tours, but it looks like another big work. It would involve the need to travel across the globe along with the journalist. What do you think? If you are interested, I would be happy to set up a meeting between you, the journalist and his agent while you're in California. Let me know ASAP."

Sipping her drink, Annabeth considered the project. The man was well known and admired. She was personally a fan of his stories and used to watch him each time she was home in the mornings. It could be a great assignment.

The other factor that made her initially want to refuse and then caused her to strongly consider was Christian. There would be no time to even try to hang out in Raleigh to see the man that she couldn't have. Out of habit, she glanced at her phone; he had just text last night. Annabeth had been vague about her plans, only that she was traveling for research. The last thing she wanted to hear from Christian was that he had met Uncle Thad before, or any mention of their possible family connection.

He'd offered his words of love, as always. Annabeth ignored those and just asked how everything was going at *Peaceful Pride*. Christian gave a detailed description of a rain shower that surprised them. Unina had nervously attempted to herd all the cats into the pens. Amra decided to be ornery and run the enclosure, refusing to be penned. Finally, it took releasing Luna and Nova back out to herd the young one to her pen.

Christian felt the cats would have been fine loose. It was a typical summer storm, no cause for alarm. These days everything worried Unina. The rest of them were simply placating her when it caused no harm to do so. The story may have been meant for humor or cause her to miss the "family" she'd left behind, but instead it was a reminder that things were unchanging at the sanctuary.

A reply was sent to Rikki. Annabeth agreed to meet with the journalist and his agent. Thad Emery should be the last interview she needed before she completed her biography on Celeste Barlow. It was time to put the book to bed and move on. She needed to do this in all areas of her life.

****

Thad met her outside of a small restaurant in the plaza of Sonoma. Annabeth loved the quaint, historic place. In the center of the plaza were majestic, old buildings and a large open park. Surrounding it were four connecting streets filled with restaurants, shops and wineries.

After a courteous kiss of her hand, Thad seated her at a table for two, covered in white linen. "I took the liberty of ordering a bottle of my favorite Chardonnay. It's a local winery, I've known the owners for decades." He was a tall, thin man. His wiry frame resembled his niece's now that she rarely ate. The California sun gave him a nice tan. A shock of white hair blew in the breeze, and Thad patted it down in vain.

"I am so grateful that you're willing to talk to me about Celeste." Annabeth said the name carefully, Thad noticed, and a look of distaste filled his features.

"You're used to calling her that other name." When Annabeth made to say Unina, he held up his hand. "Please don't. She will always be the star, Celeste Barlow, to me."

"So, you know that she's changed?"

A young man approached with a bottle of wine and two glasses. They remained silent while he poured. Thad tasted the wine and nodded; the young man disappeared. After a longer drink, he spoke, "Yes, I've been to North Carolina once."

"I didn't know that. Have her parents also visited?" Annabeth wondered if they were at the wedding. Why hadn't she ever asked? She was ashamed to admit that she knew the answer. The wedding wasn't a topic she wished to focus on.

"My sister and her husband went when she first opened the house. That was also when I did. We wanted to see what she'd done with the family estate. Celeste was so proud of it all." The server arrived, interrupting his reverie.

At Thad's suggestion, Annabeth ordered the same as he did, the Cobb salad. People were steadily passing their table; some would offer him a greeting. Thad was always polite, but his demeanor didn't invite them to stop for a visit. Annabeth surmised that normally the man may sit out here and converse with his neighbors, but not today.

"The house was fine. It reflected my parents' style, though on a much grander scale. The body of water in front of it gave it a Southern California flair. I was encouraged that she would come to her senses and return to us here." The older man stopped as salads were placed in front of them. After a bite or two and another long sip of wine, he continued. "She then took the three of us to the animals. It was there that I realized her focus had changed.

Celeste was so enamored with the beasts."

"That hasn't changed," Annabeth agreed. He stopped to eat and drink. "They are her complete life." Thad looked so sad that she decided it was best to switch topics. "I really want to know about the young girl who you got noticed when she performed in *To Kill a Mockingbird*."

His eyes lit up, "Did she tell you about that?"

"Yes, she said she got the acting bug from you and you were the one who brought important people to see her in the play."

By now the salads were eaten, the wine drank. "Let's go to my home. This conversation will be so much better if you can see her things."

They tussled a bit over the check. Annabeth finally convinced him that it was a business expense for her. Together they walked back to his place. He pointed out shops she should check out and the perfect place for dinner.

Inside his century home, he took her up shining wooden steps to the second floor. The door to the first room on the right was closed. Thad opened it with a flourish. Inside, the room was painted white, though barely a patch of paint showed. The wall space was adorned with movie posters, framed photographs, even artfully designed collages of movie tickets. Each featured Celeste Barlow and her many films and television appearances. Magazine covers were also in frames. There were dress forms in the room adorned with outfits she'd worn either to important events or as costumes. Against one wall was a glassed-in case with lighting. Celeste's awards were locked in.

Annabeth toured the room, first with wide eyes, exclaiming recognition. On the second round, she had her camera out and took dozens of pictures. She stopped at the glass case, "Why are her awards here?"

Thad looked a bit stricken, "Because she doesn't care about them anymore. I do." How sad it must be to have watched your niece achieve all that you'd wished for yourself and then for her, to reject it all.

They sat on a pink velvet sofa that Thad said was in her dressing trailer for four films. His stories began with her first role in a Christmas pageant and continued to the last film she made before she split with Tate O'Rourke.

Annabeth's fingers ached as she scribbled notes. Her phone was recording, but she continued to write as well. Thad spoke about her stint as an animal product spokesperson as if it was a shameful job. It was clear, her uncle didn't understand her obsession with the lions. Perhaps that obsessive personality came from him, his focus was the actress, Celeste Barlow.

It had been three hours since they walked into the room. Annabeth could see that the older man was tired. They both stood, "Thank you for today. I'm honored that you shared this room with me. Your words will bring the great actress to life."

The statement caused him to choke up and the dignified man uncharacteristically hugged Annabeth. Soon they headed back down to his front door. She said farewell and moved down the tree- lined street in Sonoma County.

The day had been exhausting. Thad Emery was a fount of

information but his sadness over his niece was palpable. What would he think if he knew what state Unina was really in? Perhaps Annabeth should tell him when the book was complete to not read it. No, he was certain to add it to the glass case. Any publicity photos would be framed and put on the walls.

She stopped at a bar on the main square and went in. The tourists were filling the wineries, this place seemed to be reserved for the locals. Annabeth sat on a stool and ordered a Corona. When the bartender held a lime over the opening and tilted his head in a question, she nearly broke down in tears. The night of the storm came back crystal clear. She missed them all.

After the drink, she stopped at the local patisserie and picked up a croissant sandwich for her evening meal. Up in her loft, Annabeth began writing down her thoughts. Soon, the words turned into pages for the manuscript. Thad's words flowed from her. By the time California's sun was long gone, Annabeth felt satisfied with her chapters about Celeste's acting career.

She stepped from the tiny table she was using for a desk and walked around the room. Outside the window, she could still see people moving in and out of the winery below. Part of her wanted to join them, maybe drink enough wine to come back here and fall into a drunken sleep.

Annabeth was doing all the right things on the outside. She completed a thorough interview today and then turned around and put it down in strong, effective words. Tomorrow she would head to LA and meet with two men who were wanting her to commit to another project. This was what Annabeth from Chelsea,

New York did. Her life was all about being a writer, getting the best story.

The woman inside was hurting. In that unique place that smelled of exotic animals and was so warm that her hair curled, she'd found something she hadn't realized she was missing. Annabeth wanted to wallow in the sorrow she was feeling. She was alone, that was normal. For the first time, she was painfully lonely. This was hard.

She moved to the stiff, gray sofa and stretched out on it. Tears rolled from her eyes and dropped into her ears. Annabeth Muldoon would get up tomorrow, pack her bag and head to another city. She would have the meeting and plan four to six months capturing the life of another. When the research was done, the writing would begin.

But she didn't want to. If things were different, she'd tell herself to take a vacation. Writing a book was hard work. The traveling was wearing. Vacation was not what she needed; the downtime would only be a reminder of who she missed. Those last nights in North Carolina she'd slept in the arms of a man.

Oh sure, she could go downstairs now and find a man to hold for a night, that wasn't the answer. Annabeth gave in to her misery and continued to cry. Her heart was giving her pains she'd never felt before. *This is just a process*, she told herself. Heartbreak goes away. People get used to being alone. She could do it.

Tomorrow, she would send her new pages to the editors. Hopefully, this would satisfy them. After that, she'd meet with the journalist. Together they could discuss how she would spend the next year. Annabeth wouldn't have time to miss Christian and the sanctuary. Soon, it would be just a memory.

# Chapter 31

Franklin Griffin, known as Frank, and his agent Daniel Nelson had a dinner meeting with Annabeth in a restaurant at the top of a five-star hotel in Los Angeles. Everything they discussed was pleasing. Frank was friendly and gracious. He had read her first three books and she was flattered with his praise. It was a true compliment from a man so knowledgeable.

His plans for the start of the next year should coincide with her availability. His year would begin in eastern Europe. Annabeth liked the idea. She explained that the research on his past could be done afterwards. Frank and his agent had no problem with this.

As everyone else had said, Daniel was certain her current book would be a big success. She would be busy with publicity at the end of this year. He was willing to wait instead of looking for someone else. Annabeth had been around a couple of different agents as of late. She liked this man.

Frank really appealed to her as a good subject. This man of 57 was bright, witty and not at all arrogant. When he discussed the places and people, he hoped to cover in the next year it was with great excitement. Annabeth knew doing this story would keep her busy.

In the morning, she climbed on another plane to New York. Rikki had scheduled a meeting with the editors the following day. Annabeth was suddenly feeling eager to get Unina's book over with. The ending was not satisfying. Actually, two ends weren't. As she once again leaned back in her seat on a plane, she knew the ending of her romance was also disappointing. One moment they were making love in the pond, the next day, she snuck back to New York.

****

Kerry Whitcomb and Drew Van Atta led Annabeth and Rikki into a conference room. This wasn't her first time here. Each of her previous books followed a similar pattern. This was the meeting where the editors would tell her what they liked, what they disliked and what they wanted changed or added.

Her rock biography practically wrote itself. The band members were all good about talking to her. The story progressed naturally and hit a major climax when they suffered a near fatal moment. The editors weren't acting as excited as then; they clutched notes and skimmed through their laptops. Annabeth tried to sip her coffee, but it barely touched her lips before she set the mug back down

Kerry scrolled through her files, "Well Annabeth, Celeste Barlow's change is fascinating." She shook her head, "I can't believe she went from selling out at the box office to giving herself a South African name."

Drew opened a folder and shuffled through the photos that Annabeth had taken. "These lion shots are amazing. I loved the story where the bird got in the pen and Celeste was almost killed." He kept his eyes on the photos.

Kerry stuck out her painted scarlet lips in a pout, "I had tears when Duchess died."

"It was a very hard time," Annabeth agreed.

Now Drew looked up, running a hand over his close cropped, gray hair. "But it's not quite right."

Annabeth felt her stomach clench.

Rikki spoke up, "What do you mean?"

"The ending isn't enough," he responded.

Kerry focused on her screen and joined in, "Things returning to normal isn't enough."

"Well, some things changed. They brought new interns in to help keep her safe because Udok had to return to the university to make money." The name sounded foreign on Annabeth's tongue. She hated that she sounded a tad defensive.

"But what if that's not enough money to keep the sanctuary afloat?" Drew looked skeptical.

"That's the point of the book, to make money. She can't say if they make it until we see how the book sells." Rikki came to her defense.

The editors nodded. Drew looked at his folder and back up as if he suddenly had an idea. Annabeth was certain that the two had planned this. "What's the money going to go for? Will she get another lion to replace the one she lost?"

Kerry took her cue, "And what if the money isn't enough? What will they do with the lions?"

Drew looked again at one of the possible cover photos. It was the shot of Unina and the adult female lions, all on the ground together. "Bet she has some crazy ideas."

Without thinking, Annabeth nodded and mumbled, "I'm sure."

"That's what we want to see; a sort of prediction ending."

"She can get those written up," Rikki answered.

"She needs to go back," Drew said. "I want her to get these questions answered by Celeste." He chuckled, "Didn't I read that the woman refuses to use a cell phone or computer anymore?" Both editors laughed at the absurdity of such an idea.

Annabeth's mind focused on the fact that they were saying she was headed back to *Peaceful Pride*. She wasn't certain she had the fortitude to do so.

The two women said goodbye to the editors and headed out. Rikki pushed the button to the elevator. When the door slid open, Annabeth followed her in. Once they were alone, Rikki spoke, "This isn't a setback. Don't let their words get to you." Her voice was placating.

"No, they're right. The conclusion sucks. I didn't know how to end it."

Her agent focused on her phone, but nodded, "So you'll go back and get what they want."

Picturing the scene of her return to *Peaceful Pride*, Annabeth groaned, "Oh yeah, a fabulous idea."

Her agent looked up, "They don't want you to come back?" She looked concerned.

With a shrug, Annabeth answered, "Some may be very pleased, while others not so much."

This got Rikki's full attention. "Who did you sleep with?"

Was she that transparent? Considering her confession of her affair with Trent Crosby of The Jack Corey Band, it shouldn't come as too much of a surprise she guessed. Did she really want to get into it with her agent? She looked over at Rikki; she was waiting expectantly. "Maybe I got involved with the vet."

"You mean her husband?" Rikki was not pleased. "Come on, Annabeth, that's not cool."

"He's not her husband. Haven't you read the pages?"

It was Rikki's turn to look guilty, "Not all of it, they were so eager to grab it. You're a big deal now, I didn't need to." She shoved her phone in her purse as the elevator came to a stop. They walked toward the lobby. "Now tell me about this affair."

"I just told you it wasn't an affair." The word annoyed Annabeth, "In fact, Christian was declaring his love before I returned to New York."

"But you came anyway," Rikki's tone indicated that Annabeth was incapable of love.

She bristled in offense, "I came back because I had a job to do."

Her agent was quick to apologize, "Of course. I'm sorry. Let's go get lunch and you can tell me all about it. Besides I want to hear more about your plans with Frank Griffin."

Annabeth had a flashback of MJ discussing how an agent will

do anything to please the client. She shook her head, "No, I need to make arrangements."

"Okay." Rikki started to move away, then considered, "Is that why you think Celeste may not want you back?"

And that was the question. Annabeth wasn't certain of the answer.

****

That night, she curled up on the couch and text Christian. *Met with the editors today.*

*Good evening, sweetheart. Did they love your book?*

*Not quite.*

*Why not?*

*They say the ending is wrong. They want more.*

*What do they expect you to write about?*

*I guess speculation about what would happen with the money or what would happen without it.*

*Aren't the answers to those obvious?*

*They want to hear it from Unina.*

*Shit. She'll love that conversation.*

*I know.*

There was a moment's lull, then Christian seemed to consider the situation, *Does that mean you're coming back?*

At that moment, Annabeth almost decided that she couldn't do it. She'd spent the last week fighting the notion of feeling anything for him. Hadn't she just made plans to spend the next year traveling with Frank Griffin? This would defeat the purpose of that. Why hadn't she said no? Annabeth knew why, she had to finish this book. Even Christian needed her to make it the best she could. She may not be able to give him anything else, but she could give the sanctuary some much needed funds. *Yes, I guess so.*

*Don't sound so happy. I am thrilled.*

Annabeth wished she didn't delight in his words. She was desperate to see him again as well. *I am too, for some reasons.*

*That's much better. Don't worry. I'll be with you when you ask her those questions.*

*Thank you.* She wasn't completely convinced that the two of them together would make it better for Unina. They chatted a little more, and she promised to let him know when she scheduled a flight. He repeated his words of love, she only responded with a cowardly heart emoji.

# Chapter 32

The line of departing passengers dispersed at the entrance to the airport from the plane. Annabeth followed those headed to the baggage claim. She'd convinced herself that this time she wouldn't need to pack much. The trip to North Carolina would be brief.

In reality, she knew that was questionable. Despite copious notes and further research, the best way to end the book was unclear. She hoped that Unina would discuss these things with her, and she could write a satisfying ending. She'd already had a conversation over the phone with MJ about it. The agent agreed that if necessary, she too would fly in this week.

The suitcases and duffels began their spinning journey toward the waiting travelers. Annabeth was watching for her own hard-shelled wine-colored suitcase, when she felt a hand on her shoulder. She turned to see Christian standing next to her. She couldn't hide her joy at seeing him. "What are you doing here?"

"Rumor had it that you were on this flight." He pulled her in for an embrace.

"Shannon has been telling my secrets," her hug contradicted her protest.

Soon they were side by side in his Rover. It had that comforting familiarity that Annabeth needed as she returned to *Peaceful Pride.* It warmed her insides as she looked across at the lovely man behind the wheel. They'd only been together for ten minutes and she already knew something that would change her life. She wasn't ready to give him up. If she'd stayed in New York forever, maybe she could have tamped down these feelings. Now that they were just a few feet apart, Annabeth knew she would fight for this.

The conclusion of the book didn't feel like the top priority. That would be a problem. Before her resolve slipped completely away, Annabeth looked out at the highway and gave herself an inner pep talk. *Meet with Unina and finish the book as quickly as possible. Once that's done then you can deal with this man and what he means to you.*

****

She had returned, this was Unina's thought as she watched Ben's face when he answered his phone. He'd smiled and said, "I'll be right up."

Now he looked at her as he was shoving his phone back into the pocket of his worn jeans. "Erika will be down in less than ten minutes. I'll head up to the house."

"Big plans?" Unina asked coolly.

"Shannon fried chicken," he moved toward the flat bed then

stopped and looked back, "I'll have Erika bring you down a plate."

"Thank you, that would be nice. See that she gets some for herself as well." Unina liked Erika. This new young intern was already so attached to the lions. They loved going into the pen together. Max seemed enamored with her. He would eagerly lean into Erika, demanding that she run her fingers through his unruly mane.

Alone for a change, Unina considered going in with the lions, but it wasn't worth the fight it would cause. Instead, she dropped onto the grass next to the fence. The humans at *Peaceful Pride* were always hovering, and it was exhausting. Most days, Unina felt more like one of the lions than like the people. She was very aware that Udok had commanded someone be with her at all times. When she'd first realized it, she railed at him.

Who did he think he was? *Peaceful Pride* was her sanctuary not his. She designed it, had it built and taken ownership of the lions. He had no right to take control of her handling of the sanctuary or the cats. His response to that had been a haughty, "Fine, buy my investment out and hire a full-time vet. I'll gladly leave."

She nearly wept in frustration remembering those words. He knew she didn't have the means to do those things. She'd resorted to nastiness, "Are you looking for an easy out so you can follow Annabeth to New York?"

Udok's eyes narrowed, "Don't bring her into this." He seemed truly upset. Did he think it was serious between him and the writer?

She watched the two young cats chase after a dragonfly. Their paws ineffectually swatted at the insect. Beau spoiled their fun; with a quick snap of his jaws, he ate the flying bug.

"You naughty man," Unina called out to him. With no remorse, he padded over to her and leaned his head against the fence.

Her hands mindlessly pet him. Now Annabeth had returned to *Peaceful Pride*. MJ phoned and explained why she needed to come back. Apparently, the editors wanted a different ending to the book. Well, guess what? She'd like a different ending too. Her film career brought her millions of dollars. How could this place have drained her funds in such a short time?

Udok would say that she overdid the luxuries, but the lions deserved it. Their previous lives had been atrocious. She rose from the ground and walked to the building. Her iPad was plugged in near the nightstand.

She opened her video. It had been a while since she'd watched the footage of the mother lion being shot. Tears stung at the corners of Unina's eyes. Okay, she would meet with Annabeth. The biography needed to be completed, published and sold. The money that MJ promised it would bring in would keep *Peaceful Pride* safe.

****

The group greeted Annabeth as if she was a missing member of the family. Indeed, she felt as if she'd returned home. Every one of them hugged her.

Shannon prepared a feast; fried chicken, mashed potatoes, fresh ears of corn. The piping hot biscuits were no longer real contraband, because according to Christian, Unina hadn't returned to the house for more than a few minutes at a time since Annabeth left.

After she'd packed up the basket of food for Erika to take down to the enclosures, Shannon ordered them all to sit around the big table. They passed the platters.

No one seemed to care that Christian sat near Annabeth, an obvious position of affection. She recalled that first morning when she'd come down to breakfast to discover that he was the handsome man she'd flirted with at the Cantina the night before. At that time, she thought he was married to Unina and once again she'd been interested in someone else's husband. He wasn't her husband. He'd been no one's husband. Why did that idea warm her belly?

Ben wanted to know about New York City. It was one place he wished to go someday. Christian surprised her when he said he'd been there a few times. Annabeth admitted that like any other local, she wasn't a regular visitor to the tourist highlights.

Ben nodded, "I get it. I've never spent a single night at the Outer Banks."

Christian squeezed Annabeth's leg under the table and grinned widely, "That, my friend, is a night that you'll never forget."

She changed the subject. "How are things at the sanctuary?"

Abe swallowed a bite of potatoes and spoke, "Good, but we had to dismiss Shaun."

"I thought he was doing well."

Christian responded, "He was until Abe found Unina alone in

the pen, while Shaun was inside the building having lunch."

"Well, that's terrifying," Annabeth shook her head.

Ben picked up the conversation, "Yep. We installed alarms at each gate. When the gate is opened, we get a signal on our phones." He pulled his out to show her. "Everyone of us here can be notified if someone is going in."

"Yes, and with a quick text, we can make certain she's not alone. Erika knows to text us before they go in, so no one has to rush down there," Christian added.

"Are you looking for another intern?"

"I've got someone coming out tomorrow," Abe answered.

Annabeth appreciated that they were working well as a team to keep Unina safe. It was unfortunate though, that they had to add this to their list of responsibilities. In the back of her mind, the reporter in her kicked in, this would be a good thing to add to Unina's current life for the book.

Shannon turned to her, as if reading her mind, "What more do you need to finish the biography?"

"Well, my editors want to know the two sides of the future."

Ben raised an eyebrow, "The two sides?"

"If the book sells well and brings in money or not."

Christian looked confident, "It will make money. I've read your stuff, it's superb."

"Thank you," she glanced at him to give a grateful smile, but his bright eyes on her caused her to get lost for a moment. She gave herself a mental shake and turned to the others. Shannon looked amused. "I'm only asking those questions because we don't have a strong conclusion."

****

After dinner, Ben and Abe were headed home. Shannon would see her mother and spend the night. When the last one pulled out of the garage, Annabeth looked at Christian suspiciously, "Did you ask them to leave us alone tonight?" His grin told all. "That's embarrassing."

He rested his hands on her hips, "No my darling, it's not. They all love you and are thrilled that you're back here making grumpy me happy."

Annabeth placed a soft kiss on his mouth, "Have you been a grouch?"

"The worst. The whole alarm thing was hideous. I won't even tell you about the screaming match we got into."

"You and Unina?"

"Of course. She said I could leave whenever I wanted. I said that she was welcome to buy me out and replace me." They both knew she couldn't. He looked at Annabeth, the reality of his obligation here clouded her face. "No, we will not let these things ruin tonight. Come here." Soon they were wrapped around each other, their kiss long lasting. "I have missed you, my love."

"I missed you too."

Christian let go of Annabeth, except for her hand and began walking out of the kitchen. She followed him as they headed up the stairs and to his room.

****

They'd made quick, passionate love then laid in one another's arms as the sun disappeared outside. "Do you want to go for a swim?" he asked, his head against the top of hers.

"No, too much effort. Let's go out on the terrace. I love the open country."

He pulled on his boxers; she wrapped a silk robe around her, and they headed out to the lounge chairs. "Let me run down and get us some wine," Christian offered.

"That'd be nice," Annabeth murmured, and he left the terrace. She sat alone and listened to the sounds of the night. Locusts, birds and the occasional noise of a big cat snuffling or snarling. The nocturnal creatures were exploring their pasture.

It was bad that she felt such a sense of homecoming here. As much as she'd admitted to herself that she wanted something with Christian, the obstacles they faced were still insurmountable. Would Unina be comfortable if Annabeth made her life here? That seemed impossible.

# Chapter 33

Annabeth walked alone down the trail to the enclosure. She'd snuck out of Christian's bed, grabbed her things and showered in her own bathroom. He'd mentioned, last night, that he would accompany her to talk with Unina. It was clear that the other woman still held some animosity toward her. The need to discuss financial success or failure would not be easy.

As she moved toward the heart of the sanctuary, Annabeth was disappointed in herself. She hoped, after meeting with the editors, that she could create a better conclusion for the book. She'd even returned to the passing of Duchess in the completed pages. Perhaps that could be the strong ending?

It wasn't the place to quit. If Unina gained a new appreciation for life and began to spend time with the other people, that would have been a good conclusion. Even better would have been if the tragedy reminded her that because of the low funds, they could not have the technology that would have alerted them to the accident quicker. Then, she might have chosen to open the sanctuary to paying visitors or sought a partner to invest. These did not happen.

Last night, Annabeth learned one change that occurred in her absence. They installed gate alarms. Needless to say, Unina was incensed. This sounded as if she had lost control of *Peaceful Pride*. Christian said the argument escalated into a shouting match that resulted in a few of the lions snarling at the fence. Since then, the two of them only spoke when necessary.

These were the reasons that Annabeth went alone. If she stood any chance of getting good answers from Unina, it would be without Christian. Unina was rolling the wagon of food toward the chutes. The pride of lions swiftly appeared on the other side of the fence. Behind her, Erika pushed the back of the wagon. Was Unina too weak to do it by herself?

Setting her bag on the bench, Annabeth joined the two women, "May I help?"

Unina didn't even turn, "No, we've got it. While you're here for a short while, I don't want you interacting with the cats. They consider you a stranger again."

The words stung, but Annabeth moved to the bench and sat down. She pulled out her notebook and wrote about what was going on and the words she had just heard. Despite Unina's statement that she was a stranger to the cats, Luna and Nova eagerly finished their chunks of meat and stopped at the fence in front of her. It was obvious that they were urging her to come over for a scratch. Her hand itched to touch them, but Annabeth remained seated.

Unina finished the feeding procedure. Erika went back inside with the wagon. The other woman stood at the fence with her back to Annabeth. Okay, she would have to treat this like a first-time interview; no familiarity with the lions. There would be absolutely no reference to anything Christian or the others had said. MJ would be her only other source of knowledge. She'd won Unina over before, she'd have to do it again.

"Would this be a good time to ask you a few questions for your book?" Unina turned slightly. Annabeth could see that she'd already scored points by reminding her that the story was hers.

"Okay," Unina said, still not making eye contact.

Annabeth looked at her notes and gave Unina an approximated dollar amount that her last two biographies made for the subjects of the books. It hit its mark. Unina's eyes were big when she turned to her. "That's a nice amount." She moved toward the bench and sat down next to her. Today, she was dressed in a large *Peaceful Pride* shirt and she'd rolled the sleeves up to her shoulders. Only the hem of a pair of very baggy khaki shorts peeked beneath the voluminous shirt. Her arms and legs were bone thin.

"I think your story will appeal to an even larger reader population. Initially, it will attract those who follow celebrities, but then animal lovers and activists will want to hear the story of *Peaceful Pride*."

"I can see that." She had Unina's full attention.

Annabeth focused on her notebook, pen ready to write, not wishing to appear too familiar. "So, would you speculate on what things you would do if your finances were increased that amount?"

The next forty minutes were spent as pleasantly as the first time the two women talked on Unina's terrace. Though she seemed to have lost touch with most humans, she had quite a bit of knowledge about what improvements could be made that would increase the health of the lions while also offering some cost-cutting measures. Annabeth told Unina that she was very impressed with her ideas.

Unina shrugged it off, "Actually I owe a lot of it to the new interns. Because they're forced to spend so much time with me, we talk a lot. Nights can be long, and sometimes they're working on homework. It's fascinating to hear the ideas they have." Annabeth made copious notes. "They have researched things we can plant in the pen that could improve the pasture. Erika is determined that we should have our own chickens." Unina shuddered, "I could never butcher one. She even thought we should have cattle or goats. Her next project is to do a price breakdown between butchering our own and purchasing meat."

These were unexpected gems for the book. Annabeth was happy to have positive material. "Would you add to the pride?"

The other woman was silent for a moment. When she spoke, her voice was sad, "As much as I would like to, I concede that it's not a wise decision. Our pride is a comfortable family and the number of lions is all we should have for the size of our enclosure." She added in a tone of confidentiality, "But if I ever heard of a single lion that was living in neglectful or abusive conditions, I would try to bring that lion here."

Annabeth nodded. Now was the time to move the conversation

to the other side of the discussion. “So Unina, this is a difficult topic. If for any reason the book never made it to print, and you had no new means of income, can you speculate on what would happen to *Peaceful Pride*?”

“That’s a horrible question to ask,” Unina wrapped her arms around her waist and considered. “If we had no new means of money, what would happen? Well, Udok is back at the college that’s helping.”

Annabeth knew his income was only covering the household expenses. “Is there a loan you could take?”

“I don’t know.”

“I’m sorry, I know this is difficult. My editors just wondered if you considered the future both ways.”

It ruined the good moment. Unina stood. Her expression when she looked at Annabeth was one of irritation, “I don’t wish to discuss this any further.” She walked toward the building, then turned halfway, “Maybe never. A prediction of gloom and doom will have those who think I’m doing the wrong thing hope for my demise. That’s not how I want this to end.” Unina disappeared into the building.

As Annabeth looked at the lions in various spots of the yard; all sleeping, she couldn’t blame her. She also wanted two things that couldn’t happen together; she wanted *Peaceful Pride* to support itself and she wanted Christian Mendoza for herself.

Walking to the house, Annabeth thought about last night. It was time to own up to the fact that she was in love with this man. They spoke to one another and touched one another as true partners do. This return to North Carolina cemented what two weeks ago she thought she'd successfully escaped; he was the man she wanted to be with. It was too late to deny it.

Christian was waiting for her by the pond. He'd had a morning class but was already home. Annabeth walked to him and without a moment's hesitation, leaned over his chair and planted a kiss on his lips. He responded by pulling her down on his lap, "I don't know what changed your mind, but I'm loving it." They kissed again. As their lips parted, he looked seriously at her, "I love you."

She sighed, and he looked about to turn away when she whispered, "I love you too, dammit."

"Not the sentiment I was hoping for, but I'll take it," he gave her a satisfied smile.

"I'm sorry, it's just that the logistics of this seem impossible."

"Let's not worry about that right now."

Annabeth smiled in agreement, "Okay. There's more to focus on."

"How'd the interview go?" Christian let her go as she stood then sat on the other chair.

"Not bad," she reached for the water bottle he'd left on the table. Unscrewing the cap, she took a slow drink. "She was reasonably friendly and informative." He raised his eyebrows in surprise but waited in silence for her to continue. "We discussed things the interns have told her about raising your own food."

His expression showed his doubt, "At least it's something for the book. Was she willing to talk about what she'd do if there wasn't money?"

"No."

"I thought not. What now?"

"I will ask similar questions to the rest of you. Hopefully, your combined answers will help."

Christian stood and reached for her hand, pulling her up next to him, "That's fine, but not now. We'll save that for pillow talk. What do you want to do with the rest of the day?"

"You don't have to work at the enclosure?"

"Yes, there's a few things I need to do, but before or after I have a few hours to spare."

Annabeth considered; she would use his time there to question the others up here. What did she want to do with Christian?

"Let's go into the city. Show me more of your North Carolina world beyond these fences."

Christian's eyes lit up, "Do you even want to see the college?"

"Yes."

He stopped, "Is this for the book?"

Now it was her turn to put her arms around his waist, "I promise, this is because I want to know your life, the place you've lived for so many years." She touched his cheek, drawing him in for a kiss. "I just admitted something big, trust my intentions."

"Yes, you finally did. For the record, I think you've loved me as long as I've loved you."

"Damn, Dr. Mendoza, you've certainly got an ego."

He laughed heartily, his head tilting up to the sun. She watched him, her own joy bubbling up. This gorgeous man was hers. Amazing!

****

They agreed that they would both get their work done and then meet for an outing. He changed from his "professor" clothes into shorts and a *Peaceful Pride* shirt. Annabeth gave him a quick kiss before they arrived in the kitchen.

Shannon was there, her usual domain. He briefly greeted her then headed to the garage to grab a vehicle to take him to the lions. Annabeth perched on her favorite barstool, pen and paper in hand.

"I take it this is more than a friendly conversation?" Shannon eyed her possessions.

"Do you mind? I want to ask all of you the same things that I asked Unina."

"Okay," Shannon said after only a moment's hesitation. "Would you like something to drink?"

Annabeth stood, "I'm here bothering you, you're not to be waiting on me. I'll make coffee, you sit."

The other woman smiled, "Well that sounds much better." She settled onto the stool opposite of Annabeth's. "While you're up, put some of those cinnamon rolls on a plate for us." She motioned to a covered pan on the counter.

"I should've known that given the chance you'd be bossy," Annabeth laughed as she prepared their food.

Shannon's answers to the questions were more practical and what she suspected all the other members of *Peaceful Pride* would say when questioned. The windfall of money that the book would hopefully bring in should pay off debts, make any necessary repairs and stock up on supplies they needed. She also hoped that if this financial gain could assure them that the sanctuary would thrive, that a much wiser plan would be created to keep them fluid. Her suggestions never directly blamed decisions that Unina made early on, but it was clear that things were not handled wisely.

The questions that focused on no new money caused tears to form at the corners of her eyes. "I know that my time with the lions is rare, but those cats deserve this good life. There have been so many times this year, that I've considered that they could end up in similar conditions to where they came from and it's a tragic thought. What that would do to Unina is incomprehensible. It could be as drastic as some sort of hospitalization. The unfortunate part of this is that she refuses to look at viable alternatives."

"Such as opening the place to the public?" Annabeth suggested.

"Yes," Shannon shook her head, "I know that step would be difficult for all of us. I can't imagine having people driving onto the property every day. Trash left. Bathrooms having to be maintained. But I know that places like ours make good money doing this." She looked up at Annabeth, her expression grim, "I think we may have reached that point." Using her coffee cup to gesture across the table, "Unless you write a blockbuster and put us in the black."

****

Annabeth was fortunate. In the next two hours, both Abe and Ben stopped at the house. Each time she heard the kitchen door open, Annabeth raced to it and commandeered the *Peaceful Pride* member to join her at the counter for an interview. Shannon assisted her by demanding they be as agreeable as she and by plying them with coffee and cinnamon rolls.

When Christian opened that same door, Annabeth was satisfied with her research for the day. He was her final interview subject, but they'd arranged to have that discussion later tonight when they were alone in his room. The thought of them at the location made her smile.

Christian refused Shannon's offer for the snack she'd given the others. "I need to get changed." He put his hand on Annabeth's shoulder, "I promised to show this woman our lovely city."

# Chapter 34

The lions were spread throughout the field, eating their dinners. They learned to respect one another and take their own meals to a private location. Even Amra and Kyra were beginning to put space between themselves at mealtime. Unina was sad to see that they were headed to adulthood. She would miss having little ones.

Her children were all growing up. In a rare moment of self-reflection, she realized bitterly that humans grow into adulthood much slower than these cats. If she'd gotten to have her own children, they would still be with her; needing her attention, her affection, learning from her. Sorrow from deep within her soul bubbled up to the surface.

Life was so unfair. She considered this afternoon when Udok was doing a check on the cats. He whistled while he cleaned Beau's ears. When Max shoved him down, Udok laughed and called the cat affectionate Spanish names. He was happy.

Unina knew the source of this happiness was the return of

Annabeth. She would bet that while she was down here watching the cats have an evening meal and munching on her own slices of deli turkey and cucumbers, that they were on a date.

Why did she care? When she met the veterinarian from the university, Unina thought he was the perfect match for her. His extensive knowledge of the cats and immediate interest in them filled a missing need in the sanctuary. He had been so kind. She was lonely in North Carolina; it was the most natural thing in the world to sleep with him. His romantic overtures were a welcome change from the solitude of *Peaceful Pride*. Her cousins helped if she paid them well. When they didn't want to do the hard work, she sent them away.

Udok was charming, he seemed to like her and most importantly he could care for the lions. When Mable died, she was ripped apart. He had been so gentle and caring that it seemed as if she couldn't refuse his offer of marriage. Unina was convinced that he truly understood what she needed in the relationship when he turned a portion of the storage shed into an efficiency apartment. It was his way of saying that he respected her need to be with the cats more than him.

On the night of their wedding, he proved otherwise. She was shocked at his anger when she left the reception. With all the fuss of getting ready for the wedding and then the ceremony itself, she hadn't been to the pens in over six hours! He'd been so nasty when he showed up at the enclosure. The wedding had been a mistake. Unina was so relieved to find out they were not married. She happily signed him on as her legal partner for the sanctuary. He didn't try to be romantic again. That had been a relief.

For a while, he'd brought a few women to the house. It was a sad attempt at making her jealous. Her irritation at it had nothing to do with that, she didn't like strangers around the sanctuary.

This thing with Annabeth was different. She could see a change in him. Hadn't he recently threatened to leave? When Annabeth was here for such a long stretch of time, it was obvious that she was learning the roles of a caregiver with the cats.

What if they tried to buy her out? Her heart lurched at the thought. They wouldn't do that. As much as she disliked Annabeth's questioning; prying into her life, she knew it was for a good reason. The woman was a smart and kind woman.

But could she stand it if Annabeth moved in here with Christian? What if they had children? Unina didn't think she could watch them with babies. Babies. She looked out in the field; dinner was over.

"Erika, come let's go play with my children."

****

Christian and Annabeth intended to hit all his favorite spots around Raleigh. However, they shared a common interest, unknown to them, and it consumed their late afternoon and early evening.

He'd missed lunch and was starving. Annabeth was more than happy to stop somewhere. Christian insisted they needed to find new places to make memories at. He knew of a unique pub where the wall behind the bar was adorned with many beer taps. It made an artistic display of various shapes and colors. He insisted they had delicious food as well as one of the largest beer selections he'd ever seen. Annabeth always enjoyed trying a new brew.

They went into the establishment and sat at the bar. She wanted to get a good look at the taps. Above them, on the wall were three large televisions with live sporting events on two and a news network on the third.

While they examined the menu and ordered their first beer, on the screen directly above them, the US Open tennis tournament was starting. Annabeth clapped her hands, "I didn't even realize it had started. I love watching this!"

Christian grinned, "I do too. I've always had a secret dream of attending."

"Me too!" Another commonality.

Two hours later, they'd each had a few beers, shared as many appetizers as they could eat and together cheered on the tennis players. By the time the Open was over, they were full and exhausted. Christian yawned and looked at his watch, "I think we just ate our way through lunch and dinner. What's next?"

Annabeth stifled her own yawn and felt her stomach push against her skinny jeans. "I don't think I could handle any more activities."

He reached his hand under her hair and rested it on the back of her neck, "Well, if I had to go back home and take a nap with you or turn in early, I guess I would." Their lips met for a quick kiss.

"It wouldn't be the worst thing," Annabeth agreed.

****

The next morning, Christian didn't have any classes. Annabeth cornered him when they were alone in the kitchen having breakfast. "I know you have to go down to the lions. Ben's been there since Erika left. She insists that she'll be back after her ten o'clock class. I think she may be a mini Unina."

Christian laughed as he lifted his coffee cup to his lips, "I think you know more about this place than me."

"Not exactly. Last night we forgot to talk." He grinned. "But since we're alone now, I want to take this time to ask you the same questions that I've been asking everyone."

He swallowed his drink, and sat the cup on the counter, "Okay, shoot."

Annabeth opened her phone and hit record. She knew she could dictate it all to herself later. "The first thing I've been asking is what changes do you see happening if the book is successful and provides *Peaceful Pride* with a nice little nest egg?"

"First off, my love, it will be a success. You're a marvelous writer. And, I also believe that the money it brings in will be more than a little nest egg. Celeste Barlow is a big name and so is your reputation."

"Thank you."

"So, what would I see happening?" he considered for a moment. "I think resources would allow us to investigate wiser ways to spend our money."

"How so?"

"Well, if we are operating on something other than panicked

poverty, then Unina has to listen to the professionals on the best way to provide the necessary food for the cats. We can also investigate better security measures and a trained staff. I know she'll always be down there, but I'd like her presence to be more of a figurehead leadership than required care." Annabeth thought this was a brilliant idea.

Now Christian looked at her, his eyes were serious. "If this book makes the sanctuary lucrative, then my dream would be to replace myself with a hired veterinarian and a director of the sanctuary. Those two individuals would run the place for her."

Annabeth's pulse quickened. She was almost afraid to ask the question on her mind. "What would you do?"

He put his hands over hers, "I would go wherever you wished to live."

The tears that stung the back of Annabeth's eyes were joyful. She struggled not to reveal the hope in her expression. "You'd leave the lions?"

His tone was somber, "Yes. I love them and getting to care for these exotic animals was beyond anything I ever imagined doing." Christian looked down, "But that dream came with a cost. I haven't been happy here for a long time. That is until," now his eyes met hers, "you showed up here."

A single tear won the battle and rolled down her cheek. "Thank you," she whispered.

Christian leaned his head close and kissed her. "I want to be where you are."

Annabeth shook her head, "I don't think we could make a life here with Unina."

His serious expression was taken over by his grin, "You've thought about it!"

"Of course, I have."

His arms reached to her, but Annabeth firmly pushed them off her. "Not yet, that's only half the questions."

"Okay, I can wait. What's next?"

"If for whatever reason, there was no money, then what?"

"I don't see that happening, but I know you must ask." Christian was quiet for a moment. Annabeth got up and fixed herself another cup of coffee and refilled his.

As she took the first sip, he spoke, "If no new money comes in, then we are in deep trouble. There's not a lending company on the east coast that would give us a loan. We have no way of making any new money to pay it off. The sanctuary cannot continue this way. It would have to change fast."

"Let's say Unina let you make the decision on how to handle it, what would you do?"

His expression was wistful. After more coffee, Christian answered, "I would look into opening this place to the public. The publicity that we would get could also lead to corporate sponsors for events and even larger items in the sanctuary. Corporations love to put their names on new displays or education centers. There's a lot we could do." Annabeth saw in the shine of his eyes that these were things he'd hoped for in the past. Had he approached Unina with these ideas? Most likely yes, and without question she would have shot them all down. Poor Unina did not understand that loving those six lions was not enough. She built them a luxurious place of freedom, but the means to keep it going were slipping through their hands.

Annabeth and Christian shared a long embrace and a few kisses when she was done with the interview. They'd both revealed some important thoughts of a future together.

Now, he needed to go down the trail to the one place that made their future together seem implausible. Annabeth stood on the front porch and watched the utility vehicle he was driving move toward the pens. At that moment it seemed they were all stuck in an unmoving pattern. She was wrong, change was rolling in at full force.

# Chapter 35

They sat in the clustered circle of chairs and couches; Shannon was on one corner of the worn leather couch. Christian sat at the other corner with Annabeth curled so close that her knees were bent and draped over his. Ben sat in a recliner, next to him in the other seat was Abe. He still had a towel draped around his neck from a quick shower.

It was black outside, sunrise was still over an hour away, the room was completely dark. The group seemed unaware of this as they looked at Abe and he began to speak. "When I arrived at the enclosure, Erika warned me that Unina was not feeling well. She'd whispered as she left, that she thought it was more emotional than physical. I walked around the building and saw her lying on the grass by the fence. Luna and Nova were on the opposite side, their fur pressed against the links. Her hands were touching them, and it sounded like she was humming. I chose not to disturb her and went to the building to check on the shipment of medical supplies that arrived."

He glanced at Christian, "They shorted us ear drops again." Abe paused; realizing the story he was sharing. He rubbed his face roughly, "I'm sorry, I don't know why the hell I said that."

Christian leaned forward and patted his knee, "It's okay."

Abe took a deep but ragged breath and continued, "I inventoried supplies and put them away. When I came out, Unina stood up. She looked terrible; dark circles under her eyes. She's gotten so skinny, she never eats." His words caused him to choke slightly. The group remained silent.

"'Let's go in,' she said. Her voice was so quiet that I moved closer to hear her. When I got near her, I could see she had dirt and grass in her hair."

Nodding his head, Christian said, "I told her this morning that she needed to clean up."

"I suggested that she go take a shower, while I circled the pen to check the lions. I could see she didn't want to, so I promised we'd go in afterwards. When she came out, I had food on the table. 'It's close to feeding time, let's eat, feed them and then we can spend a nice long time in the pen.' We sat down, but she barely ate more than a few bites of leftover chicken and a slice of tomato."

Annabeth listened to the trivial details. Abe needed to say these things first. He needed to tell all of it.

"While we sat there, she asked me if I would stay here when I was an Udoktela. I said I wasn't sure. I'd want a full-time position somewhere. She said, 'If Udok leaves, you could be ours.'"

"Shit!" Christian whispered. Annabeth felt her heart drop.

Abe looked at Christian as if defending himself, "I told Unina that you wouldn't leave this place. It's your life. She got quiet, so I figured that's what she wanted to hear. I finished eating, and we began loading the feed wagon. I could hear the lions starting to get restless. They knew it was feeding time. We fed each one with no problems. As we watched them eat, Unina turned to me and said, 'These are my babies, my children. No one else loves them like I do. No one understands them.' I didn't know where this was coming from, but I just agreed with her. I told her it would be okay. We would give them time to finish their meal and then she could be with them." Abe paused.

"She sat down on the bench and watched them while I returned the wagon to the building. I noticed when I came out that Max still had a good portion of his meat bone beside him but had quit eating and was chewing at his paw. As I watched, it looked like maybe a nail was snagged, and it was annoying him. The others were finished. Most got a drink, then settled down for a nap. Unina waited a while and was quiet. It wasn't long before she said, 'I want to be with my babies.' I said I'd get a training stick, and we'd go in."

Abe stopped and took a deep breath, preparing to take them through the next moments. "The stick wasn't on its hook by the door. I searched and just as I found it on the counter, the alarm went off. I still took the time to grab the stick. As I got to the door, I saw her. Unina was already in the pen. She was moving through the grass slowly when she stumbled on something."

His voice was rough, "By now, I was at the gate. I saw her look down. It was like we both knew at once what she'd tripped on. Max was next to her in a flash." Abe began to cry, but didn't stop talking, "He snarled and only swiped at her once. She went down. He didn't even look at her, just picked up his bone and stalked away."

The words coming out of his mouth were barely audible, "One swipe of his paw was all it took." At last he dropped his face in his hands and sobbed. Shannon crossed to the space between them. She sat at his feet, holding his shoulders, her head pressed against his.

"She's so damn skinny," Ben said then broke into a sob

Christian pulled Annabeth's faced against his shoulder. They were both crying.

"And you carried her out?" Ben asked, when he gained composure.

Abe sat up, wiped his eyes, and cleared his throat, "I had to. None of the cats were aware of what happened. Unina was quiet. I had to get her out no matter what. I couldn't risk it if she began to bleed heavily." He broke again and puffed air from his cheeks. "I took the stick and headed toward her. It was so hard not to run, but that would have attracted attention. When I got to her, I could see that his claws struck across her throat and chest."

Shannon still at his feet, rubbed his legs, "Oh, Abraham, what that must've been like."

"I picked her up. Beau and the older girls were catching the scent in the air."

"Blood," Christian nodded.

"Thank God she was light enough that I could still send commands and wave the stick to keep them from coming near."

He was silent, remembering the scene. "I got her out of the pen and laid her on the bench."

Now he looked at Christian, "That's when I dialed 911 and then called you."

Annabeth remembered that moment well. She and Christian were sitting on his bed. He'd been reading assignments from his students on his laptop. She was writing new pages from the interviews.

Christian received the signal that the gate was opened, but knew Abe was with Unina. As usual, he'd received a text letting him know that they would be both going in, so he'd not been concerned. When his phone buzzed, he responded with a quick, "What's up?" His tone changed instantly, and he was shouting profanities and repeating the word *No*. He'd jumped off the bed and headed to the door.

Annabeth followed at his heels. He clicked off the call. When they reached the stairs, he turned, "Unina's been injured." He raced down the steps. At the bottom he turned again, "Abe's pretty sure she's dead."

Shannon was in the back of the house watching television. They called out to her. She would wait at the gate for the police and emergency people and call Ben.

Christian didn't bother with the slower vehicles, instead they jumped in his Range Rover. Gravel flew as they raced down the trail. When they reached the enclosures, they were met with a grisly sight.

Abe was kneeling by Unina. Both were covered in blood. He

stood as they approached. Tears made a trail through the blood on his face. “She’s dead, Udok.” Christian and Annabeth looked down at the fragile woman, she was definitely gone. Her eyes were closed, had Abe had to do that? Though she was covered in blood, it was obvious her throat was torn open. Breathing would have stopped. The slice also appeared to follow where her heart would be.

Annabeth stepped back, not wanting tears to drip on Unina. She prayed it had been quick.

# Chapter 36

The arrival of the Emergency Squad and the Sheriff's department made this already horrible event worse. As these men and women moved about in their roles; EMT's checking out Unina, placing her in a stretcher and law enforcement officers photographing the scene and taking everyone's statement, the lions were uncontrollably upset.

Max and Beau both sprayed urine at more than one official. The bench which held Unina was close to them and they were nervously territorial. The females' instincts warned them that something was wrong. Luna and Nova paced the gates, and when they crossed paths with one of the nervous males, he would snarl and swipe at them with a paw. The concerned females would respond in kind. At least three times, Christian had to smack the fence with the stick and order them to "Go!"

Abe was sitting on a chair brought out of the building. An EMT offered him a warm blanket and it was hung across his shoulders; in an attempt to stop his uncontrollable shivering. Just when

Annabeth thought he was fairly calm, one EMT said to the other, "Call the time of death."

And just like that, the world changed; Celeste Unina Barlow was gone forever.

****

Now the five remaining human inhabitants of *Peaceful Pride* stood almost as one. Each took a turn at pulling Abe into his or her arms for an embrace. Christian held him the longest. "I'm so sorry. I brought you here as a young student and have held you to this place longer than I should have."

Abe's voice was ragged, but he shook his head, "Not true, Udok. I love this place. I love those cats. I adored Unina." He broke down again, "I'm so sorry I failed her."

The group rushed in, holding him in an awkward hug, each hand or arm grasping him. "No," they murmured adding strong words to convince him otherwise. "You did everything right tonight."

At last he pulled himself together. "Thank you, guys."

Shannon took his forearm, "Young man, you need to sleep, for hours. Go upstairs and get some rest."

Christian walked into the kitchen and pulled a pill bottle out of the cupboard. Annabeth recognized it as the one that Shannon sometimes took a pill out of and added to Unina's smoothie. He tapped two into his hand and walked to Abe.

"This is not a request, it's an order. Take these and go to bed. Unfortunately, there's still more to deal with. The Occupational Safety and Health Administration and the U.S. Department of

Agriculture will be here to investigate tomorrow. You'll need to be well rested to go through all of this again."

****

It was true, a possible killing by an exotic animal in captivity must be investigated. Animal sanctuaries shut down for such a thing. Christian discussed this with Annabeth when they'd at last crawled into his bed as the sun was rising. "She wasn't mauled to death, he walked away after just a swipe. I hope that's clear on the autopsy. Abe's word won't be enough to convince an investigator."

"Too bad you don't have video cameras."

He gave her a wry smile, "I guess you can add that to things we'd improve with money."

Annabeth kissed him. They both settled in on their own sides of the bed. The night had been too emotionally draining, and they needed their own space to unwind. Her mind was spinning. He'd brought up something that she hadn't even considered; the book.

****

Rikki was full of opinions on the book when Annabeth called her in the morning. Christian was at the pens with Abe and Ben. The investigators were due to arrive at any minute.

Shannon was in the house, so Annabeth crossed the driveway to the pond. She suspected how this conversation would go and she didn't want anyone to hear her responses.

Rikki crowed aloud at the news, "Damn girl, you know how to pick them. How could you possibly have once again been there when a major news story broke out?"

Though she knew this was exactly what her agent would say,

Annabeth got defensive, “What the hell, Rikki. A woman that I’ve spent nearly two months with is dead. I was there last night next to her body when they took it away.”

“Ah shit, shit, shit, I’m sorry,” Rikki’s voice was remorseful. “You know I’m sorry that you were there. Tell me all about it.”

Annabeth knew there was no reason to hold back. Soon she would be putting it all down as words and sending it to her. Unable to sit, she paced the circumference of the pond and talked. The words spewed from her mouth. She didn’t realize until she’d finally stopped, that she was crying. Rikki’s voice on the line was uncharacteristically consoling, “Ah Annabeth, damn. That’s the saddest thing I’ve ever heard. Crap, just like that.”

Gaining control of her emotions, Annabeth agreed, “It sure was.”

Her agent was silent. When she spoke, Rikki’s words were hesitant, “I know you’re going through a lot, especially being involved with Christian, but are you writing any of this down?”

She wanted to be angry, but Annabeth knew that Rikki was right. “Yes, I’ve made notes on everything.”

“Good, keep doing that. With the investigation and the funeral and everything to follow, you’ll have so much more to write. Kerry and Drew will lose their minds. How dare they question your writing again. This book will blow the Jack Corey one out of the water.”

It was hopeless, Rikki was an agent first. “Okay, I’ve got to go. I’ll send you pages as I write them.”

Her agent seemed to realize the coarseness of her last

statement, "Do you want me to come to North Carolina and be with you for the funeral?"

Annabeth had to admit, that was reasonably kind. "Unnecessary, but thanks for the offer, Rikki. I'll keep in touch."

She clicked off the call and watched the officials' trucks pull through the gates and down the trail. Poor Christian.

She was about to return to the house when her phone buzzed again; it was MJ. Another agent, but this one just lost her client. She was sobbing, "What the hell happened, Annabeth?"

Once again, Annabeth circuited the pond and shared the details of the night before. Occasionally, she could hear MJ respond in sadness. When she was done, it was silent on the other end, "MJ?"

"Damn her. She knew better. She wasted her gift. Celeste could still be winning Oscars, but she chose those stupid lions." MJ cried a bit more. Finally, she seemed to regain some composure, "Is the press there yet?"

"No, which I'm surprised about."

"I'll make a statement."

"I don't know if Christian's ready for that."

Now MJ's voice was outraged, "This is not up to Christian Mendoza. This is about Unina! Wait, no more of that name. From now on, she's Celeste Barlow. The world needs to know they lost Celeste not Unina." With that MJ clicked off the call.

*And so, it begins,* Annabeth thought as she headed to the house. She better warn Shannon that the press would return in swarms.

****

Within the hour, the first local news van settled at the gate. Shannon stood nearby, issuing orders that the television van stay outside the gates when others came through. The reporter tossed a few questions at her, but Shannon turned her back on the woman and walked to the house.

Annabeth pulled a bike from the garage and rode down to the pens. The three men of *Peaceful Pride* huddled together talking. The lions were in their usual lounging positions, apparently the trauma of last night and strangers here today did not interest them.

When Christian saw her, he strode to her in quick steps. Immediately he wrapped his arms around her and held tight for a long moment. "The investigators say the ME's report matches Abe's story. The case seems to be cut and dried. We are very lucky."

He pulled back and gave her a kiss. She touched his cheek and sighed, "Not as lucky as you think. While you were down here, MJ called. She's already released a statement and the first news van is at the gate."

"That publicity whore would!" His raised voice alerted Ben who joined them. Abe remained near the fence; it was obvious he was still suffering. Christian explained to Ben about the press.

"Call her and tell her to make another statement that drones are dangerous around the cats," Ben suggested.

"Great idea," responded Christian. Before he could get his phone out of his pocket, Annabeth was on hers.

MJ answered on the first ring. She told her that the investigation was closed and about the drones. MJ was back in business mode, “So you’ve got a lot of writing to do.” It wasn’t a question.

Annabeth didn’t want to discuss this with the two men watching her, “Yes, I do.”

“Good, this should be a bestseller.” The agent hung up. Annabeth tried to tell herself that MJ’s reaction was just to cover her own grief. Afterall, the two women had been lovers, hadn’t they?

She looked at Christian, “We need to discuss something else.”

Ben took the hint, “I’ll go tell Abe what’s going on.” He moved away.

“This doesn’t seem like the right time to bring this up, but things are happening fast. Who’s making decisions here? MJ will run the show for Unina if you don’t. What exactly is the legal state of things?’

Christian sighed and clasped his hands together behind his head, looking up. “Oh shit, here it comes.” He looked at her, “I’m certain that it falls to me to make all legal decisions. We signed those documents when we didn’t get married.”

“Do you have a lawyer?”

“Not really.”

“Then let’s make some calls and see how quickly we can get one to look at your papers. You need to know. And, you need to decide on the funeral before MJ does.”

“I don’t care what she does about that.”

"You will if she expects you to pay for it. She'll have half of North Carolina and as many celebrities at it as possible."

Christian hugged her again, "I can't believe how lucky I am that you came back to me right before this happened. I need you so much."

"You've got me," she whispered, reaching for one of his hands.

# Chapter 37

Dr. Ava Johnson, from the university, had a cousin who was a lawyer in town, she convinced him to go to the sanctuary as quick as possible. The good news was that Christian was correct. The papers they both signed made him the legal owner and controller of *Peaceful Pride*.

Annabeth urged him the next morning to walk out of the gate and give a press conference. She stood by his side but advised him to not acknowledge her as anything, but the person hired to write the biography of Celeste Barlow. By now, the national media joined the local press. She received some ribbing from a couple of reporters for once again being at the scene of the action. Christian's words offered enough sensation. He gave a briefly detailed story of how Celeste died, never referring to her poor judgement of going in alone or Abe's absence. He said many kind things about her passion for her cats and all lions around the world.

The press was doubly excited when one asked him about his

wife, and he revealed that they were never married. The questions continued about what his part at the sanctuary was and what would happen now. Christian spoke well; he was, after all, an educated veterinarian as well as a college professor. "We will continue to make this place a haven for the six lions that were Celeste's babies. She loved the cats and showed a compassion like no other when she took all that she had to build a place where they could live out their days as they deserved to."

When the reporters quit hounding him with questions, Christian stepped off the makeshift platform that Ben put together. He and Annabeth walked back through the gate. Ben closed it tight. Shannon, Abe and Erika were there as well. As the group headed to the house, Christian reached for Annabeth's hand and she held it tight.

The familiar group gathered around the table, ignoring the food placed there. Ben crossed the room to the cupboard and pulled out two bottles of liquor. "Unina liked her vodka, let's have one for her."

"Or two or three," Christian nodded.

They drank and shared memories. There was even laughter at stories of the lions. Abe recalled the moment when Celeste ran into the pen to get the bird. They all agreed she was a stubborn woman.

Abe looked at Annabeth, "Are you going to write this into the book?" Everyone was quiet, as if they'd forgotten her original purpose for being there.

She knew this would come up, but she wasn't prepared for it.

"Yes, I will let you," Annabeth looked at Abe first and then around to the others, "and any of you read what I say before I send it. I want to handle it in the most respectful way."

Erika, who had been inconsolable for days, was drunk, "The book is going to sell now."

Christian clinked his glass against hers, "Yes, it is, Celeste found a way to care for her lions after all."

****

It was Shannon who arranged the funeral for Celeste Unina Barlow. She was the woman who'd probably known her best for the past few years. Shannon also knew the funeral director, the cemetery director and everyone else she needed to know.

Annabeth greeted Thad along with his sister and her husband; Celeste's parents. There were a few strangers with the family. Christian said they were the cousins. MJ spoke politely to them all, then stepped away. Shannon embraced the siblings. She and Celeste's mother had been a few years apart in school.

Thad had held Annabeth for a long moment. When he stood back, his eyes were full of tears. "You write the best book you've ever written. My sweet angel needs to be immortalized."

# Chapter 38

The sounds of the traffic below were distracting as Annabeth struggled to focus on her writing. This attempt at new material was a strain. She heard cars moving and the squeals and shouts of children.

With a sigh, she closed her laptop and stood up. It'd been two hours since she sat down, so Annabeth stretched her arms and neck. At the open door, the smell of food wafted in from somewhere. Her stomach rumbled.

A horn sounding brought her back to the sights below. She stepped out on the terrace to see the activity. Cars were moving at a steady pace on the road. Visitors to *Peaceful Pride* made the trek down the now paved road which led to a massive parking lot.

It had been two years since Celeste Unina Barlow died in the lions' pen. Things changed to such an extreme that if her soul could look down and glimpse the sanctuary, she might not recognize it.

They opened *Peaceful Pride* to the public just under a year ago. The parking lot was not the only thing that had been added.

Besides the lion sanctuary, four Bengal tigers lived in a similar habitat.

Christian began restructuring the place shortly after Celeste died. The amount of publicity they received brought them to the attention of other sanctuaries. One, in particular, was dealing with similar issues of expenses. Together they combined their resources and now *Peaceful Pride* had two prides; one of lions and one of tigers.

Annabeth's book did exactly what Christian predicted it would. It flew to the top of the bestseller list. Soon they received royalties that helped pay for the changes being made.

Abe stayed on, now a full veterinarian. Annabeth admired him for being able to remain where he'd witnessed such a tragic event. He was the one who pushed for the education center. They built the gorgeous cedar and glass structure on the hill between the house and the lion pen. Inside, docents educated visitors on the plight of wild cats in their native countries as well as the problem with captive exotic animal ownership.

There was a special section with countless photos of Celeste and her cats. Video footage of her interactions with the lions constantly streamed. Even Duchess got her own memorial area.

To add to it all, Annabeth was in the final editing phase of a children's book about Unina and her lions. Rikki found an incredible illustrator, and she was satisfied with what they were accomplishing. Soon the book would be available in the gift shop. Annabeth also wanted the volunteers to read it with the children in the education center. The profits would go to Africa to help the lions there. The center would please Celeste, Annabeth thought.

****

At the railing of the terrace, she held a pair of binoculars to her eyes, scanning the crowd. Her husband did not appear to be anywhere in sight. She decided to get some lunch and then head down to the sanctuary to look for him. As she stepped back into their room, Christian walked in.

He stepped to her, "Hello my beautiful wife. Ready to take a break from writing?"

She crossed the room until they were together, "Yes, I am. Writing at a child's reading level is a real challenge for me."

He laughed and pulled her close, "I simply don't believe it. You can do anything you want."

When the dust had settled at the sanctuary, after all that followed Unina's death, Annabeth and Christian had decisions to make. They were reminded that the world can change in an instant. Their love deserved a chance.

She wasn't ready to give up her career as a biographer. Once again Rikki was flooding her email with suggestions. Annabeth knew that she would, someday, go immerse herself in another's world for the purpose of telling their story. She had passed the Franklin Griffin biography to another writer.

These past two years were about getting her life with Christian, and what was now their sanctuary, settled. "How's the animal world?" Annabeth took his hand and led him out in the hallway.

"Just fine. Busy, but not too busy." When they first opened, they were swarmed with press and people waiting in endless lines on the road to get in. Unina's sensational death had everyone wanting to see where she'd spent her last years.

Christian's opportunity to leave *Peaceful Pride* and start over presented itself when people began to approach him with an interest in combining sanctuaries or investing in his. He and Annabeth spent an extensive amount of time exploring the possibilities.

In the end, she told him that the path he chose was up to him. She was committed to their relationship and would be wherever he decided to be. Christian realized his heart was there with his six lions and those who'd helped him survive the difficult times.

Now he took his wife's hand as they moved down the steps. Through the front door they couldn't see the traffic. They'd erected a privacy fence around the house.

"How's the fence across the road coming along?" Annabeth looked out the door.

"The crew was there, but Ben needed help fixing some gates at the enclosure."

She gave him a flirty smile, "Okay, but until they completely enclose the pond with a privacy fence, there will be no swimming for us."

He turned to face her, his hands around her waist. "It seems like forever ago when I told you that we'd be a happy ending."

Annabeth kissed Christian, "How very right you were."

Linda Van Meter is the author of *Worth Losing, Whispered Regrets, and After The Show*. She is the mother of three and grandmother of three. Linda lives in Ohio with her husband. She teaches Language Arts, Creative Writing and Communication to high school students.

Follow Linda on Facebook: @ldvanmeter
Twitter: @lldvmeter
Instagram: lindadvm81
Email: lindadvm81@gmail.com

Made in the USA
Lexington, KY
24 November 2019

57618565R00175